the cats
came back

TITLES BY SOFIE KELLY

curiosity thrilled the cat
sleight of paw
copycat killing
cat trick
final catcall
a midwinter's tail
faux paw
paws and effect
a tale of two kitties
the cats came back

the cats came back

A MAGICAL CATS MYSTERY

SOFIE KELLY

BERKLEY PRIME CRIME
new york

BERKLEY PRIME CRIME
Published by Berkley
An imprint of Penguin Random House LLC
375 Hudson Street, New York, New York 10014

Library of Congress Cataloging-in-Publication Data

Names: Kelly, Sofie, 1958– author.
Title: The cats came back / Sofie Kelly.
Description: First edition. | New York : Berkley Prime Crime, 2018. |
Series: Magical cats ; 10
Identifiers: LCCN 2018014151| ISBN 9780399584596 (hardcover) |
ISBN 9780399584602 (ebook)
Subjects: LCSH: Cat owners—Fiction. | Women librarians—Fiction. |
Cats—Fiction. | Murder—Investigation—Fiction. | BISAC: FICTION /
Mystery & Detective / Women Sleuths. | GSAFD: Mystery fiction.
Classification: LCC PR9199.4.K453 C39 2018 | DDC 813/.6—dc23
LC record available at https://lccn.loc.gov/2018014151

First Edition: September 2018

Printed in the United States of America
1   3   5   7   9   10   8   6   4   2

Cover art by Tristan Elwell
Cover design by Rita Frangie
Book design by Kelly Lipovich

acknowledgments

This is the tenth book in the Magical Cats Mysteries, an achievement that didn't seem possible when the series began and that wouldn't have happened without so many wonderful, supportive readers. Thanks to all of you.

My agent, Kim Lionetti, is and has always been one of my biggest cheerleaders. Thanks, Kim!

This book in particular, and the series in general, has benefitted from the talents of my editor at Berkley, Jessica Wade, who always makes me look good. Thanks go as well to Tara O'Connor, for getting the word out about Kathleen, Hercules and Owen's latest adventures.

And, as always, thanks to Patrick and Lauren. So happy you're my tribe!

the cats
came back

chapter 1

The body was on the front seat of my truck, about halfway between the passenger door and the cloth grocery bag I'd left in the middle of the seat.

"Not again," I muttered, setting the box of glasses I was holding in the bed of the truck. I glanced at my watch. I couldn't exactly leave the body where it was, but I didn't want to be late, either.

A flash of movement registered at the edge of my vision. I let out a breath as what I'd caught a glimpse of came into focus. A second corpse, small, furry and rodentlike, just like the one on the seat, appeared to be hovering about three inches above the hood of the truck.

I narrowed my eyes in the general direction of the seemingly levitating body. "Very nice, Owen," I said. "I'm sure Everett will be happy to learn that the offender who's been digging up his onion sets has been dealt with."

Everett Henderson, my backyard neighbor, had been waging a war all summer long against a persistent and aggressive vole that seemed to be digging up whatever he planted just as quickly as he planted it—for sport, Everett insisted. His wife, Rebecca, had tried to convince him that if he'd just leave the vole one small area to dig in, it would leave the rest of the garden alone. But Everett wasn't willing to concede one square inch of the yard to what he called "a thieving interloper." He'd tried tenting the entire garden with netting, setting out a perimeter of mothballs, putting a large owl statue on an overturned galvanized bucket in the middle of the bed and even spraying a boundary around the garden of a pest control product that allegedly contained fox urine. The vole had been undeterred. It had, however, met its match in Owen, it seemed.

Just then the small gray-and-white tabby appeared—literally—on the hood of the truck, holding the dead vole in his mouth. There had been a time when Owen's ability to appear and disappear at will had been disconcerting; now it was just something he did, a quirk, like the way he had to inspect his food before he ate it or how he loved to ride shotgun in the truck. There was a gleam of satisfaction in his golden eyes as he looked at me. I felt sorry for the dead rodent. It had never stood a chance against the cat.

Owen and his brother, Hercules, had spent the early part of their lives—at least as far as I knew—out at Wisteria Hill, Everett Henderson's former family homestead. Both cats were excellent hunters, a skill that had most likely been honed during that time.

I pointed toward the backyard. "We don't want to keep Ruby waiting," I said, making a hurry-up gesture with one finger. Normally, since it was Thursday, I would have already been on my way to tai chi class, but it had been canceled. My friend Maggie Adams, who was the instructor, was over at the Stratton Theatre, supervising the installation of artwork from the artists' co-op that she was past president of.

Owen immediately jumped down to the driveway and headed for the backyard, the dead vole still firmly in his mouth, passing Hercules on the path that wound around the side of the house. They exchanged a silent glance, the kind of mute exchange I'd seen pass between them dozens of times. Sometimes I wondered if they used a kind of mental telepathy to communicate. Given their other skills the idea really wasn't that far-fetched.

Hercules launched himself onto the hood of the truck in his brother's place. He gave himself a shake and then padded over to me. "Mrrr," he said, cocking his head to one side, and it seemed to me there was a question in the sound.

I reached over to stroke the soft black fur on the top of his head. "Yes," I said. "I think Everett's garden may be safe, at least for now." I glanced at the front seat, where the other furry corpse still lay. Whatever it was, it didn't look like another vole. I turned my attention back to Hercules. "We have to leave in a minute." I tipped my head toward the windshield. "Could you move that so I don't have to go get a shovel?"

He craned his neck to see what I was gesturing at, then he

walked through the windshield, landing lightly on the front seat. Unlike Owen, Hercules couldn't become invisible on a whim. He could, however, walk through walls, doors and windows, through pretty much any obstruction that got in his way.

The first time I'd seen him do that, I thought I'd imagined it. I thought I was overtired, that my eyes were playing tricks on me or I needed glasses. My knees had started to shake so hard that I'd had to sit down on the floor before I fell down. That time Hercules had vanished into one of the library's meeting rooms. He hadn't darted past me. He had walked through the solid wooden door to the small meeting room just as though it wasn't there, and it almost seemed as though there had been a faint *pop* as the end of his tail had disappeared.

I remembered how I had pressed my hands on the door, pushing at the smooth wood, looking for some kind of secret opening or hidden panel. But the door had been thick and unyielding. The second time I'd witnessed the cat walk through a solid wall, I'd been afraid I was having some sort of mental breakdown. Now, like Owen's disappearing act, it was just Hercules being Hercules.

It had never felt like a good idea for anyone to find out what the cats could do, so I'd always kept that piece of information to myself. I hadn't told anyone, including Marcus. Detective Marcus Gordon was logical, sensible and practical—and very handsome. I was crazy about him. I couldn't keep this kind of secret from him much longer, especially since I'd discovered his cat, Micah, shared Owen's talent for disappearing. The fact that all three cats came from the old Henderson estate had to have something to do with their abilities. I just had no idea what.

The little black-and-white furball was sniffing Owen's second victim now. He nudged the corpse with his nose and finally picked it up in his mouth, making his way over to the open driver's door, where he dropped his burden on the edge of the seat. He made a face, crinkling his nose and scraping his tongue against his teeth as though he were trying to get rid of a bad taste. He looked up at me, green eyes slightly annoyed.

"What?" I said. I knew that look.

He poked the body with one white-tipped paw. I leaned down for a closer look.

The furry corpse wasn't a corpse at all, I realized. It was actually a large, dark gray pom-pom made out of some kind of faux fur material.

"Okay, where did that come from?" I asked. I slipped a covered elastic from my wrist and smoothed my hair back off my face into a ponytail. I'd had the long, dark layers trimmed over the weekend, but my hair was still long enough to pull it back when I wanted to.

The cat gave me a blank stare. He didn't seem to have any idea, either. Then I remembered that last night when Maggie had stopped by, she'd had a bag of items from fiber artist Ella King that were going to the artists' co-op store that Maggie helped manage.

Owen adored Maggie; he had a pack rat streak that went with his natural cat inquisitiveness and he wasn't above swiping something that took his fancy. From time to time I'd caught him raiding Everett and Rebecca's recycling bin. Had he swiped the fuzzy ball from Maggie's bag?

I picked up the pom-pom and leaned around the door of the truck. "Owen," I called.

In a moment he poked his head around the side of the house. Part of a dried leaf was stuck to his left ear. *What?* his expression seemed to say.

I held up my hand, the ball of gray fur dangling from between my thumb and index finger. "Explain this," I said.

The cat made his way over to me, making low muttering noises in the back of his throat. He jumped up onto the front seat next to Hercules, glaring at his brother as though he thought he'd been ratted out. Hercules pointedly moved sideways onto the passenger side of the truck, lifting his chin and gazing out the window with a bit of a self-righteous attitude.

I was still holding on to the pom-pom. Owen tried to grab it from me, coming up on his hind legs, but I'd seen his tail twitch from the corner of my eye just before he moved and for once I was faster. I whipped my hand behind my back. "Were you rooting around in Maggie's bag last night?" I said sternly.

The little gray tabby immediately ducked his head as though he'd suddenly discovered something engrossing on the blanket that covered the bench seat.

I stretched across the seat and stashed the pom-pom in the glove compartment. I was pretty sure Owen's skills didn't extend to popping that open.

"I know you love Maggie," I said. I suspected that was why he'd swiped the gray ball of faux fur. In his kitty reasoning he'd expected to be caught and that we'd make a trip to return what he'd taken and he'd be adorable and contrite.

Or maybe I was attributing too human a motive to a cat, albeit a pretty extraordinary cat. Maybe it was simply a case of Owen see, Owen like, Owen take.

I leaned in close to his furry gray face, and he tried to avoid meeting my gaze by staring down at his front paws. "You shouldn't take things that don't belong to you," I said. "We've had this discussion before, Owen."

His golden eyes met mine for a moment. He made a couple more disgruntled noises, then settled himself on the seat and looked out the windshield. I noticed he was careful to keep some space between himself and his brother.

I grabbed the small canvas backpack I had placed on the roof of the cab, along with the box of glasses that was in the bed of the truck, and reached inside to set both on the floor on the passenger side, smiling at Hercules as I did so. Then I slid behind the wheel, pulled out my keys and stuck them in the ignition. We had just enough time to get downtown to meet Ruby. Hopefully, the extra traffic from the music festival wouldn't slow us down getting across town.

The Wild Rose Summer Music Festival took place every year in late August here in Mayville Heights. Musicians and vocalists—both professional and amateur—came to town from all over the Midwest to work with several well-respected and increasingly well-known teachers and conductors. The highlight of the event was the closing concert, held in the restored Stratton Theatre with a massed orchestra and choir performing everything from classical pieces to rock-and-roll standards—but there were lots of other performances before that. I'd taken in one of the lunchtime events just a couple of days before. The festival brought a lot of tourists to town. Many people planned their vacations around it.

We started down Mountain Road, and I could see almost the entire town spread out along the river. The original settlers of Mayville Heights had taken the shortest route to get where they were going, which meant the town was laid out pretty much like a grid. Streets like Mountain Road stretched, for the most part, straight up the hill to Wild Rose Bluff, which the music festival was named for. The streets that ran from one end of Mayville Heights to the other all followed the shoreline of Lake Pepin, which was the largest lake on the Mississippi River. Much like Loch Ness in Scotland, there had been rumors that the lake was home to some kind of prehistoric creature. However, since most sightings of the creature seemed to involve the consumption of large amounts of alcohol, it was a rumor most people took with a very big grain of salt.

There was more traffic downtown on Old Main Street—not to be confused with just plain Main Street—than on a typical Thursday night, but I still made it to the Riverarts building with five minutes to spare. Ruby Blackthorne's art studio was in the big brick building. The former school had been converted into working space for Mayville Heights' artist community a number of years ago, a joint project of the artists' co-op and the town. The partnership between the co-op and the town had been good for everyone. Not only were the artists responsible for bringing more tourists to town to take workshops and buy artwork, they'd also helped reverse a trend that other small towns were seeing: populations that skewed increasingly older as young people headed for more opportunities in the city. As my friend Burtis Chapman liked to put it, those places were getting older and grayer by the day. Thanks to Ruby and Maggie and the other artists, that wasn't happening in Mayville Heights.

Ruby was just coming out of the back door of Riverarts when I pulled into the small parking lot. I backed into Maggie's spot while Hercules looked out the passenger-side window and Owen craned his neck to see over the dashboard.

"Stay here for a minute," I said to the boys.

Hercules twitched his whiskers at me. Owen basically ignored me, starting across my lap as though he were going to go right out the driver's door—assuming he could figure out how to use his paws to open it.

I put one hand on his back. "Where are you going?" I asked.

"Mrr," he muttered as he tried to wriggle out of my grasp.

"I want to give Ruby the glasses she asked to borrow and find out where she wants to shoot. You can wait for a minute."

He lifted his head to look at me, ears twitching in annoyance.

Ruby was on her way over to the truck, smiling.

I bent my head close to the cat. "I know what you're thinking," I whispered, in case Ruby somehow had bionic hearing. "It wouldn't be good if this whole photo session had to disappear." I put a little emphasis on the last word.

Hercules meowed at his brother. A warning maybe to just let it go? Owen made a huffy sound through his nose, his way of letting me know that he was doing what I wanted under duress. But he did sit back down on the seat.

"Thank you," I said. I leaned over, grabbed the box of glasses and got out of the truck.

Ruby smiled. "Oh, hey, you remembered," she said. "Thanks." She took the box from me, peering inside.

"Are you sure those will be enough?"

"Yeah, this is great," she said. "How did you end up with so many drinking glasses, anyway? Did you go a little crazy at a yard sale or something?"

I smiled back at her. "I didn't. It had to be the person who lived in my house before me—or maybe it was Lita."

Lita was Everett Henderson's assistant. Not only was Everett my neighbor, he had also hired me to supervise the renovations at the library for its centennial. My little farmhouse was one of the benefits that came with the job. It was almost four years now since I'd come to Mayville Heights. The head-librarian position had been a temporary eighteen-month appointment, but when the time was up I found myself wanting to stay in the job. Luckily, the library board had felt the same way.

"I bet it was Lita," Ruby said. "She was a Girl Scout. I think she had pretty much every badge they give out. Isn't their motto 'Be Prepared'?"

"'A Girl Scout is ready to help out wherever she is needed,'" I recited. "'Willingness to serve is not enough; you must know how to do the job well, even in an emergency.'"

Ruby raised an eyebrow at me. I felt my cheeks get warm. "It's from the Girl Scout manual. I read it somewhere."

Her smile stretched into a grin. "Kathleen, you're better than the Web. I know you're always a reliable source." She leaned around me and waved at the driver's window of the truck.

Owen was standing up on his back legs, front paws on the door, looking at Ruby through the side window.

She held up a finger. "Give me a second," she said. I knew she was talking to Owen, not to me.

I wasn't the least bit surprised when the cat bobbed his head in acknowledgment as though he'd understood—and I was certain he had—and then sat down.

Ruby didn't seem surprised, either. I wasn't the only one who talked to the cats like they were . . . well, people. Everyone seemed to accept that Owen and Hercules were more than just everyday cats, although no one else knew exactly how extraordinary they really were.

Ruby tipped her head to one side and looked up at the sky. I'd seen her do that enough times to know she was considering the light. "It's not going to be dark for a while," she said. "I've been wanting to try some photos just before sunset. When the sun is low in the sky the shadows are softer and longer. I think I can get some really dynamic images." She held the box of glasses against her chest with one hand and gestured with the other as if she were painting in the air. "So is it okay if we do the inside shots first?"

"Do whatever works for you," I said.

A few weeks earlier Ruby had taken a photo of Owen and Hercules on the steps of the library, seemingly studying a map of Mayville Heights. Maggie had created the hand-drawn, incredibly detailed map of the town, and it had turned out to be very popular with tourists, even more so after another artist,

Ray Nightingale, posted Ruby's photo of the boys online and it went viral. Tourists actually came into the library building looking for the cats. Now Ruby was doing a series of photos with them for a calendar to promote Mayville Heights and the surrounding area. Everett Henderson was funding the project.

Both cats loved having their picture taken, although Owen was by far the bigger ham. Ruby had photographed each cat in the past, using the photos as the basis for two oversized acrylic pop-art portraits she'd painted. Both had been auctioned off as fundraisers for the cat rescue organization Cat People.

No one seemed surprised that Ruby could get Owen and Hercules to pose for her even though cats didn't exactly have a reputation for doing what you wanted them to do when you wanted them to do it—or ever doing it at all.

"As long as I've known Ruby she's had a rapport with animals," Maggie had said the night before, sitting at my kitchen table, licking chocolate icing from a cheesecake brownie off her thumb while Owen sat adoringly at her feet. "And anyway, Owen and Hercules aren't regular everyday cats," she'd continued, sneaking a tiny bite of her dessert to her furry gray shadow— something that would have landed her in the doghouse, pun intended, if our friend Roma had been around. Maggie had caught me watching her, and both she and Owen had looked up at me, faux innocence in her green and his golden eyes.

"Owen and Hercules are special," Maggie had added, an edge of self-righteousness in her voice as though that "specialness" explained everything from how photogenic they were to how Owen deserved a piece of her brownie.

You don't know the half of it, I'd thought.

I got both cats out of the truck now. Hercules agreeably climbed into the cat carrier. I left the top panel unzipped so he could poke his head out and slung the bag over my shoulder. I decided to carry Owen because of the two, he was the more likely to disappear—figuratively and literally. The cats had been feral and didn't like to be touched by anyone other than me, so Ruby didn't offer to help. I closed the door of the truck with my hip, and we followed Ruby into the building.

"How's practice going?" I asked as we headed up the stairs. As in previous years, Ruby was in the festival choir, and this year she was also performing with Everett's granddaughter— Ami Lester—and cabaret singer Emme Finley.

Ruby rolled her eyes. "Just like every other year. Right now we sound like crap. Nobody knows their parts, and I swear there's half a dozen people who couldn't carry a tune no matter how big a bucket you gave them."

"It can't be that bad," I said. The massed choir was the highlight of the final concert. In my experience it always sounded wonderful.

Ruby had a dozen years of voice training and had worked as a singer and dancer at a resort for several years during college. "It can be and it is," she said as we rounded the second-floor landing. "We were doing warm-ups this morning and—I'm not making this up"—she put her free hand over her heart—"I could hear dogs howling."

Owen made a face, scrunching up his whiskers. An unfortunate encounter with Harrison Taylor's German shepherd, Boris, had left him with a pretty low opinion of any and all dogs.

I shot her a skeptical look.

She shrugged. "Okay, so it was only one dog, and in all fairness he had treed a squirrel in the parking lot, which might have been the reason he was howling, but my point is still the same. Right now we stink." She shifted the box of glasses onto her hip and tucked her hair behind her ear with her free hand. She was wearing it longer and layered, just brushing her shoulders. It was dyed a rich copper color, like a newly minted penny, instead of her usual neon-colored streaks.

Hercules craned his neck in Ruby's direction and gave a murp of concern. At least that's what it sounded like to me. Last year I'd bought a CD of the final festival concert. Whenever I played it Hercules would listen with his head tipped to one side, eyes closed. I didn't think I was imagining that he liked what he heard. Hercules was much more of a music lover than Owen. He shared my love for Mr. Barry Manilow, something Owen decidedly didn't.

Ruby leaned around me and smiled at Hercules. She'd once seen him "listening" to the CD in my office. "Don't worry," she said. "We'll be ready."

The cat's green eyes flicked to me.

"Uncle Mickey will work his magic," I said by way of reassurance.

Ruby nodded.

Uncle Mickey was family friend Michel Demarque, brilliant conductor, composer, pianist and world-class flirt. My mother, Thea Paulson, was an actor and a director. Mom and Michel had worked together on a Stephen Sondheim musical many years ago in Vermont and stayed in touch—much to my dad's chagrin. Michel reminded me of actor Hugh Jackman—dark eyes in a wonderfully expressive face and the ability to command the attention of every room he stepped into.

Ruby talked more about some of the pieces—a mix of classical and contemporary—that they were working on as we continued up the stairs to her studio. "I'm looking forward to the concert," I said.

Hercules meowed loudly from my hip.

I laughed. "Apparently so is Hercules."

Ruby grinned at the cat. "Don't worry," she said. "I'll set aside a CD for you."

Owen twisted restlessly in my arms. I had the feeling all the talk about the festival was boring him. Ruby unlocked the door to her studio and I set him down. He made a quick circuit of the space and then looked expectantly at Ruby.

"There," she said, pointing at a length of counter space. The town map was spread on the paint-spattered surface. I moved to pick Owen up, but he launched himself onto the counter before I could, landing lightly on the center of the map. He shook himself and began to check out the various art supplies that were spread out over the dark wood surface. I took Hercules over, lifted him out of the cat carrier bag and set him down next to his brother.

He put each white-tipped paw down gingerly.

"It's okay," I said softly. "I don't see any wet paint."

Ruby had set the box of glasses on a chair and was bringing her tripod over to the counter. "Everything is clean and dry. I promise," she said, as much to Hercules as to me. She knew all about his distaste for wet or dirty feet.

I smoothed the fur on the top of his head. "You look very handsome," I whispered.

Owen's golden eyes darted in my direction.

"You too," I said, reaching over to give him a little scratch between his ears.

He immediately took a couple of passes at his face with a paw.

I took several steps back, snagged a stool and sat down out of the way where I could watch Ruby work.

She fastened her camera to the base of the tripod and then got busy posing Owen and Hercules. I was fascinated by the process every time. Since she couldn't actually pick the cats up or move them around, Ruby would tap the counter with a finger or direct them with a quick hand motion. And most of the time they seemed to understand what she wanted. She talked quietly to them all the time, just the way I suspected she would have done if she'd been working with people. Once, when neither cat seemed to want to go where she wanted them to, Ruby looked through the viewfinder of her camera and then muttered, "Yeah, okay, you're right. That works better."

Finally, she straightened up, linking both hands on top of her head, stretching out her neck and shoulders. Then she grabbed her backpack and pulled out a small brown paper bag with a fold-over top. "Roma-approved," she said, holding up the bag so I could see that it held the organic cat crackers made by one of Roma's friends who, like her, was a veterinarian.

"Yes, go ahead," I said.

Ruby poured a little pile of the treats in front of each cat. "Good job, guys," she said. She took the camera off the tripod and brought it over to me. "What do you think?" she asked, scrolling through the images.

"I know I'm biased," I said. "But they're all wonderful. You're a great photographer."

She smiled. "Owen and Hercules are very photogenic. Don't tell anyone, but I swear they're easier to work with than some people. This calendar is going to be amazing."

Owen lifted his head and seemed to smile in our direction as though he'd understood the compliment. And he probably had.

After the cats had finished eating and had cleaned the cracker crumbs from their whiskers, we moved outside. Ruby wanted to take some photos in front of the building. She'd just taken several shots on the grass near the flagpole when I caught sight of two people coming up the sidewalk.

As they got closer I realized the two women were Emme Finley and Miranda Moore. Emme, who was in her early thirties, was a popular cabaret singer from Chicago. Her friend Miranda Moore worked as her assistant. Ruby had introduced us at the library. As part of the festival, several of the musicians taking part were giving public lectures at the library as a way to generate more interest in the festival. Emme had given a talk about rhythm. She was an engaging speaker, and although I couldn't carry a tune even if I used both hands, I'd been fascinated.

Emme smiled as she came level with us. She was tall, at least an inch above my own five-six, but she didn't move with the self-consciousness some tall women did. Her thick dark brown hair was loose on her shoulders. She had strong features and the kind of knowing smile that made you think she had a secret, but if you sat next to her, maybe she'd whisper it in your ear.

Miranda looked so much like her that they could have easily been mistaken for sisters. They were almost the same height and they had the same hair color, although Miranda's hair looked like it had been dyed brown, while I was fairly certain Emme's was the color she'd been born with. Miranda's eyes were blue-gray, while Emme's were hazel. The most obvious difference between them was the small mole above the left corner of Emme's mouth.

"Hi, Kathleen," Emme said. "Are we interrupting?"

Ruby had been down on one knee, trying to get a shot, but she straightened up now. "You're not interrupting anything," she said. "We have to take five for hair and makeup." She pointed toward Owen, who had sat down and was meticulously cleaning his tail.

Hercules, meanwhile, was making his way across the grass to me. I took a couple of steps forward, bent and picked him up. "Merow?" he said quizzically, cocking his head and eyeing the two women with curiosity.

"Ruby's friends," I said in a low voice in case he was wondering who they were.

Emme looked from Hercules to Ruby. "Are these your cats that Ruby has been photographing?"

I nodded, giving Herc a scratch behind his right ear. "This is Hercules." I gestured at Owen with my elbow. "And that's Owen."

Emme reached a hand in Hercules's direction.

"Not a good idea," Ruby said, shaking her head. "They used to be feral. The only person who can touch those two is Kathleen." Her gaze flicked to me for a moment.

I nodded in confirmation.

Miranda put her hands behind her back. She leaned toward us and smiled at the little tuxedo cat in my arms. "Hello, Hercules," she said.

"Mrr," he replied.

"He's very handsome," she said to me.

As if he'd understood the words, the cat straightened in my arms, his chin coming up to show off his sleek white chest.

Ruby was showing Emme some of the photos she'd already taken. Owen was still working out whatever had messed up his tail.

"Is he named for the mythological hero or the campy Kevin Sorbo show?" Miranda asked.

"A bit of both," I said. "But mostly the TV show."

She gave me a conspiratorial smile. "I loved that show when I was a teenager. I used to pretend to be watching *Baking with Julia* on PBS. I'd change the channel really fast if I heard anyone coming." She was wearing a rose gold bracelet on her right wrist with what looked like a small locket attached. It was a very distinctive piece.

"I like your bracelet," I said.

Miranda ran her fingers over the twisted links. "Thank you. My dad died before I was born. This is the only thing I have from his side of the family."

Behind us Owen had apparently fixed whatever had annoyed him about the fur on his tail. He meowed loudly.

Ruby looked skyward again. "Owen's right. We better get back to it or we're going to lose the light."

I set Hercules down by his brother and backed up again.

Emme came to stand beside me. "Kathleen, I meant to ask you the last time I saw you. Are you by any chance related to Thea Paulson?"

"She's my mother," I said.

A smile lit up her face. "I was in the chorus of a production of *Mamma Mia!* about five years ago in Chicago."

"Mom was Rosie," I finished. "She listened to so much ABBA music, even I could do the songs." I smiled back at her. "Remember the outfit with the silver platform boots?"

Emme nodded.

"She let me wear it as my costume for Halloween." I grinned at the memory.

"I learned so much from her." The wind tousled her hair, and she brushed a strand away from her face. "Just watching her was better than taking an acting class, and she was always willing to answer any question anyone had."

That sounded like my mother. She had the ability to bring out the best in people. It's what made her a great acting partner and what was also getting her a reputation as an excellent director.

"I'll tell her you're here next time I talk to her," I said.

Ruby was trying to get Owen to put his paw on a particular place on the map that was now partially unfolded on the grass. They seemed to be having creative differences.

A bit of color came to Emme's cheeks. "I don't know if she'd even remember me."

"Mom remembers everyone she's worked with," I said. I wasn't exaggerating. I could name a production from twenty years ago, and my mother would rattle off the names of the cast and crew. My head for trivia was probably a skill I'd inherited from her.

I was about to step in and try to convince Owen to do what Ruby wanted him to when I saw Hercules make his way around his brother and place his paw on the exact spot Ruby had been trying to get Owen to "point" to. I waited for Owen to object, but all he did was sit down and cock his head to one side—his "cute" pose.

Miranda asked a question, but I didn't catch it or Ruby's answer.

I focused on Emme again. "Have you done a lot of musicals?" I asked.

She lifted her hair up off her neck for a moment before letting it fall back down again. "It's funny you asked that," she said. "You know that mostly I'm a cabaret singer?"

I nodded. "Ruby mentioned that."

"I've been thinking about stepping away from popular music and moving into doing more musicals. I had so much fun doing *Mamma Mia!*" She ducked her head for a moment and then her gaze met mine again. "I've been making plans to go back to college—I only did a year before I quit to focus on music."

"What would you study?"

"French, for one thing," she said. "I, uh, I'd like to sing Jacques Brel as his work was originally written, without someone having to write it all out phonetically for me."

I nodded. "My mother took a term of French at Boston College. She had two lines in a play that were in French, and she wanted them to sound right."

Emme nodded as though that made perfect sense to her. Ruby had told me how hard Emme had worked to have a successful music career. Her mother had died when she was small, and her father when she was just a teenager. All she had for family was her older sister, Nora.

"She has a lot more talent than I do," Ruby had said. "But somehow when I sing with her she makes me sound better."

Emme and I watched as Ruby took a few more shots. Finally, she straightened up again, rolling her neck from one shoulder to the other.

"We should get going," Emme said. "It was good to see you, Kathleen."

"You too," I said, bending to pick up the carrier bag that I'd set at my feet. "I'm looking forward to hearing you sing with Ruby and Ami."

She moved over to Miranda and touched her on the shoulder. Miranda turned, nodded at whatever her friend had said and with a wave to Ruby and a smile for me cut across the grass and headed down the sidewalk.

I walked over and scooped up Hercules, giving him one of the cat crackers I'd palmed earlier. He settled in the bag, crunching happily. I held out the other cracker to Owen, who sniffed it suspiciously before taking it in his mouth. I picked him up before he decided to go explore somewhere.

"Did you get everything you need?" I asked Ruby.

She was checking out the photos on the camera's screen. "I did. These are great," she said. She smiled at both cats. "Thanks, guys."

Hercules murped at her, which may have been "thank you," or may have meant "more crackers."

Owen bobbed his head, which pretty much translated the same way.

Ruby turned her attention to me. "Thank you, Kathleen," she said.

"Hey, I'm just chauffeur for the talent," I said.

Owen picked that moment to meow loudly.

Ruby laughed. "Well, I appreciate you driving them around. I really think this project is going to bring more visitors to town."

Owen was sniffing the pocket of my T-shirt, probably looking for more crackers.

"I hope so," I said. "Mayville Heights is my home, too."

"I'm so glad you decided to stay." She threw her arms around me, careful not to touch Owen, and I gave her a one-armed hug in return. "I'll text you with some times for the next shoot."

"Sounds good," I said. I hiked the carrier bag a little higher on my shoulder and headed for the truck.

I settled Owen and Hercules on the seat, and once I'd fastened my seat belt I turned to see both cats staring at me. I knew what the look meant.

"You did an excellent job, as usual," I said. "There's a sardine waiting at home for both of you."

Owen's gaze immediately went to the glove compartment.

I slid the key in the ignition. "There are no crackers in there. You ate them all the last time Ruby took your picture. Remember?"

He made a noise that sounded a lot like a sigh.

When we got home I set Owen on the kitchen floor and put the carrier bag beside him. Hercules climbed out as I kicked off my sandals. I got each cat the promised sardine, got out the peanut butter and stuck a piece of bread in to toast and then padded to the fridge in my bare feet for a glass of lemonade.

I sat at the kitchen table with my lemonade and toast, propping my feet on an empty chair.

Hercules finished eating first, crossed under the table and leapt onto my lap. He walked his way up my chest and looked from me to my plate. "Roma says you have too much people food," I said.

He wrinkled his nose at me.

I reached over and scratched behind his left ear, and he stretched out across my body. I glanced over at the refrigerator, where the cats' food dishes were. Owen had disappeared.

My computer was on the table. "Want to see if we can find any videos of Emme singing?" I asked Hercules.

I remembered the production of *Mamma Mia!* that Emme had been in with my mother, although I didn't remember her specifically. And at that performance I'd just attended, she'd been singing as part of a group. Now I was curious about her voice, especially since Ruby had told me how good she was.

The cat lifted his head and licked my chin. That was a yes. I reached for the laptop.

When the song ended I looked at Hercules. "Wow," I said. My toast was cold and forgotten, and the lemonade was sweating droplets of water onto the table. The cat was sitting up, one paw on the edge of the table, green eyes fixed on the computer screen.

"Good" wasn't a good enough word for Emme Finley's voice. It was incredible, a husky contralto that pulled every bit of emotion out of the song "The River" by Bruce Springsteen. I'd seen Springsteen perform the song live. It seemed like sacrilege to say Emme's version was even better.

But it was.

I got to the library earlier than usual on Friday. Michel was giving a lecture on the music of Leonard Cohen, and I wanted to make sure everything was set up. There had been a lot more interest in the talks than even I'd expected. Tickets had run out for every one of them.

The Mayville Heights Free Public Library was over a hundred years old, built back in 1912. It sat just about at the midpoint of a smooth curve of shoreline, protected from the water by a rock wall. Like many others of its vintage, it was a Carnegie library and had been built with funds donated by Scottish-American industrialist Andrew Carnegie. Everett Henderson had funded the restoration of the building—everything from the mosaic tile floors to the plaster ceiling medallion—as a gift to the town for the library's centennial. The two-story brick building had an original stained-glass window at one end and a restored copper-roofed cupola, complete with the original wrought-iron weather vane that had been placed on the roof when the library had originally been built. Every time I walked into the building, I felt a tiny surge of pride at how well it had all turned out.

Emme and Miranda came in at about one thirty. There were already some tourists wandering around waiting for the lecture to start.

"Hi," I said, walking over to meet them. "You're about half an hour early for Michel's talk, but you're welcome to wander around. And there will be cookies later." In the almost four years I'd been in Mayville Heights I'd learned everything went better with cookies.

Emme was wearing a green flowered sundress with a lacy white cotton sweater. Her hair was pulled back in a low ponytail. Miranda had on a similar dress with a pale yellow sweater, and her hair was also in a ponytail. The gold bracelet I'd noticed before was on her arm. Once again I thought how alike they looked.

"I can't stay for the lecture," Emme said. "Although Miranda is going to. I just came to give you this." She handed over a small pink envelope.

Inside there was a photograph of my mother in a white T-shirt, denim cut-offs and those silver platform boots she had let me wear for Halloween.

"It was a picture someone took at rehearsal," Emme said.

"Are you sure?" I asked. "I could have a copy made."

Emme shook her head. "No. It's yours."

"Thank you," I said. I glanced down at the photo again. "I could barely walk in those boots. How did she dance in them?"

"I have no idea," Emme said. "I wear heels when I perform, but I spend most of my time sitting down." She stuck out her leg. She was wearing a pair of flat red sandals. "These are more my speed. Miranda's the one who can glide around in heels." She gestured at her friend, who was wearing a pair of lime-green retro wedge lace-up espadrilles. I realized that without the heels Miranda was a couple of inches shorter than her friend.

Emme had her cell phone in her hand, and she glanced down at the screen. "I'm sorry. I have to go. I have a practice to get to," she said. "I'm really glad you like the photo." She glanced at Miranda. "Have fun. I'll see you later." She headed for the door.

I turned to Miranda. "Please feel free to look around or use one of the computers." I gestured at the desk where Mary Lowe was checking out a stack of picture books for a slightly frazzled mom with a squirming toddler on her hip. "Mary can answer any questions you have."

"Could I help you with anything?" Miranda asked. She gestured at the stack of festival brochures in my hand. "I could put one of those on every chair if you'd like."

I smiled at her. "Well, that would be a help," I said.

She held out her hand and I gave her the brochures. "It's not that I don't like your library, but I'm really bad at waiting. I'd rather be doing something."

"Don't say that too loudly or Mary will have you shelving books," I teased as we headed for the meeting room.

Miranda smiled back at me. "I worked in the school library when I was in high school. I know the Dewey decimal system. The nine hundreds are history and geography. Four hundreds are language and the two hundreds are religion." She ticked off each one on a finger. "Am I right?"

"Yes, yes and yes," I said. "I'm impressed."

"I just have a head for random pieces of information. I can quote poetry I learned back in the eighth grade." She played with a button on the front of her sweater with one hand. *"When you are old and gray and full of sleep,"* she recited, her voice low and quiet.

"And nodding by the fire, take down this book," I continued. "William Butler Yeats. Again, impressive."

A grin stretched across her face. "You too," she said.

I nodded, feeling my cheeks get warm. "Knowing a bunch of random information can actually be useful when you're a librarian."

"It's also a pretty good way to avoid ever having to pay for your own coffee," Miranda said. She started moving along the first row of chairs, setting a brochure on each seat.

I made a face at her as I moved the coffee table a little to the right. "I'm not following."

Miranda looked up at me. "Emme said your parents are actors."

"They are."

"So you know that there's usually some kind of card game or trivia game going on backstage at a production. It's the same at a club."

I laughed, nodding knowingly. "Okay, I get it now." Not only was there often some kind of game going on backstage, there was often some kind of wager involved as well.

Miranda made short work of putting out the festival brochures. Then she helped me set up a large poster that featured information about what the library offered aside from books, with details on the programs planned for the fall. We talked about the festival in particular and music in general. I was impressed by how much she knew about the latter, especially old rock and roll. Miranda was smart and funny, and it struck me that when Emme was around she seemed to just fade into the background, letting her friend take center stage to shine.

"I love your cats," Miranda said as we headed up to the lunchroom on the second floor to bring down the coffee cups. "Ruby showed us all the photos she's taken so far. They're both so photogenic."

"They're both little hams," I said.

"How did you end up with them?" she asked. "You said they were feral."

"I lived in Boston before I came here," I said as we reached the top of the stairs. "I sold most of my things, including my car, before I left. So when I first got here, I explored the town on foot." We started down the hall. "I was exploring out at Wisteria Hill—it's the old Henderson estate just outside of town. Owen and Hercules were just kittens then. Two little balls of fur, really. When I headed home they followed me. Twice I took them back. The third time I brought them home with me."

Miranda brushed a stray strand of hair off her face. "So it's kind of like they picked you."

"It's exactly like that," I said. As far-fetched as it sounded, I did believe it. Given everything else I'd learned about Owen and Hercules, them choosing me, not the other way around, really wasn't that far-fetched after all.

We'd just gotten to the bottom of the stairs with our trays

of cups when Michel walked in. There were easily a couple dozen people hovering near the meeting room.

"I'll go put these out," Miranda said.

I smiled. "Thanks," I said.

She headed across the mosaic tile floor, and I set my own tray down on the circulation desk and went over to say hello to Michel, aka Uncle Mickey.

He caught my hand in both of his. "Kathleen, it's good to see you," he said.

"You too," I said. He only seemed to get more handsome with age.

He looked over my shoulder at the people gathered outside the meeting room. "Are they all waiting to hear me talk?"

"Well, we do have cookies," I teased. "But I think they're here for you."

One eyebrow went up and he smiled. "I supposed it would be a bit disingenuous of me to say I didn't expect all these people."

He was wearing jeans and a white shirt with the sleeves rolled back, and I could see why women threw themselves at him. He was a very attractive, charismatic man, but to me Michel Demarque was always going to be Uncle Mickey, who taught me to sing "Frère Jacques" as a round and bought me mugs of hot chocolate with whipped cream and shavings of bittersweet chocolate.

The talk went even better than I'd hoped. Every chair was filled, and Michel was his usual funny, self-deprecating self. Across the room Ruby gave me a thumbs-up. We had several events planned with the artists' co-op, and given how well this collaboration with the festival had gone, I felt good about them.

I grabbed one of the two coffee carafes. It was just about empty. As I moved around the clusters of people so I could take it upstairs for a refill, I glanced out the window. The meeting room overlooked part of the parking lot.

Two people caught my eye. One was a bearded man in a faded black ball cap. The other was a woman. *Was that Emme?* I stopped and took a step backward for a better look. *It definitely was Emme out there.* I recognized her dress and her red sandals. *What was she doing in our parking lot, other than arguing with a man I'd never seen before?*

chapter 2

When I came back downstairs with a full pot of coffee, Emme and the man she'd been arguing with were gone. I knew from Ruby that the pressures of the festival and some strong-willed "artistes" sometimes made for a volatile combination, although up until now the artistic disagreements had stayed at the Stratton Theatre. This was the first time, as far as I knew, that one had spilled over to my library parking lot.

Michel answered questions for close to forty-five minutes. "I had no idea there'd be this kind of turnout," he said, giving me a satisfied smile. "Thank you for organizing everything."

"You're welcome," I said. "You made it easy. There are lots of people who want to hear what the esteemed Michel Demarque has to say about the late Leonard Cohen." I gave him a teasing smile.

"I am full of information." He raised an eyebrow. "Or some people would just say I'm full of it, period."

I laughed and he put an arm around my shoulder, giving me a quick hug. "Let me take you to lunch tomorrow," he said. "We haven't had a chance to catch up since I got here."

I knew that part of "catching up" would be a conversation about my mother. He still had a soft spot for her, and while she didn't encourage his feelings, she didn't exactly discourage them, either. Mom mostly seemed amused by the idea that Dad was jealous of the conductor when it hadn't bothered him at all when she'd shamelessly flirted—in a movie—with Denzel Washington.

Mom and Dad had married, divorced and then secretly rekindled their relationship before marrying for the second time. The presence of my younger brother and sister at the ceremony, so to speak, Mom glowing Madonna-like with her hands resting on her round belly, was proof that she and Dad just couldn't stay away from each other.

"I'd love to have lunch with you," I said.

The library closed early on Saturdays. Michel and I agreed to meet at Eric's Place the next afternoon at quarter after one, and he said good-bye.

Someone tapped me on the shoulder. I turned around to find Miranda standing there. "Wow," she said. "I had no idea Michel was such a wonderful storyteller."

I smiled. "His father is French but his mother is Irish. I think Michel inherited his way with words, so to speak, from his Irish side."

"I'm looking forward to the next talk," she said.

I nodded. "So am I."

"I have somewhere I have to be," she said. "It was good to see you, Kathleen."

"You too," I said.

Mia Janes, my part-time student, had arrived for her shift, and the two of us put the chairs away and cleaned up the meeting room. Mia was leaving for college soon and I was dreading the idea of replacing her. We'd gotten closer when her grandfather was killed, and it wouldn't be the same when I didn't see her almost every day.

She set the large poster about the library's upcoming events against the wall and folded the easel. Maggie had made it for me out of some reclaimed wood we'd found in the old carriage house out at Wisteria Hill. Mia caught me watching her and smiled. "I'm going to miss you, too," she said, grabbing the easel with one hand and reaching down for the poster with the other.

The rest of the day was busy, especially for a Friday in August. I was tired by the time I got home. Owen and Hercules were waiting in the kitchen. Marcus had stopped in to check on them and, knowing him, had probably given them some kind of treat. But that didn't mean they weren't going to try to wheedle another out of me.

I was sitting at the table with a glass of lemonade and one of the last remaining chocolate cheesecake brownies when my cell phone rang. It was Ruby.

"Hey, Kathleen," she said. "I know it's very late notice, but are Owen and Hercules available for another quick shoot to-morrow?" I could hear a piano in the background, which made me think she was still at the theater.

"I could make later in the afternoon work," I said.

"Any chance evening would work for them?" She was talking about both cats like they were people.

"They have nothing on their calendar." Marcus was work-ing on a case—he hadn't been able to share the details—and I'd seen very little of him all week. I didn't think things were going to change in the next twenty-four hours, so I had noth-ing planned for Saturday night.

"How about the marina about eight? I'll meet you at the far end of the lot, by the stairs to the lookout."

"We'll be there," I said.

"Thanks, Kathleen." I could feel her smile through the phone. "See you then."

I set the phone back on the table and reached for my lem-onade. Both cats were eyeing me, curiosity in their eyes. "Ruby," I said.

Owen immediately began to wash his face.

"You don't know that was about more pictures."

He paused his paw in midair and meowed at me.

"Okay, so it was, but there's no way you could have known that." He went back to washing his face after giving me a look that could best be described as condescending.

Saturday morning was busy at the library, plus I ended up hav-ing to make a quick trip over to Henderson Holdings to drop off some paperwork for Everett. So I was happy to finally sink onto a chair at a window table at Eric's and let Michel charm me a little. He asked about my life, told me how much he liked being in Mayville Heights for the festival and gave me an old photo of Mom and me. I was touched that he'd taken the time to find the picture. I was going to put it on the refrigerator the way I'd done with the one Emme had given me.

"You look so much like Thea," he said.

I smiled across the table at him. "I've always thought that both Ethan and Sara look more like Mom than I do." I glanced down at the photo again. "But you're right, here we do look a lot alike." The similarities were less about actual physical features and more about mannerisms. We had the same smile, the same way of tipping our head to one side, the same thoughtful expression in our eyes.

"Thank you for this," I said, tucking the photograph carefully in my bag.

He turned his coffee cup in a slow circle on the table. "How is your mom?" he asked. "I caught some of the episodes when she was doing that soap last fall. She was great."

"They want her back again," I said. Mom's appearances on the daytime drama *The Wild and Wonderful* had brought her a devoted and vocal group of fans that had been clamoring for a return visit to the show since her most recent appearance last fall.

"I'm not surprised," he said. "Do you think she'd be interested in doing TV full-time?"

I shook my head. I knew the show had offered her a two-year deal but Mom had turned it down. "Her heart is always going to be onstage."

"I've been talking to the festival organizers about adding a workshop on stage presence. I have some very talented singers who don't seem to have any idea how to work the stage or the audience—or even what to do with their hands." He smiled. "Now that you're living here maybe I can entice your mother to come and teach it for me another year."

I tried to imagine having my mother in town for a week or more. Mags would love being able to talk about *The Wild and Wonderful* with her. The show was Maggie's secret vice. Owen and Hercules would follow Mom adoringly around the house—and not only because she tended to ignore Roma's rules about what they should eat. And big, burly Burtis Chapman would likely invite her for breakfast at Fern's Diner and flirt outrageously. It wouldn't be boring.

Michel and I talked for a few more minutes and then he glanced at his watch. "I have to get back to the theater." I reached for my purse but he shook his head. "You're my guest, my dear. I invited you."

"Thank you," I said. We both got to our feet and I hugged him.

"I'll see you soon, Kathleen," he said.

I left the truck where I'd parked it—just a couple of doors down from the café—and walked up the street to the artists' co-op store. I was meeting Maggie, and we were headed to Red Wing to check out a huge neighborhood yard sale.

The yard sale turned out to be a great success as far as Maggie was concerned. We loaded a vintage dressmaker's dummy, an old Underwood typewriter and a royal-blue metal steamer trunk into the bed of the truck, securing them in place with the straps and bungee cords I kept for exactly that purpose. She also had a brown paper shopping bag full of old photos and postcards. The only thing I bought was a movie poster of *West Side Story*. We were planning a week of classic movie musicals in the fall, and I'd managed to snag several posters at different flea markets and yard sales in the area.

I took Maggie and her treasures to Riverarts, and we managed to get everything up the stairs to her top-floor studio. "Thanks for coming with me," she said. "And for lugging everything back here."

"It was fun," I said. "I can't wait to see what you do with everything." I left with a promise that we'd get together soon and finalize the last few details for Roma's upcoming wedding shower.

I headed home to have supper with Owen and Hercules. I spread the movie poster on the table to have a closer look at it. It was in excellent shape—just a couple of creases near one corner.

Hercules jumped up onto a chair and craned his neck as though he were checking out the poster. "Mrr," he said, which I decided to take as his kitty seal of approval.

Owen, on the other hand, was pretty much indifferent to my find. It might have been because he liked movie musicals about as much as he liked the music of Barry Manilow. Or it might have been because although he sometimes seemed to act like a person, he was still a cat.

I ate supper, brushed my teeth and my hair and then went

downstairs to the living room. I sat in the big chair and reached for the phone. Talking to Michel about Mom had left me missing her. Owen leapt up onto the footstool, cocked his head to one side and gave me a quizzical look.

"I'm calling Boston," I said.

He seemed to take my words as an invitation. He launched himself from the footstool, landing in my lap, where he kneaded my leg with his paws.

"Claws," I reminded him as I shifted so he could get settled. Once we both seemed comfortable—me with one leg tucked underneath me and Owen sprawled half on his back—I reached for the phone again.

My brother, Ethan, answered. "Hey, Kath, how's life in the land of lumberjacks and Bigfoot?" Ethan loved to tease me about living "in the middle of nowhere" as he put it. He'd bought me Bigfoot pajamas, a pair of Bigfoot slippers and a red T-shirt with the words *I'm a Lumberjack and I'm Okay* emblazoned on the front, a reference to the Monty Python song. I'd worn it to the Winterfest supper back in February. It had been a big hit.

"When are you going to come see me and find out for yourself?" I asked.

"Maybe sooner than you think," he said. "There's a chance we might do a short tour out your way this winter."

"That's great," I said. Ethan was a drummer. He taught jazz drumming back in Boston and he was also in a band, The Flaming Gerbils. They'd gone out on tour several times up and down the East Coast and up into Canada.

Owen lifted his head and his golden eyes gleamed with curiosity.

"When and where?"

"February, probably. Milwaukee, maybe Chicago, Springfield, Des Moines, Kansas City, maybe Minneapolis."

"If you don't make it to Minneapolis, I can see you in Des Moines or Milwaukee," I said. "And maybe you could come spend a few days with me. You keep saying you're going to."

I heard him exhale on the other end of the phone. "I know. I swear I really do want to see you, it just seems like there's always more stuff I have to do. There's my students and the band. I've been writing a lot and Sara has some ideas for our next video. Some days it's midnight and I honest to God don't know where the day went." It was impossible to miss the enthusiasm in his voice. "There's a really good chance that everything will work out for February."

"I hope so," I said.

Owen looked at me and yawned.

"Is Mom around?" I asked.

Ethan laughed. "Yeah, she's right here. She's been hovering ever since she figured out it was you." I heard my mom's voice say something in the background. "Here she is. Love you," Ethan said.

"You too!"

"Hi, sweetie." It seemed as though I could feel the warmth of my mother's voice through the phone.

"Hi, Mom," I said.

"How are you? How are Owen and Hercules, and Marcus?

Oh, and Maggie? And what about the festival? Have you seen Michel?"

"Fine, fine, fine and fine, going well and yes, we had lunch today."

Owen lifted his head again, nudged the phone with his nose and murped softly.

"And Owen says hello."

"Let me talk to him."

Owen was eyeing the phone as though he'd somehow heard what she'd said.

"Mom, he's a cat," I said.

"I'm aware of that," she said. "What's your point?"

I shook my head. This was an argument I wasn't going to win. And it wasn't like Owen hadn't "talked" on the phone before. "Hang on a sec," I said. I put the phone to Owen's ear. "She wants to talk to you," I said. No, this wasn't weird.

I had no idea what my mother was saying to Owen, but he seemed to be listening intently and he meowed twice. Finally he turned his head and looked at me.

Nope. Not weird at all.

"So tell me about the festival," Mom said now that her conversation with the cat was over. "Has your Uncle Mickey charmed most of Mayville Heights by now?" I pictured her in the kitchen at home, holding the phone to her ear with both elbows propped on the counter.

"From what Ruby tells me, it's going well," I said. "And based on the reception his talk at the library got, I think Uncle Mickey has charmed at least half the state."

Mom laughed.

"Do you remember when you did *Mamma Mia!*?" I asked.

Owen stretched, yawned again and then jumped down and headed to the kitchen.

"Which time?"

"The first one."

"Umm, I do," she said. "Those platform boots did great things for my legs, but I almost broke my ankle learning to dance in them."

"Do you remember a young woman named Emme Finley? She was in the chorus."

"Gorgeous voice. Tall. Dark hair—I think it was all her own. Why? Is she there at the festival?"

"She is. She's going to be singing with Ruby and Everett's granddaughter, Ami."

"Oh, sweetie, I'd love to hear them. Will you get me a copy of the CD?"

"Of course," I said, nodding even though she couldn't see me.

We talked for a few more minutes. I told Mom about the two photos I'd gotten from Emme and Michel and promised I'd make a copy of each of them and send them to her.

"Give Dad a big hug for me," I said. "I love you."

"I love you, too, Katydid," she said. She blew me a kiss and we hung up.

It was about five to eight when I pulled into the marina driveway. I parked the truck at the far end of the parking lot. The view out over the river was beautiful, even though it was almost dark. Several sailboats, navigation lights shining like tiny stars, were slicing their way through the water, the breeze curving and filling their sails.

Marcus had called just as we were about to head out the door. He was at the station doing paperwork after helping break up a smuggling operation that had been moving knockoff health supplements from Minnesota into Wisconsin and on to Chicago and likely farther east. He sounded tired but I could also hear the satisfaction in his voice. For now, at least, the bad guys had lost, the good guys had won and some dangerous products were out of circulation.

I'd imagined him leaning against the wall in the hallway at the police station, where he usually went for a bit of privacy when he called me, one long leg crossed over the other, his dark, wavy hair mussed because he'd run his hands through it so many times.

"I'm going to be a while," he said. "I'm sorry. I feel like I haven't seen you all week."

"Hey, it's okay," I said, happy just to hear his voice. I explained about the photo shoot with Ruby.

"Owen and Hercules are turning into celebrities," he said.

"Maggie says if we're lucky maybe they'll be invited onto *The Tonight Show*."

Marcus laughed. "And let me guess. They'd give everyone little pawprint autographs."

"Something like that," I said.

Both cats were in the porch, waiting not very patiently. Hercules meowed loudly, annoyance in his green eyes. "I have to get going," I said, sliding a foot into my canvas shoes. "If you get away before midnight, please call me."

He'd promised he would and said good-bye. I thought about how we'd butted heads when we first met. If someone had told me we'd end up falling in love, I would have thought they were crazy.

I saw Ruby coming across the grass now as I held the bag open for Hercules to get in. Owen tried to climb over me, making the process more complicated.

"Wait, please," I said.

He made a grumble of protest but sat down on the seat again.

Hercules got settled and I backed out of the truck, holding the cat carrier bag with one hand and scooping up Owen with the other.

Ruby caught sight of us and smiled. "Perfect timing," she said.

"The key to a happy life," I said. "At least according to my dad."

"I thought the key to a happy life was cute shoes and lots of chocolate," she countered.

I smiled back at her. "That works, too."

"Thanks for coming on such short notice," she said. "I got thinking last night that the marina is something that could attract tourists." She waved a hand in the direction of the water. "It's quiet. It's beautiful. I think it's exactly what people from the 'big city'"—she made air quotes around the words—"are looking for."

I nodded. "The first week I was here I walked up to the first lookout three times, and there was still snow on the ground." I smiled at the memory. I'd been amazed at how peaceful it was to stand by the wooden railing and just let my mind wander.

"I'd like to take some photos of both cats up on the lookout and over on the grass as well," Ruby said, gesturing back over her shoulder. "I want to see how it will work with the flash and the parking lot lights. And maybe a few of them actually on the stairs; I mean, if they feel like doing that."

"Where do you want to start?" I asked. Owen was getting restless. He kept craning his neck toward the water. Was he watching the sailboats? Somehow I didn't think so.

"How about on the grass first?" She gestured at a red metal bench. "Maybe there?"

We walked over to the bench and I set Owen down first. Instead of taking a couple of swipes at his fur he looked past me out toward the water again. I put the carrier bag down, and Hercules climbed out, shook himself and then followed his brother's gaze. I looked back over my shoulder, wondering what they were looking at, but I didn't see anything other than the boats.

I knew Ruby was trying to create some kind of special effect with the parking lot lights, so I just took a few steps back and let her get to work.

Every shot seemed to take a long time. Or maybe we were just spoiled by how easy the previous photo shoots had been. Twice Ruby stopped and took a couple of deep, cleansing breaths, the way Maggie had taught us to do at tai chi class to get centered. I wondered if there was some way I could get Owen and Hercules to do the same thing.

Both cats were distracted, looking over in the direction of the water multiple times. I took a few steps away from the bench to see if I could see what had taken their attention, but I couldn't see anything anywhere that would interest a cat.

Ruby was lying on her stomach on the grass, trying to get a photograph of Hercules walking in front of the bench, but it wasn't working. He kept stopping, staring out across the grass and then turning his gaze back to Ruby.

The third time he did it she gave an exasperated sigh and got to her feet, brushing grass and dirt off the front of her cut-offs. "Is there something out by the water you want me to see?" she said to the cat.

Owen was still sitting on the bench where Ruby had taken the last photo of him. "Merow," he immediately said. Hercules turned to look at his brother and they exchanged a look.

Hercules turned back to Ruby and meowed.

"Okay," she said. She looked at me. "Just give me a minute."

Before I could bend down and pick up Hercules he started purposefully across the grass.

"All right, I'll just follow you." Ruby shrugged and trailed the little tuxedo cat.

I sat down next to Owen and put a hand on his gray fur just in case he got the idea to go after them. He looked at me and then leaned to the right so he could watch his brother's progress, but he made no move to follow.

Hercules kept moving until he reached the edge of the green space where the bank dipped down to the water's edge. A chill fingered its way up the back of my neck. I remembered having to jump down over a similar embankment, across from the hotel, trying to escape a killer. I put my free hand on my stomach and took a slow deep breath and then another.

Owen made a soft murp and nudged my hand.

"I'm okay," I said. I leaned sideways, just the way the cat had, to see where Ruby and Hercules were. Hercules had stopped walking. He was next to a small scrub of waist-high bushes at the edge of the embankment. Ruby took a step forward, leaning down to look at something. Her body went rigid.

My chest tightened; the feeling was like being laced into an old-fashioned corset. For a moment I couldn't get my breath. Whatever Ruby was looking at, it wasn't good. I picked up Owen and got to my feet, grabbed the carrier with my other hand and headed across the grass.

Ruby was pale, one hand clenching the strap of her camera so tightly her knuckles were white against her skin. She pointed at a cluster of wild black currant bushes. "I think . . . there's a body, right there," she said.

"Are you sure?" I asked. I wasn't doubting her. I just really wanted her to be wrong.

She exhaled softly. "Yes . . . I think."

"I'll look," I said. I'd seen dead bodies before. I put Owen down next to his brother. "Stay with Ruby, please," I whispered to both of them.

I made my way closer to the bushes, watching carefully where I stepped. I could see what easily could have been mistaken for a pile of discarded clothing—the sleeve of a white sweater, a striped skirt or dress and rope-heeled shoes, but experience told me I was looking at a body. I moved closer, part of me hoping against hope that it was just someone who'd had too much to drink and passed out, even as some other part of me was aware of the way the body was crumpled in on itself and that there was no indication the person was breathing. I tasted something sour and bitter at the back of my throat.

I tugged a branch out of the way so I could get a better look at what was in front of me. For a moment the image blurred out of focus as though I'd suddenly stuck my head underwater. I forced myself to take a second look.

It was Emme Finley. She'd worn that candy-striped sundress with its bright yellow, blue, red, green and white stripes at the noon-hour concert I'd taken in on Tuesday—with that same white sweater.

It looked like there was some blood in her hair. I reached down and touched two fingers to the side of her neck. The skin was cool and mottled under my touch. It confirmed what I already knew: She was dead.

chapter 3

I closed my eyes for a moment and mentally wished Emme's spirit a safe journey. Then I picked my way out of the bushes, trying to step where I'd put my feet when I'd made my way over to the body in the first place.

Ruby's eyes were locked on my face. "Kathleen, please tell me that's not . . ." She swallowed hard. ". . . Emme."

I shook my head. It was difficult to hold back the tears, but it wouldn't do me or Ruby or even Emme any good to just sit on the grass and cry—even though that's what I wanted to do.

Ruby held up her phone. "I called nine-one-one," she said. Her voice was raspy with emotion.

I cleared my throat. "I'm . . . uh . . . going to put Owen and Hercules in the truck. I'll be right back."

The cats had stationed themselves on either side of Ruby

while I'd checked on the body. Neither one objected when I picked them up and headed across the grass. I unlocked the driver's door and set them both on the front seat. "Please just stay here," I said.

Hercules meowed and Owen nudged my hand with his head. It almost seemed like they understood.

I walked back to Ruby. She was standing in the same spot, looking out across the water, arms folded over her chest, shoulders hunched a little. "She bought that sweater at the co-op store," she said. She didn't look at me. "I was with her. It was one of Ella's."

Ella King was a talented knitter. Everything she created was one of a kind.

"I thought it was her but I wanted to be wrong."

"Me too," I said.

We stood there in silence until a police car came down the street and turned into the marina driveway, lights flashing, siren silent. It cut across the parking lot and pulled in next to my truck. Officer Stephen Keller got out of the driver's side. He was a big man, ex-military, as his square-shouldered stance suggested. He gave me a nod of recognition.

"She's over . . . there," I said, gesturing in the direction of the clump of black currant bushes.

"Wait here, please," he said. He moved past me to go check the body.

I looked back toward the street and felt a rush of relief to see Marcus's SUV waiting to turn into the marina. He parked on the other side of my truck. As he got out from behind the wheel, he gave me just the barest hint of a smile.

"I'll be right back," I said to Ruby.

She glanced back and caught sight of Marcus. "I'm okay," she said.

I met Marcus at the edge of the grass. He was wearing jeans and a gray T-shirt and he needed a shave.

"Are you all right?" he asked, concern pulling lines tight around his mouth and blue eyes. "And what about Ruby? When I heard there was a nine-one-one call out here . . ." He swiped a hand across his mouth.

"We're fine," I said.

He gave my arm a quick squeeze. "I'm glad. Tell me what happened."

I explained how distracted the cats had been and how Ruby had finally followed Hercules over to the embankment. "I checked to make sure it was a body and not someone just passed out or asleep."

"Owen and Hercules probably caught the scent of—"

"I know," I interrupted. I didn't want him to finish the sentence. "Her name is Emme Finley," I continued. "She's here for the festival. Ruby and I know her."

He glanced in the direction of Officer Keller. "You know how this works, Kathleen," he said.

I nodded. "I do."

He walked over to join the other police officer. I rejoined Ruby. The two men spoke for a moment, then Keller led the way to the body.

Marcus took a quick look, then pulled a pair of blue latex gloves from his pocket and bent down for a closer view of the body. I tried not to think of it as Emme Finley lying there.

"What could have happened to her?" Ruby said. Her arms were still folded over her midsection as if she were hugging herself.

"I don't know," I said, tucking a stray strand of hair back behind my ear. "Maybe she fell and hit her head. Maybe she had some kind of medical problem." I hadn't seen any obvious signs of injury on Emme's body other than the bit of blood in her hair, but I hadn't looked any closer than I needed to be sure she wasn't alive. I didn't say that maybe foul play was involved. I hated even thinking it.

"I wasn't even sure . . . I mean, you know how people dump things along here. Even when I thought I recognized the sweater I wasn't certain. Then I saw a foot."

I nodded. "She was wearing that sweater and the same striped sundress at the lunchtime concert on Tuesday."

Ruby looked at me, and I could see it was taking as much effort for her not to cry as it was for me. "I wanted to be wrong."

I reached for her hand and gave it a squeeze. The image of the foot slipped halfway out of the green espadrille was etched into my brain.

A green lace-up espadrille.

I flashed back to the conversation I'd had on Friday at the library with Emme when she'd shown me her pretty red flat sandals: *These are more my speed. Miranda's the one who can glide around in heels.*

"What is it?" Ruby asked.

Something must have shown on my face.

"It's not Emme," I said.

"Yes it is," she said. "I told you, Ella made that sweater. I was with Emme when she bought it. And you said she was wearing that dress at the concert."

I started shaking my head before she'd finished speaking. "You saw the shoe. It had a heel. At least two inches."

Ruby looked lost. "Why does that matter?" she asked.

I pressed both hands to my face and blew out a breath. "Because yesterday Emme told me she only wore heels when she was performing. And because yesterday Miranda was wearing a pair of shoes just like those." I looked over my shoulder in the direction of Marcus and Stephen Keller.

The color drained from Ruby's face. "You mean that's Miranda?"

"I think so," I said.

Ruby made a helpless gesture with one hand. "Miranda? That doesn't make sense. She's nice. Kind. *Young.* She and Emme are like sisters."

Marcus was on his way over to us. "I have a few more questions," he said as he joined us.

"We were wrong," I blurted out. "That's not Emme Finley."

His blue eyes darted from me to Ruby and back again. "What makes you say that?"

I explained about the shoe.

It was getting darker. Marcus raked a hand back through his hair.

"Emme has a tattoo," Ruby said. "A bird, just the outline of one really." She held up her thumb and index finger about an inch apart. "About this big."

"Where is it?" Marcus asked.

Ruby put three fingers on her left shoulder blade. "Right here."

"And she has a beauty mark, just to the left of her mouth," I added, touching my face.

"I'll be right back," Marcus said. He walked over to Officer Keller again, and both men approached the body. I saw Marcus pull a pen from his pocket and nudge the neck edge of the white sweater aside. Keller leaned in for a closer look.

The muscles in my shoulders were tight. I didn't want it to be Emme lying there dead, but I didn't want it to be Miranda, either.

Marcus finally straightened up and looked in our direction. I could tell from his face that it wasn't Emme Finley's body there in the bushes.

"It's not Emme, is it?" I asked as he rejoined us.

"I don't think so. There's no tattoo on the left shoulder. No mole on her face, either."

"It's Miranda," Ruby said. She was rubbing her left arm with her other hand.

"Why do you think so?" Marcus asked, his forehead furrowed.

"They look a lot alike," I said. "They could be sisters."

"Do you know where Ms. Finley is staying?" Marcus said.

"Her sister—she's Emme's manager—came with her. They rented an apartment just down the street from the Stratton. Miranda was staying with them. She's kind of Emme's assistant. You know the building that the Gunnersons own?"

"I know it," Marcus said. He hadn't written anything down.

Because of his dyslexia he made fewer notes than most other police officers.

I took a deep breath and let it out. "So now what?" I said.

"I'm going to send a car over to check on Ms. Finley."

Ruby pulled her phone out of her pocket. "I have her number right here. I can just call her."

Marcus held up a hand. "Don't. Please," he said.

She frowned. "Why?"

"Because right now we're not sure who that is."

Ruby gave an almost imperceptible nod.

Marcus looked at me. "Kathleen, do you feel up to taking another look at the . . . body? Maybe we can clear this up."

"I'll do it," Ruby said, even as I nodded.

"You don't have to." I cleared my throat. "I've . . . been in this circumstance before."

She gave me what passed for a smile at this moment. "It's okay, Kath, I'm not going to fall apart. And I've spent more time with Emme and Miranda than you have." She looked at Marcus. "Let's do it."

Marcus led her back across the grass. I waited, hands stuffed in my pockets. Officer Keller leaned over the body and carefully moved part of the black currant bush to one side. Marcus said something to Ruby. She nodded, squared her shoulders and stepped closer. She studied the body for a long moment, then looked up at Marcus.

Ruby's expression was serious, lips pressed together, as she walked back over to me. Her gaze met mine and she nodded. "You were right. It's Miranda."

I sighed. "I didn't want it to be Emme. But I didn't want it to be her, either."

"I know," she said. She looked around. "What I don't get is what Miranda was doing here. And why was she wearing Emme's clothes?"

"They were best friends, so they might have borrowed each other's clothes. And maybe Miranda came to look at the boats or to climb up to the lookout."

"Climb up to the lookout in those shoes?" Ruby made a face. "I don't think so. Anyway, why would she be here all by herself?"

It was a good question. I didn't have a good answer.

Marcus was headed back to join us again. More vehicles were arriving in the parking lot. He glanced past us and then his gaze settled on my face. "Both of you can go now." He switched all his attention to Ruby. "I'm going to want to talk to you again," he said. "Probably in the morning."

Ruby folded her arms over her chest again. "I'll be at the shop."

Marcus glanced at me. "I'll try to call you later. I can't promise."

I nodded. "That's okay."

Ruby and I headed toward the truck. "Did you walk?" I asked. "I can give you a ride home or take you back to your studio."

"What?" She shook her head. "I'm sorry. No, I drove." She gestured at the gray-shingled marina building. "I'm parked over there." She sighed. "I was just thinking about how awful this is going to be for Emme. She and Miranda grew up together in the same town. They're more like sisters than friends."

"Do you know anything about Miranda's family?" I asked, fishing my keys out of my pocket.

"She doesn't really have one. Her mother is dead. She has a stepfather and a couple of stepbrothers, but she told me they aren't close."

I remembered Miranda telling me when I'd noticed her bracelet that her father had died before she was born.

"Emme told me that after graduation she moved to Chicago with her sister to attend Chicago State and Miranda went with them. Miranda took some sort of administrative assistant course and then got a job. She is . . . was a whiz with numbers. When that job disappeared she became Emme's assistant. She was a nice person. Why would someone want to kill her?"

We had reached the truck and I glanced back to see Marcus talking with Officer Keller again.

"Whoever killed her must have thought she was Emme," Ruby said.

I hesitated, unsure how to answer her.

"C'mon, Kathleen, there was blood in her hair. I know you had to have seen it."

I had seen it, although I didn't know what had caused it to be there. "She could have fallen and hit her head. You said yourself that she wasn't wearing the right footwear to be walking along that embankment."

Ruby was already shaking her head. "If Miranda fell and hit her head, then we couldn't have seen any blood. She would have been lying on the side that was injured."

The same thing had occurred to me. I just didn't want to believe that someone had murdered Miranda. "Marcus will figure it out," I said.

Ruby pulled a hand over her neck. "I should have told him. Emme had had problems with an ex just before they came for the festival. Some overeager fan took photos of her with the guy at some club. Her ex's name is Derrick . . . something. I don't remember his last name." She made a face. "He's a hustler, all charm and no depth, at least according to Emme's sister, Nora. Anyway, a couple of the pictures turned up on the club's Facebook page and their website, and then they got posted some other places. It looked like Emme was drunk, but she doesn't drink. Some people called her a hypocrite for saying she didn't drink, and the whole thing just got blown way out of proportion. I think it might be what ended the relationship with Elliot, the guy she'd recently been seeing. He's a history professor. A little—uptight, if you know what I mean. Rumor had it he was pretty angry about those photos."

I could see she was beginning to get frazzled. I felt a little frayed around the edges myself. "You can tell Marcus in the morning," I said.

She pulled a hand back through her hair. "Kathleen, it's possible this Derrick guy is here, in Mayville Heights. Nora thought she saw him a couple of days ago. Maybe he attacked Miranda because he thought she was Emme. Or maybe Miranda was trying to keep him away from Emme, and he attacked her on purpose." She suddenly stopped talking. Tears filled her eyes and she tipped her head back so they wouldn't spill over. "This is just like Agatha all over again," she managed to choke out.

I wrapped my arms around her. Agatha Shepherd was the first person to believe in Ruby's artistic talent and the first one to encourage the would-be juvenile delinquent to make something with her art and her life. She had been killed in an alley downtown, and to make things even worse for Ruby, she'd been a suspect for a while. "Come back to the house and have tea with me and the furballs," I offered.

Ruby broke out of the hug and swiped away a stray tear with one hand. "You don't like tea," she said.

"I like iced tea," I said. "And I have lemonade. And brownies. I think." Owen and Hercules were watching us from the driver's-side window of the truck. "Please come."

"Okay," she said, giving me a small smile. "I'll follow you."

I nodded and she started across the lot toward her car.

I unlocked the driver's door of the truck and climbed inside. Owen and Hercules backed across the seat far enough to let me get in. They were both watching me.

"It's Miranda," I said, sticking the key in the ignition.

They exchanged a look, then Hercules meowed softly. "I know," I said. "I liked her, too."

Owen put a paw on my leg. Hercules tipped his head to one side. I didn't try to pretend that they didn't understand what I was saying. "Ruby's coming back to the house with us."

Owen gave a murp of what I took to be approval. As I started the truck Hercules turned and looked out the passenger window. "We'll probably see Marcus for breakfast," I said. He turned back around and settled himself on the seat.

I was just getting out of the truck as Ruby pulled into the driveway behind me. Hercules jumped down from the seat and headed for the back door. Owen waited for Ruby.

"Hey, Owen." She smiled down at him.

"Mrrr," he said in reply before starting around the side of the house.

Hercules was waiting on the top step. I was glad he hadn't decided to go inside before I'd had a chance to open the door.

Once we were inside I flipped on the kitchen light and hung the cat bag on one of the hooks by the door.

Owen had clearly appointed himself Ruby's guardian for the evening. "Have a seat," I said to Ruby, gesturing in the direction of the table.

She pulled out one of the retro chrome chairs and sat down, kicking off one Birkenstock and pulling her leg underneath her. Owen stationed himself by the chair. Hercules was sitting by his food dish, looking pointedly in my direction.

I got each cat three of my homemade sardine crackers and put fresh water in their dishes. Hercules murped his thanks and decided on a drink first. Owen nudged his pile of crackers over and sniffed each one suspiciously.

"He still does that," Ruby said, leaning sideways to watch Owen's obsessive pre-eating ritual.

"He does," I said, reaching for a towel to dry my hands. "Roma thinks he may have eaten something out at Wisteria Hill that made him sick when he was a kitten. She says that may have made him a little . . . fanatical about his food."

Owen lifted his head and shot me a glare when I used the word "fanatical." Ruby smiled again and my own sadness eased a little. "It's okay, Owen," she stage-whispered. "Just because you're a little paranoid doesn't mean people aren't out to get you."

He wrinkled his whiskers at her and went back to his crackers.

I poured us each a tall, icy glass of lemonade and put the last two cream cheese brownies on a plate, then I took a seat at the table as well.

Ruby took a long drink, then set the glass back on the table and sighed. "I keep hoping this is all going to be a mistake somehow," she said, the smile fading from her face. "That your phone or mine is going to ring and somehow the last hour just didn't happen."

I pulled up one leg and propped my chin on my knee. "I keep thinking about Miranda at the library just a day ago. She knows . . . knew the Dewey decimal system." I had to take a drink from my own glass to get rid of the lump that had suddenly appeared at the back of my throat.

Ruby had set one brownie on her napkin. She broke it into several pieces and ate one. "That's good," she said.

"Thanks. I've been trying different brownie recipes," I said. "Trying to come up with the ultimate one."

She took another bite. "This one is right up there." We sat in silence for a minute and then Ruby said, "I think she had a bad relationship with her stepbrothers."

I knew she meant Miranda.

She shifted in her seat. "Sometimes she'd refer to herself as Cinderella, and I heard her say something about her 'Ugly Stepbrothers' once when she was talking to Emme and Nora. It seemed to be some kind of inside thing. Oh, Nora is Emme's sister. You knew that, right?"

I nodded as I reached for the other brownie.

"Emme is pretty popular in Chicago. She has this really devoted fan base. Wherever she goes some of them always show up. Sometimes Miranda would step in and deflect people so Emme could go out to dinner in peace. They didn't always take it well. A few people got pretty abusive."

Both my mother and father had had to deal with zealous fans—Mom from her soap role and Dad from his gig as a dancing raisin in a series of commercials that had become cult classics—but they'd never had to deal with people who were that fanatical.

"Do you think any of those fans could have shown up here?" I asked.

"I don't think so," Ruby said. "Emme didn't mention anything, and no one bothered us any of the times we were out together."

We talked about the festival for a few minutes and then Ruby stretched her arms up over her head and yawned. "I should go," she said. She got to her feet. "Thank you for everything—for the lemonade, for the brownies, for the company. I needed it."

She gave me a hug.

"Thank you for coming," I said. "I needed it, too."

She said good night to Owen and Hercules and promised to send me any photos that turned out. Then she left, giving a little wave as she went past the sunporch windows.

I went back into the kitchen and dropped into Ruby's chair.

Hercules launched himself into my lap, walked his front paws up my chest and nuzzled my chin. "I liked Miranda," I said. He murped his agreement. "Why would somebody kill her?"

I'd stayed away from how and why Miranda had died with Ruby, but I'd seen enough of that blood on her head to know it probably hadn't been an accident.

chapter 4

I was making coffee the next morning when Marcus stopped in. The ends of his hair were still damp from his shower, and when he pulled me close I caught the scent of his citrusy after-shave lotion. There were dark shadows like faint bruises under his eyes, and he'd missed a spot on his chin when he'd shaved.

"I can't stay," he said after he'd kissed me, "but I didn't want to go all day without seeing you."

"Did you have breakfast?" I asked.

He pulled a hand through his hair. "I'll grab something later."

"Three minutes," I said, holding up three fingers. "I can scramble an egg and make an English muffin." The whole wheat English muffin I'd been going to use for my own breakfast was already in the toaster. I reached over and pushed the lever down.

"You don't have to do this," Marcus objected.

I stood on tiptoe and kissed him. "Breakfast is the most important meal of the day," I said. Then I went to the fridge and got the eggs and spinach.

"I can stop at Eric's," he said.

I stopped long enough to kiss him again. "Yes, you can."

He made an exasperated sound that reminded me of Owen when he couldn't find one of his catnip chickens. "You're not listening to me."

I rinsed a handful of spinach under the tap, then took a step back and kissed him for the fourth time before returning to the sink to shake the water off the spinach. "I'm listening. You just haven't changed my mind."

One corner of his mouth twitched with the promise of a smile. "Well, you do keep kissing me. Why would I stop trying?"

I turned, moved as though I was going to kiss him for the fifth time and then turned back around, picked up an egg and broke it into the bowl I'd gotten out to make my own breakfast. "Point taken," I said.

He laughed and sat down. Hercules wandered in, murped a hello at Marcus and went over to his dish. I'd already put his breakfast out.

"Where's your brother?" I asked. I hadn't seen Owen since I'd gotten up. Hercules lifted his head long enough to shoot a look at the basement door.

Owen had his own little lair in the basement. Maggie said

that made him sound like some kind of criminal mastermind. Given that he'd swiped most of the stuff he had down there, including a scarf that had been Maggie's and some bits of paper that had come from Rebecca's recycling bin, I didn't think the term was that far off.

I turned the heat on under my cast-iron frying pan and added some dill and pepper to the egg. Out of the corner of my eye I saw Marcus check his phone and make a face.

"How's the case?"

"Which one?" he asked.

"Miranda Moore's murder."

"I didn't say she was murdered."

The toaster popped and I reached for the English muffin. "I know you didn't," I said. "But she was. I saw . . . blood in her hair."

"That's for the medical examiner's office to decide. Right now all we're doing is gathering evidence." He glanced at his watch. "I'm sorry, but I do need to get going. I have to head over to the marina to see if I can get their security footage. I suspect they're going to be difficult and make me get a warrant."

I noticed he hadn't actually said the words, that it wasn't murder, but he was in what I thought of as police-officer mode and I knew he wasn't going to tell me anything more.

I put the egg sandwich together, filled my stainless-steel travel mug with coffee and gave both to Marcus. In return I got a long, slow kiss that made me think I definitely needed to cook him breakfast more often.

A few minutes after Marcus left, the basement door swung

open and Owen poked his furry head out. He looked around the kitchen, blinking his golden eyes.

"Good morning, sunshine," I said.

He gave an offhand meow that I decided was a "good morning" in return and made his way over to his breakfast. Hercules had just finished eating and was about to wash his face. He paused, one paw in the air, and they exchanged one of their looks. I saw Owen's ear twitch and smiled, thinking of Maggie joking that this seemingly silent way the boys had for communicating was actually them doing semaphore with their ears.

Owen glanced at the door to the porch and then his gaze came to me.

"Meow?" he said.

"Marcus didn't really say anything," I replied, stretching my legs out onto the chair across from me.

The cat might not have been asking what I learned from Marcus, but then again he might have been. It wouldn't be the first time that Owen and Hercules had ended up involved in one of Marcus's investigations. And my answer seemed to satisfy him. He dropped his head and began to suspiciously sniff his food.

I spent the morning working outside, weeding my flowerbeds, picking tomatoes and soliciting the cats' opinion on whether or not we should have another raised bed in the backyard so we could expand the vegetable garden next year. Hercules seemed enthusiastic; Owen was indifferent.

After lunch I headed down to Riverarts. Maggie was dyeing fabric for a new project. "It smells like cinnamon in here," I said, dropping my bag on a stool. I'd made blueberry muffins and brought four with me.

Maggie was peering into a pot that was simmering on the small two-burner stove that she'd added to her studio just a few weeks before. She lifted her head. There was a smudge of yellow-orange on her chin. "It's probably the marigolds," she said. "They kind of have a spicy smell when you boil them."

I looked at the big speckled black pot. I had a similar one in my kitchen. "That's not lunch, is it?" I asked. I raised an eyebrow at her à la *Star Trek*'s Mr. Spock. "I know I said I was trying to eat more fiber."

She laughed and pushed a stray blond curl off her face with the heel of her hand. "No, it's not lunch, but they do feed marigolds to chickens. They make their egg yolks a deeper yellow."

"I'll keep that in mind," I said, smiling back at her.

The grin faded from her face. "I heard what happened last night. Are you okay?"

I nodded, exhaling slowly. "I'm okay. Have you talked to Ruby? Is she all right?"

"I saw her a little while ago. She was on her way to a sort of unofficial meeting over at the Stratton. Just to see what people want to do." Maggie gave the contents of the pot a stir with a large wooden spoon.

"Do you think they're going to cancel the rest of the festival?"

"I can see why they'd want to," she said. "But I hope they

don't. People are going to be upset. Sad. If they keep the festival going, it gives everyone something to focus on, somewhere to use that energy."

The organizers of the music festival met first thing Monday morning and decided to continue. The final concert would be dedicated to Miranda. Emme, however, didn't feel she could sing under the circumstances, so she resigned from the event. Ruby stopped into the library to share the news.

"I couldn't change her mind," she said. She played with a knotted bracelet on her left wrist. "I don't know, maybe it's selfish of me wanting her to stay. I just thought . . . maybe we could sing something for Miranda at the final concert."

I put a hand on her arm. "I don't think it's selfish. Emme just has to work through her grief in her own way. And maybe you and Ami could still do a song for Miranda. You could talk to Emme's sister, Nora. Maybe she could tell you what songs Miranda liked."

Ruby nodded. "I like that idea. I'll see what Ami says. Thanks." She was still fingering the knotted cord around her wrist. "Kathleen, do you remember if Miranda was wearing a gold bracelet when we . . . when we found her?"

I shook my head. "I don't. Why do you ask?"

"Emme asked me about it. She said Miranda wore it all the time but it wasn't with . . . her."

"You could ask Marcus," I said. "Maybe the police have it."

"That's a good idea."

There was a moment of silence filled only by the sound of

the printer in the computer area. Ruby cleared her throat. "Kathleen, I kind of hate to ask this, but I need a favor."

"Sure," I said. "What is it?"

She exhaled softly. "Gunnerson's Funeral Home is taking care of the arrangements for . . . Miranda. I don't know anything yet about a service. The thing is, the police still have the apartment sealed off. Could you, uh, ask Marcus if Nora and I could just go get an outfit for her? Nora says there's a dress that Miranda was going to wear for the final concert."

I nodded. "Of course. I'll go up to my office right now and try him. I'll text you and let you know what he says, but I'm sure he can work something out."

Ruby smiled. "Thanks," she said. She hugged me. "I'll talk to you soon."

I got Marcus's voice mail when I called. I left a message explaining what Ruby needed. He called me back about an hour later. "Give me Ruby's number. I can take them over right after supper."

"Thanks," I said. I recited Ruby's cell number from memory.

"I have to work late tonight," he said. "I'm sorry. I was hoping to see you."

I nodded even though he couldn't see me. "I figured you would. Call me later if you have time. I love you."

"Love you, too," he said.

I was sitting in one of my big wooden Adirondack chairs after supper that evening, watching Owen prowl around the yard like he was inspecting the mowing job Harry Taylor had done earlier in the day, when Ami Lester came across the grass. I knew she was staying with Rebecca and Everett, her grandfather. We'd waved across the backyard a couple of times since she'd arrived, but I hadn't had a chance to talk to her.

"Hi," I said, getting to my feet.

"Hi, Kathleen," she said. "Are you busy?"

I shook my head. "No. I was just sitting here thinking that I should see if there are any more tomatoes ready to be picked." I gestured at the chair next to mine. "Please. Sit down."

Ami took the other Adirondack chair. She was wearing cutoff jean shorts, a black-and-gold-striped tank top and Birkenstocks. Her long, strawberry-blond hair was twisted into a loose knot. She wasn't wearing any makeup and a frown creased her forehead.

"You heard that the festival is going on after all," she said.

I nodded. "I did."

"Ruby and Emme and I were supposed to be singing together, so we kind of spent a lot of our off time together. Miranda, too. I mean, she was bit older, but we liked a lot of the same music and it turned out we were both watching that show *Restless Days*. So we kind of got to be friends." I saw the first hint of a smile on her face. "Mostly because of the show at first. Ruby and Emme wanted to practice one night, and I didn't, because I wanted to see the new episode. They didn't see what the big deal was and then Miranda said, 'But Angelo's coming back,' and I said, 'You mean you don't think he's dead?' and we started talking about what was going to happen next and we were just friends after that." She cleared her throat. "That's why I'm here."

"Okay," I said, looking uncertainly at her.

"I need you to find the person who killed her."

It was the last thing I'd expected her to say. Hercules had come from somewhere, and now he settled himself by my feet, leaning against my leg, his green eyes focused on Ami, seemingly following our conversation. "Ami, the police are already doing that," I said.

She shook her head. "They have other cases, and people aren't going to talk to them the way they'll talk to you."

I started to say something but she held up one hand. "It's true, Kathleen. Rebbie says you have a way of getting people to tell you things, and that's important because some of the people at the festival were street performers for years. They don't like the police and they're not going to talk to them." "Rebbie" was what she called Rebecca and had since she was a little girl. They had always been close.

"I'm not a detective," I said. "Investigating a murder takes more than just getting people to talk to you."

"You figured out who killed Ruby's teacher Agatha Shepherd and what happened to Roma's father. It's because of you that my great-grandmother's name was cleared."

Everything Ami had said was true up to a point. What was also true was that the cost of getting involved in those cases had been very high. It had almost destroyed my relationship with Marcus before it really even got started.

I felt bad about what had happened to Miranda, but I had no idea how to figure out who had killed her. If it had been a case of mistaken identity, if she was dead because someone mistook her for Emme, it was going to be even harder to catch the killer.

"Ami, I'm sorry," I began.

She shook her head again, holding up both hands as though she could somehow stop my "no" before I even got the word out. "Please, Kathleen. You're good at this kind of thing. You see inside people. You see connections other people don't."

I was pretty sure Rebecca had told her that. She'd told me more than once that I had a knack for reading people. I'd spent a lot of time around theater people growing up, watching my parents and other actors turn a character on the page into a three-dimensional person. I'd learned a lot about human nature from that.

I glanced down at Hercules. His green eyes met mine and then he looked toward Ami. I was pretty sure what he thought I should do.

"I don't want Miranda's murder to get pushed aside because she's not from here and she has no one to speak up for her," Ami said, a determined set to her mouth.

"And no one will let that happen," I said. "I can't help you, but I will keep my eyes and ears open and I'll share anything I learn with Marcus."

She sighed and got to her feet, wiping her hands on the front of her shorts. "Okay, I can live with that for now," she said. "But please think about what I said." She gave Hercules a small smile and headed back across the yard to Rebecca and Everett's house.

I looked down at the cat. He was looking up at me, eyes narrowed, a sour expression on his face.

"I'm not a detective," I said. "And you know Marcus is good

76

at what he does." Once again, here I was, explaining myself to a cat.

Hercules continued to glare at me, making it clear that he didn't like my explanation.

"And I don't want to put him in a difficult spot," I added. "What else could I do?"

He made a huffy sound through his nose, flicked his tail at me and stalked toward the house. It wasn't hard to guess what he thought I should do.

chapter 5

Marcus stopped in at the library Tuesday morning to bring me coffee and a lemon-blueberry muffin. He was tight-lipped about the case other than to say there was nothing new.

After he was gone I stood for a moment in front of the big window behind my desk and looked out over the water. I had always thought one of the most beautiful parts of the town was the waterfront, with all the elm and black walnut trees that lined the shore, and the Riverwalk trail that made its way from the old warehouses at the point, past the downtown shops and businesses, all the way out beyond the marina. I'd walked the path dozens of times. Was it possible that Miranda's death was just a random act of violence? Was the Riverwalk not as safe as I thought it was?

Maggie and I met Roma for a late lunch at Eric's to talk about the wedding. The small restaurant was busy. It was good to see that the music festival was bringing people to town.

Over bowls of Eric's taco salad, Roma showed us a photo Ella King had texted her of our bridesmaid dresses. We had to go out for one last fitting.

"That's beautiful," Maggie said, bending her head over the image. Our dresses were simple floor-length sheaths that complemented Roma's wedding gown, which Ella was also making. The sleeveless chiffon dresses featured a jewel neckline and a deep V at the back. Ella had suggested a satiny ribbon tie at the waist. Roma had chosen a soft sage green that went well with Maggie's green eyes and blond curls and equally well with my darker eyes and hair.

"Are you sure you're both happy with Ella's design?" Roma asked. "And the color?"

"Yes," I said.

Maggie nodded her agreement.

"Because if you want sleeves, Ella can add them."

I put my hand on her arm. "We don't need sleeves. The design is perfect. The color is perfect."

"You're going to be a perfect bride and it's going to be a perfect wedding," Maggie added.

Roma put a hand on her chest. "I'm actually getting married," she said, as though it had just occurred to her.

I smiled. "That's what happens when you propose to someone in the middle of my kitchen."

She smiled back at me. "I did do that, didn't I?" She pointed at both of us then. "I almost forgot. I brought the readings with me." She reached for her bag by her feet, pulled out a blue file folder and handed a sheet of paper to Maggie and another to me.

Maggie scanned the page, then she looked up. "I like this," she said. "'How Falling in Love Is Like Owning a Dog.'"

"Don't tell that to Owen," I teased. My own reading was a piece from the Bible, the story of Ruth and Naomi.

"What's Sydney reading?" Maggie asked. Sydney was Eddie's ten-year-old daughter from his first marriage.

Roma shook her head. "I don't know. Neither does Eddie. She won't tell us. It's supposed to be a surprise." She smiled. "I'm so lucky she's okay with us getting married."

"Given how hard she tried to get the two of you together, I think she's more than okay with it," Maggie said, folding the sheet of paper she'd been holding in half and putting it in her messenger bag.

"When does Olivia get here?" I asked. Roma's daughter, who was a biologist and commercial diver working on a TV show for the Exploration Channel, was coming to spend some time with her mother before the wedding. Roma was overjoyed. Her face lit up every time she talked about Olivia.

"She'll be here next week," she said. "I can't wait to see her. I think she's been feeling a little left out of the wedding planning. I talked to her a couple of days ago, and she didn't seem that enthusiastic about her dress."

"Don't worry," I said. "There are still things she can help with once she gets here." Maggie and I were hosting a wedding shower for Roma.

"You're not going overboard with the shower, remember?" Roma said.

I gave Maggie a blank look. "I don't remember agreeing to that, do you?"

She wrinkled her nose at me. "Doesn't ring a bell."

Roma shook her head. Her gaze went from me to Maggie and something in her expression changed. "I don't know how to say thank you for everything that you've both done, from helping me find the perfect dress when I thought I didn't even care about having a wedding dress to telling me to follow my heart"—she gestured at me—"to getting the two of us together in the first place." She looked at Maggie.

"That's what friends are for," I said, reaching for my coffee. "And how many people have a how-we-got-together story like yours and Eddie's? Do you remember the night we moved Faux Eddie to the community center?"

Maggie had created the very lifelike figure of Eddie for a Winterfest display.

Roma laughed. "I don't think I'll ever forget it. You and Maggie hijacked my SUV. And not for the first time."

Maggie was gesturing with her fork because her mouth was full of food. When she could speak she said, "You wanted to cut my Eddie into pieces." She mock glared at Roma.

"His feet were hanging out the back of the car," Roma retorted. "It looked like I was driving a dead body around."

I snagged a tortilla chip from my bowl. "Do you remember how cold it was that night?" I asked. "And we were afraid it was going to snow." I grinned at the memory.

It had been pretty clear that Faux Eddie wasn't going to fit in the back of Roma's SUV. The legs were hanging out, almost touching the driveway.

"Could we take his legs off?" I'd asked.

Maggie had looked at me, aghast. "Take Eddie's legs off? How?"

"I have a hacksaw under the front seat," Roma had chimed in oh-so-not-helpfully.

I remembered how Maggie had put a protective hand on mannequin Eddie's thigh.

"Do your legs detach?" she'd asked.

Roma had suggested wrapping "Eddie" in plastic and tying him to the roof. I was pretty sure that would get us pulled over by the police before we'd even driven a block. Luckily, we'd managed to get the mannequin turned around and positioned in the front passenger seat with the seat belt holding him in place.

Roma had walked around to the front of the vehicle and looked through the windshield. "He looks so real."

Faux Eddie had looked so real it started a rumor that he and Roma were an item. The real Eddie got in touch with her and pretty soon they were a couple.

She shook her head now. "I spent way too much time worried about things that weren't important."

"It doesn't matter," Maggie said, reaching for the little metal teapot. She lifted the lid and peered thoughtfully inside, then looked up at us. "Sometimes love takes the long way home."

Roma smiled. "That's beautiful."

Out of the corner of my eye I saw Ami and Ruby walk by, heading in the direction of the theater. I hadn't been able to stop thinking about my conversation with Ami. Part of me did want to help her. I just didn't see how I could do that.

I realized then that Maggie was saying something. She had leaned over into my line of sight. "I'm sorry," I said, shaking my head. "What did you say?"

"Where were you?" she asked.

I reached for my coffee cup and leaned against the back of my chair with a sigh. "I'm sorry. I just saw Ruby and Ami walking by."

"I'm glad they're going to continue with the festival," Maggie said. "But that doesn't make what happened any less sad."

"Does Marcus have any leads at all?" Roma asked.

"Not that he's telling me," I said. "I know he's been talking to everyone who's taking part in the festival, but I don't think he's come up with anything." Given that I'd barely seen Marcus since Ruby and Hercules had discovered Miranda's body and when I did he was distant and distracted, I was pretty sure I was right about how the case was going. Was Ami right? Would I have better luck talking to people?

Maggie was still eyeing me, a thoughtful expression in her green eyes. "What aren't you telling us?" she said.

I hesitated for a moment, but only a moment. "Ami came over last night. She asked me if I'd . . . investigate Miranda's murder."

"What did you say?" Roma asked.

"I told her no," I said. "I'm not a detective. Marcus is and he's good at it."

"Marcus being good at his job doesn't somehow mean that you're not good at figuring this kind of thing out yourself," Roma said.

I looked at her, surprised. "Wait a minute. Are you saying I should have said yes?"

Roma shook her head. "No. We're on your side." She glanced at Maggie, who nodded. "And if you'd said yes to Ami, we'd be on your side." She studied me for a moment. I could tell from the slight frown on her face that she was debating whether or not to say something else.

I waited.

Finally, she seemed to find the words she'd been looking for. "Kathleen, you were the one who figured out what happened to Thomas." She meant Thomas Karlsson, her birth father.

I opened my mouth to respond, but Roma held up one hand. "I'm not trying to say that Marcus and the rest of the police department wouldn't have figured it out, but the point is that you did it first. You're good at reading people. That doesn't mean you have to get involved in what happened to Miranda Moore. It doesn't mean you have to say yes to Ami, either." She looked at Maggie. "I had a point and now I don't remember what it was."

Maggie smiled. "Bride brain," she said. She turned to me. "Do what feels right to you. We have your back if you need us. Just don't make a decision based on whether or not you think Marcus is going to get his man panties in a wad."

"His what?" I said. The expression was so unlike Maggie. Beside me Roma's lips were twitching as she tried not to laugh.

"Brady and I were over at his dad's place playing pinball last night. Burtis was upset about something to do with one of those big tents they rent. He's pretty much all bluster, but I think he was getting on Lita's nerves. She told him not to get his man panties in a wad. I guess the expression just stuck in my brain."

"Okay," I said slowly. "I promise I won't make any decisions based on whether or not I think Marcus is walking around with bunched-up underwear."

That did it. Roma started to laugh. "I'm sorry," she said, waving a hand in the air. "I just got this mental image of—" She started to laugh even harder, leaning her head on one hand.

I wondered whom she'd gotten a mental picture of and decided I was probably happier not knowing.

We decided against dessert. We paid our bills and I hugged them both. "I'll see you tonight at class," I said. Maggie and Roma headed out together. I waited long enough to grab a take-out cup of coffee and then headed back to the library.

It was a gorgeous afternoon, just a few wisps of clouds in the sky and the sun sparkling on the water. I had the urge to turn around, run after Mags and Roma and play hooky for the rest of the day. But Roma had animals that needed her expert care, Maggie was working on a new project for the tourist alliance and I had a meeting with Lita about the library budget. I thought about the night the three of us had moved Faux Eddie, the night that the rumors that the real Eddie was seeing someone in Mayville Heights had started. Maggie was right. I could count on both of them, and I hoped they knew they could count on me.

As I followed the gentle curve of the road back toward the library I thought about Emme Finley. It certainly seemed like she and Miranda had had the same sort of friendship. I knew I'd be devastated if anything happened to Maggie or Roma—or Lise, my best friend back in Boston. I felt sympathy for Emme. And I told myself it was only natural, under the circumstances, that I felt a little niggling twist of uncertainty about saying no to Ami.

It was a busy afternoon at the library. Several tourists came in just to see the building, and I found myself giving a group of them an impromptu talk about the history of the library. We had a group of day-campers come in for a tour and several stories. The little ones were enchanted by Mia, who did all the voices from a guinea pig named Einstein to a lion with a case of back-to-school nerves. I left just after five and headed home for supper and some time with Owen and Hercules, and then, because it was such a nice night, I walked down to tai chi.

Rebecca was at the top of the stairs, sitting on the long, low wooden bench underneath the coat hooks. She smiled at me as I came up the last three steps, and I realized that she had been waiting for me, waiting to repeat Ami's plea.

I sat down next to her, set my bag on the floor and returned her smile. "I'm listening. Go ahead," I said.

She tipped her head to one side, pulling a gauzy lavender scarf from around her neck. "Am I that transparent?" she asked.

"No," I said. "It's just that I know how much you love Ami." Ami was Everett's only grandchild. Everett, a widower, had raised Ami after the death of her parents in a car accident when she was four. Even though he and Rebecca had been apart for most of Ami's life, she and Rebecca had formed a tight bond, as strong as any biological connection.

Rebecca nodded. "I do. And I'm not casting any aspersions on Marcus or the department, it's just that you have a way of finding things out."

I'd heard that so many times in the past day and a half I was beginning to feel like the Amazing Renaldo, the 1-900 so-called Psychic to the Stars from late-night TV.

"Please," Rebecca said. She didn't say anything else, but her blue eyes stayed locked on my face.

I think on some level I'd known from the beginning, from the moment Ami had sat down in my blue Adirondack chair and asked for my help, that I was going to say yes. I sighed softly. "I'll see what I can find out, but I'm not making any promises." I held up a hand. "And I'm not taking Ami's money. Or yours."

"I understand," she said with a solemn nod. She got to her feet. "I hope this isn't going to cause any problems with Marcus."

I shook my head. "It'll be okay."

Maggie poked her head around the door then. "Hi," she said. "We're almost ready to start." She had a gleam in her eye that told me she was going to work us hard.

I was right. By the time we finished the complete form at the end of the class, my T-shirt was damp and sticking to my body. Ruby crossed the floor, mopping sweat off her neck with a towel. "Hey, Kathleen, I'd still like to try to get some shots of Owen and Hercules along the walkway. Do you think we could reschedule for after supper tomorrow night?"

"I can't think of any reason why not," I said. "I'll check my calendar when I get home, and if there's a problem I'll text you."

"Sounds good," she said.

I waited for Maggie to lock up, and we made a quick trip out to the Kings' to try on our dresses. Other than a slight adjustment to the hem on my dress, they were perfect. When we got back in the truck, I handed Maggie my phone. "This is the final guest list for Roma's shower," I said. "Everybody we invited is coming."

"That doesn't surprise me. Everyone loves Roma." She scanned the names, then handed the phone back to me.

"Have you talked to Pearl?" I asked, digging out my keys. Roma's mom was thrilled that her daughter and Eddie were getting married. She was already referring to Eddie's daughter, Sydney, as her granddaughter.

Maggie nodded. "I did. She'll be here."

"Have we forgotten anything?"

Maggie smiled. "How many lists have you made in the last month?"

I ducked my head. "No comment."

That made her laugh. "We haven't forgotten anything, Kath. The shower is going to be wonderful. I promise."

I dropped Maggie at her apartment and headed home.

Hercules was waiting on the back steps. I reached down to stroke his fur, and he wrinkled his nose at me, taking in my sweat-blotched shirt.

"It's not that bad," I said, grabbing the edge of the shirt and pulling it away from my body.

"Mrr," he said, still making a face. Hercules was particular about his own hygiene—and mine, too, it seemed.

I unlocked the doors and Hercules went ahead of me into the kitchen. I told him about Rebecca waiting for me at tai chi and how I'd agreed to see what I could find out as I made toast with peanut butter and poured a glass of lemonade.

Hercules listened thoughtfully it seemed to me, his green eyes locked on my face, although it may have been the toast and not my words that really had his attention. When I sat down at the table he jumped onto my lap. "I thought I was too sweaty and offensive for you," I teased, stroking his dark fur.

"Mrr," he said, sending a pointed look at my plate.

"One small bite," I said. Roma was always warning me about the cats' penchant for people food over cat food, and while I felt fairly certain they didn't have the digestive systems of "normal" cats, I tried to follow her guidance, just in case.

Herc ate his treat and licked his whiskers.

"One bite," I reminded him.

He continued to stare at me, just the way Rebecca had. She wasn't the only one who challenged my ability to say no and stick to it. There was a dab of peanut butter on the edge of my thumb, and I stuck it out so he could lick it off.

"You're as bad as Rebecca," I said.

The cat glanced at me and almost seemed to smile. Both Owen and Hercules adored Rebecca. I stroked his fur again. "I have to tell Marcus," I said.

Hercules murped his agreement.

"I'm not sure how I keep getting involved in his cases, but good or bad, I'm involved. Again."

I put my hand flat on the table, and to my amusement the cat put his paw on top of it. It seemed that good or bad, he was in, too.

chapter 6

It was one of those Wednesdays at the library when it seemed as though half the population of Mayville Heights came into the building looking for something. Lunch was part of a sandwich that I ate in snatches between answering questions, searching the shelves for books and solving a small computer crisis. So much for my plan to take in another lunchtime concert at the Stratton Theatre.

"It was a good day," I said to Susan, smiling with satisfaction as I locked the main doors at the end of the day. "I love it when we have a lineup at the checkout desk and everyone is carrying a stack of books."

"Me too," she said, nudging her cat's-eye glasses up her nose. "Which reminds me, I have to grab a couple of books for the boys." As usual her hair was twisted up in a topknot, held today with an unsharpened number-two pencil, and what I was reasonably certain was a brush for applying eyeliner. I was never quite sure what was going to be poked into Susan's updo, and I was equally unsure of whether that was because she sometimes tended to be a little distracted or because she let her genius twins do her hair.

"What are they reading these days?" I asked.

Susan counted on her fingers. "*Treasure Island*, the latest Einstein book and one on robotics." She pushed a stray strand of hair off her face. "I've been dropping hints for some kind of maid-bot that will empty the dishwasher and bring me coffee in bed every morning. The boys are leaning toward a rocket that will probably set the backyard on fire." She smiled. "Five minutes and I'll be ready."

I watched her head for the stacks and wondered what it would be like to head home to a child or two. Marcus and I had talked about the future in the abstract sense but nothing more. Before we could make any kind of long-term plans, I had to tell him about Owen and Hercules and their . . . superpowers, something that I'd put off for far too long. And before I did that, I needed to tell him that I was going to see if I could find out anything about Miranda Moore's murder.

I helped Susan carry the books she'd picked out to her car. I was about to get into my truck when I heard someone call my name. Ami was cutting across the parking lot.

"Rebbie told me that you said you'd look into Miranda's murder," she said as she came level with me. She pushed her hair out of her face. "I just wanted to say thank you. So . . . thank you."

"I'm not making any promises," I warned. I didn't want to get her hopes up that I could somehow come up with answers, like a magician pulling a rabbit out of a hat.

She nodded. "I know. I just feel better knowing you're looking for answers. If I can help, you'll call me, right?"

"I will," I said.

She smiled. "Okay, so I better get to practice." She took a couple of steps backward and then turned and made her way toward the sidewalk.

I got in the truck and headed up Mountain Road. There was no sign of Owen or Hercules when I stepped into the kitchen. "I'm home," I called. After a moment there was an answering meow from the second floor, followed by another from the basement.

Hercules wandered in while I was making a salad for supper, probably drawn by the smell of the hard-boiled egg and slice of bacon I was chopping. I expected him to park himself at my feet, but instead he headed across the floor to where my messenger bag leaned against the wall under the coat hooks, and tried to get under the front flap with a paw.

"After supper," I said.

He turned and looked at me with his big green eyes, then pawed at the bag again.

"After supper," I repeated a little louder, carefully enunciating both words. I tossed the egg into my bowl along with some roasted pumpkin seeds and added dressing. Then I set the dish on the table.

Hercules had given up trying to lift the flap of my bag and was now poking a paw at the side.

I sat down and reached for my fork. "I get that you want to do some research on Miranda, but we don't have time right now, because we're meeting Ruby in a little while." I didn't turn around, but I imagined his head coming up when I said Ruby's name. After a moment I glanced down to see him at my feet. He meowed inquiringly.

"She wants to finish taking pictures down by the marina. If that's okay with you."

He immediately started to wash his face. That was one yes, I decided.

I had another bite of my salad, and then Owen's furry gray tabby face peered around the living room doorway.

"Ruby wants to take more photos," I said around a mouthful of egg, cheese and crunchy romaine lettuce.

He looked down at his chest, then looked at me again and meowed once more. It seemed to me I could hear a question in the sound.

"You look very handsome today," I said.

It seemed to be the right answer, because he disappeared (not literally) once more.

I had time to do the dishes and clean the bathroom before we left. The boys willingly climbed into the truck and settled themselves on the front seat. Owen seemed to feel I wasn't moving fast enough. He looked from me to the windshield a couple of times, grumbling just under his breath.

Ruby was waiting for us at the marina. "Hey, guys," she said as we got out of the truck. Like the last time, I was carrying Owen in my arms, and Hercules was riding in the cat carrier slung over my shoulder.

Ruby seemed more subdued and quieter than usual. Her hair was pulled back from her face, she wasn't wearing any makeup and she was dressed in a plain navy T-shirt.

"Are you sure you want to do this?" I asked. "We can go somewhere else or just take the night off if you want to."

She gave me a half smile and shrugged. Both hands were jammed in the pockets of her gray shorts. "Truthfully, I could use the distraction," she said.

Owen was eyeing her, golden eyes narrowed.

"I'm fine," she reassured him.

He seemed satisfied and used one paw to take a quick swipe at his face.

I glanced at Hercules, who was looking intently at me. Ruby had already started across the grass. I felt a bit silly, but I tipped my head toward him and whispered, "She's okay."

I saw Ruby send a quick glance in the direction of where Miranda's body had been found before she walked a bit farther up the shoreline. The boys and I followed her without comment, although Hercules looked up at me again. I wondered if I was imagining the concern in his eyes.

Ruby decided she'd work with Owen first. "Where do you want him?" I asked.

She pointed to a large rocky outcropping. "There would be good."

I set Owen down on a flat area on the top of a weathered boulder and smoothed the fur on the top of his head. Then Hercules and I stood back and watched.

Once again I couldn't help thinking how unlike most "regular" cats Owen was as he posed for Ruby, following her instructions and hand gestures—most of the time. I knew how lucky I was that Mayville Heights was the type of place where pretty much no one would think it was the least bit odd that my cats made great models.

Ruby finished with Owen as the shadows got longer, and then it was Herc's turn. I set him down by a large elm tree and was reaching to pick up Owen as a woman walked by. She looked to be in her late forties or early fifties, wearing a dark blue T-shirt dress with a pretty shawl in soft shades of blue and gray over her shoulders.

Owen bolted out of my reach and scampered across the grass, stopping a few feet in front of the woman and meowing loudly at her. The woman looked down at him, and I started toward them before she could make the mistake of trying to stroke his soft gray fur.

Ruby caught sight of the woman. "Nora?" she said.

The woman stopped. "Hello," she said to Ruby, with just a hint of a smile.

"Hang on a second," Ruby said to Hercules as though he were a person, and he obligingly sat down.

She walked over to the woman—Nora. She looked familiar, although I couldn't place her. Maybe she'd been in the library recently.

"What are you doing?" Nora asked, looking surprised to see us and the boys.

Ruby explained about the photo project.

Nora leaned forward and held out her hand to Owen. "What a beautiful cat," she said.

In that perverse way cats sometimes have, he took a couple

of steps toward her. I stepped in, putting my arm out in front of him. "I'm sorry," I said. "Owen used to be feral. He doesn't have the best social skills."

"He looks so friendly," she said.

Ruby nodded. "He is. So is Hercules." She gestured over her shoulder at the little tuxedo cat, still sitting patiently waiting for us. "As long as you stick to a strict hands-off policy."

"I'm sorry," I added.

For a moment Nora almost seemed put out, but then she recovered. "I understand," she said, smiling at Owen. "I don't like people I don't know getting handsy with me, either." She looked at me. "He really is a beautiful animal."

"Who thinks he's a person most of the time," I said, bending down to pick up the subject of the conversation. Owen continued to stare at Nora, clearly curious about the woman.

Ruby shook her head. "I'm sorry; Nora, this is my friend Kathleen Paulson." She turned to me and her voice softened. "Kathleen, this is Nora Finley."

Nora was Emme's sister. That's why she looked familiar. Emme had dropped out of the music festival. I wondered why her sister was still in town. "I'm so sorry about Miranda," I said. "I didn't know her very well, but I liked her."

Nora nodded. "Thank you," she said. "Emme and Miranda had been friends for so long Miranda felt like another little sister." She let out a breath. "And what makes it even worse is the idea that someone may have wanted Emme dead and killed Miranda by mistake."

"What?" Ruby exclaimed. She stared at Nora, then abruptly shook her head. "I'm sorry," she said. "That was rude."

Nora held up one hand. "It's all right. It's just that Miranda was wearing one of Emme's dresses along with her sweater. And they did look a lot alike. Plus, Miranda didn't have an enemy in the world, while some of Emme's fans could get . . . well, a little obsessed. It just seems to me that her death had to have been a horrible case of mistaken identity."

"Do you know why Miranda was wearing Emme's things?" I asked.

"She did her laundry and somehow a red T-shirt ended up in the washer. Her clothes all came out a rather sickening shade of pink. Since they were the same size Emme offered to lend Miranda what she needed." Nora sighed softly. "Other than that, the day just seemed like any other day, you know. We went home at about four thirty. We didn't even go out for supper. We ordered in. I keep thinking what if Emme had gone out instead?"

Up close I could see that Nora Finley was closer to fifty than forty. She wore her dark brown hair in a layered chin-length bob with long bangs. She had hazel eyes behind her tinted glasses. Her makeup had been expertly applied but couldn't quite hide the lines around her eyes and the dark circles underneath them. She looked tired, which was understandable under the circumstances.

"The police will find whoever did this," I said.

Nora's gaze darted toward the stretch of riverbank where Miranda's body had been found. "I hope so," she said. "What I really hope happens is that they find Emme's ex-boyfriend."

"The professor?" Ruby said.

Nora shook her head. "No, not Elliot. I was referring to that lowlife loser Emme briefly got mixed up with."

"Do you think he could have . . . hurt Miranda?"

"I know it's a cliché—the ex did it—but Derrick didn't take his and Emme's breakup well. And he was arrested once for a fight outside a club."

"Is Emme okay?" Ruby asked, twisting the hem of her T-shirt between her fingers. "I wish she'd stayed."

"She's all right," Nora said. "I mean, she's upset about Miranda, of course. It was just too painful for her to stay. She just—she just needs to take a few days for herself, and then we're going back to Chicago. Emme's agent has a number of club dates lined up."

Ruby looked surprised. "Does that mean she's given up on going back to school? I thought that was all set."

"She's put it aside for now," Nora said. "With everything that's happened Emme needs to get back to her life. Back to her music. It's the best thing."

Owen was squirming restlessly in my arms.

"I should let you get back to work," she said. She gave me a polite smile. "It was nice to meet you."

"You as well," I said.

"Tell Emme we're all thinking about her," Ruby said. She'd stopped playing with her shirt and stuffed her hands in her pockets again. "If she needs anything or you do . . ." She let the end of the sentence trail off.

"I will," Nora said. She turned and walked back the way she'd come.

Ruby just stood there for a moment, looking after Nora. Then she shook her head. "This is just a big mess," she said in a voice that was barely audible as she turned back to Hercules.

Since she seemed to be talking mostly to herself I didn't comment, but Owen meowed softly, seemingly in agreement.

chapter 7

Ruby wrapped up the photo session just as it was getting dark. I set the boys on the front seat of the truck and gave them each two sardine crackers. Hercules gave a meow of thanks but he looked at Ruby instead of me.

"Are you sure you're okay?" I said.

She nodded. "I am," she said. "It's just . . . strange. I can't seem to get my mind around the idea that Miranda is dead and it's because someone really wanted Emme dead."

I was having a bit of trouble with that as well. Certainly anyone who had known Emme couldn't have mistaken Miranda for her. "Nora said that Emme's ex had a history of violence."

"Can you call a bar fight a history of violence?" Ruby asked.

"I don't know," I said. "I'm sure Marcus is looking for the man. Did Emme say anything about him to you?"

She shrugged. "Not a lot. Derrick's last name is Clifton. I asked Ami. I think he was a year ahead of Emme in school. She showed me a picture of him once on her phone. Average-looking guy. Brown hair, scruffy beard." She touched the left side of her forehead. "He had a scar right here."

Aside from the scar it sounded like there was nothing distinctive about Derrick Clifton. It would be easy to walk right past him on the street.

"Did you get the sense that Emme was afraid of him?" I asked.

Ruby shook her head. "No. Truthfully, I got the sense that she was crazy about the guy. When she showed me the picture her whole face lit up. Nora, on the other hand, has no use for the guy. Protective big sister, I guess."

So Emme wasn't over her ex. That was interesting.

"I wish she hadn't left town," Ruby said. "She wrote me a note to say good-bye. I can't help thinking if we'd talked face-to-face maybe I could have convinced her to stay."

"Do you know why Nora is still here?"

"She volunteered to help with promotion for the music festival. She wanted to finish what she started. And Ami thinks she's hoping Emme will change her mind and come back. I wish she would." She held up both hands. "And I'm making myself crazy when there's nothing I can do." She gave me a hug. "I'll talk to you soon."

I slid behind the wheel and started the truck. I felt unsettled. I was acutely aware of the promise I'd made to Rebecca.

Both cats were watching me, I realized, two sets of eyes locked unblinkingly on me. "I know," I said. "I'm just not sure where to start."

I decided to stop at Eric's on the way home on the theory that if chocolate didn't help, it wouldn't hurt, either.

I found a parking spot just up the street from the café, behind an unfamiliar older Subaru.

"I won't be long," I said.

Owen looked at me and licked his whiskers. Translation: "I want whatever you're having."

The restaurant was busier than usual for a Wednesday night. I ordered a hot chocolate and Eric's chocolate pudding cake to go.

Nic raised an eyebrow. "Long day?" he asked. Nicolas Sutton was built like a hockey goalie, with a shaved head and smooth, dark skin. In reality he was a found-metal-and-paper artist who created incredible artwork. His latest piece was an eight-foot-long sturgeon made entirely from garbage found in the river.

"Kind of," I said. "How's the fish coming?"

He grinned as he reached for a take-out container. "Good. The only thing is I'm probably going to have more stuff than I can use and I hate the fact that all of it came from the water. What the heck are people thinking? Do they actually think when they throw something in the river that it's really gone?"

Before I could answer, Nic threw up his hands. "Sorry, Kathleen. I'm getting preachy again. I'll be right back with your order."

He was back in less than a minute with my food. He gestured to the domed cover of my hot chocolate. "I stuck a couple of marshmallows on top," he said. "They're like chocolate. They'll fix pretty much anything."

I thanked him and paid for my order. As I was approaching the door, I glanced out the big front window and to my surprise saw the bearded man I'd seen arguing with Emme Finley in the library parking lot hurrying up the street. He was wearing the same faded black ball cap. Could he be her mysterious ex? I couldn't see his forehead to tell if he had the scar that Ruby had mentioned Derrick Clifton had.

I hurried to get outside, but as I stepped onto the sidewalk I could see that the man was already at his car—the Subaru that was parked ahead of my truck. He slammed the lid of the trunk, used his hip to close the rear driver's-side door and then slid behind the wheel. At the same time I saw Hercules standing on his back legs, looking out the passenger window, seeming to watch the man as well, as though he'd recognized him from my description—which I knew was impossible.

The cat turned and put one paw on the dashboard, and a feeling of dread washed over me. "No, no, no, no, no," I whispered.

Hercules jumped onto the dash and walked through the windshield.

I called to him as I half ran, half walked up the sidewalk, but he ignored me. He walked down the hood of the truck and paused at the end, just above the grill, as if he was judging the distance. He glanced back over his shoulder, and then he launched himself across the space between the two vehicles and through the back window of the car just as the driver pulled away from the curb, clearly unaware that he had a stow-away.

I awkwardly ran the last few steps to the truck, slopping hot chocolate on my hand. I climbed in, jamming the take-out cup into the cup holder and wiping my hand on my shorts.

Owen looked at me as I dropped the container of chocolate pudding cake on the seat. "I'm going to buy those harnesses Roma has been talking about," I said. Roma had been after me to restrain Owen and Hercules for safety reasons when they were in the truck. Owen suddenly noticed something on the passenger floor mat that needed all his attention.

The Subaru was heading down the street. I yanked on my seat belt and pulled away from the curb. "We'll follow the guy at a distance, and when he stops again and gets out of the car we'll get your brother," I said to Owen.

The cat made a murp of what sounded like skepticism to me.

I looked over at him. "Do you have a better plan?" I asked.

He ducked his head and suddenly became very engrossed in the floor mat again. I gestured at the street ahead of us. "Whoever that is, he's not a bad guy. He has a *Save the Bees* sticker on his bumper. A violent person wouldn't be an environmentalist, would they?" I had a feeling Marcus wouldn't think much of my logic.

I glanced at my gas gauge. I really hoped the Subaru driver's next stop was somewhere closer than Minneapolis.

Luckily for me it was. After what were probably a couple of wrong turns the Subaru turned in at the marina. The driver parked on the far side of the building. I pulled in four spaces beyond him, hoping he hadn't paid much attention to my truck outside of Eric's.

"Mrr?" Owen asked. He had turned his head to look at me.

"We wait until he heads inside or wherever he's going, and then I'll go get your brother." *And hope no one we know happens to walk by,* I added silently.

From the corner of my eye I saw the driver slide out from behind the wheel of his car. Wherever Hercules had hidden himself, the man appeared not to have seen him. I sent Maggie a quick text telling her what was going on and giving her the license plate number of the car, just in case. I waited until the door to the building closed behind him, then I got out of the truck, trying not to think about how crazy this was. I went over to the car and peered through the side window. I couldn't see any sign of a small black-and-white cat.

I looked around. There was no one else around. "Hercules," I said sharply. "Get out here right now." I didn't see so much as a flick of a tail or a twitch of an ear.

I wrapped both arms up over my head and closed my eyes for a moment in frustration. This was bad. Very, very bad.

Then from behind me a gravelly male voice said, "Hey, what are you doing?" And I realized I'd been wrong before: *This* was bad.

chapter 8

I straightened up and turned around. The Subaru driver was holding a large brown envelope in one hand and his car keys in the other. He looked annoyed. I couldn't blame him for that. He was an inch or two under six feet, with salt-and-pepper hair poking out from under his ball cap, and a wiry build. I couldn't see any sign of a scar on his forehead. This was not Derrick Clifton.

"I'm sorry," I said. "But my cat's in your car." I didn't see any point in making up some elaborate story. My mother likes to say, "Tell the truth. It's a lot easier to remember."

The man frowned at me and his gaze darted to the car for a moment. "I didn't see any cat in my car." He looked skeptical.

How was I going to explain this? I had a feeling he wouldn't buy it if I told him Hercules had walked through the back window for some reason only the little cat knew.

"You were just parked downtown on Main Street," I said.

He nodded slowly.

"I don't know whether you spend much time online, but there's an ad campaign for the town—'The Cat's out of the Bag.'"

He gestured at his car. "Hang on a sec. You're saying one of those cats is in my car?"

I brushed my hair back off my face. "Hercules. Yes." I leaned sideways and pointed at the truck. "Owen, the other one, is in my truck." The little tabby's front paws were on the passenger door, and he was watching out the side window.

The man half turned to take a look at the truck. When he turned back to me he looked a little less annoyed. "Really, I don't think your cat's in my car. I would have noticed it."

I swiped a hand over my neck. A certain black-and-white feline was going to lose his sardine-cracker privileges when I finally got hold of him. I shot a glance at the car again. Where the heck was he hiding?

"Hercules is, well, pretty sneaky," I said. "We'd actually been at a photo shoot and I stopped at Eric's Place downtown. You were parked ahead of me. Hercules got out of the truck." I held out both hands. "He's fast when he wants to be."

"I did leave the back door on the driver's side open for a minute while I got something out of the trunk," the man said.

I nodded. "That's all it would take. Could I just check your backseat to put my mind at ease? Please?"

He studied me for a moment, and I tried to look normal and

nonthreatening and not at all like the owner of a cat that could walk through the back windshield of someone's car. "Oh, what the hell," he muttered. He pointed the key fob at the car. It beeped several times and I heard the door unlock. The man moved around me and opened the back door on the driver's side.

I leaned around the door and scanned the backseat. A black hard-shell guitar case leaned against the seat on the other side of the car. A furry nose and a pair of deep green eyes peered around the curve of the case.

I blew out a noisy breath, and my bangs, brushed to the side, lifted from my face. I leaned into the car. "Hercules, get over here right now," I said.

He hesitated for a moment, his black-and-white face the picture of innocence. This was more the kind of thing Owen would pull.

"Now," I said. Cat or not, the annoyance in my voice was pretty obvious. Hercules squeezed around the guitar case, jumped up to the backseat and walked across it to the open door, eyes downcast as though he were walking a tightrope and had to watch each step.

"There will be repercussions," I whispered as I picked him up. I backed out of the car and turned to face its owner. "This is Hercules," I said. "Thank you."

"Merow," the cat said.

The man actually smiled. "Hello, Hercules," he said. He looked at me. "Is it okay to pet him?"

"Actually, no, it's not," I said. "Both cats were feral. They're not good about being touched. I'm sorry."

"No problem," he said. "I've done some work with a rescue group in Chicago. I know some cats don't like to be handled by people they don't know." He shook his head again. "I can't believe he got past me."

"I think he might have been a ninja in one of his past nine lives," I said lightly.

He smiled. "So how did you end up with a couple of feral cats, if you don't mind my asking?"

"I don't mind." I gave Hercules a scratch behind his ear. He was still in the doghouse, so to speak, but I was glad to have him back. "It was when I first came to Mayville Heights. I was exploring this abandoned property. Hercules and Owen were just kittens. It's probably where Hercules learned to be so stealthy." I raised an eyebrow at the cat. He licked my chin in return. "When I started home they followed me. I really hadn't been thinking about getting a cat, and suddenly I had two."

I realized then that I hadn't introduced myself. I held Hercules with one hand, wiped the other on my shorts and held it out. "I'm Kathleen Paulson."

"Jack Spector," the man said as he shook my hand. He frowned. "I think I saw you at the library." His grip was strong without being crushing.

I nodded. "You probably did. I'm the head librarian."

"It's a beautiful building."

"Thank you," I said. "It was restored a couple of years ago for its centennial." I glanced back at the guitar case in the backseat of his car. "Are you here for the music festival?"

"Kind of," he said. "A friend of mine is taking part." He rubbed a hand over his chin. "At least she was."

"Not Emme Finley?"

He nodded and the smile faded from his face.

"You must have known Miranda," I said. "I'm sorry. What happened was horrible. I only met her a couple of times but I liked her."

"Everyone did," Jack said. "The word 'nice' is overused, but it applies . . . applied to Miranda." He ran his fingers over his bearded chin. "I couldn't believe it. I was sitting in with some buddies playing in a bar in St. Paul when I got a text with the news about Miranda. I left right away. I wanted to be here for Emme but she was already gone."

"I'm sorry Emme felt she couldn't stay," I said. "She has a wonderful voice, and I hate to think that what happened to Miranda is going to stop her from going after her dreams."

"Yeah, Miranda was kind of her biggest supporter. I don't want her to give up but she might. I know she was having second thoughts even before Miranda died." He gestured at the guitar in the backseat. "I'm actually part of her backup band." He gave his head a shake. "Ironically, Emme and I had had an argument about going after your dreams in the parking lot at your library. I was in Minneapolis and I'd come to bring her some music."

The argument I'd seen.

Jack shifted his weight from one foot to the other. "I hate the thought that she's using what happened as an excuse because she's scared, you know?"

I nodded. I did know. I glanced down at Hercules. His attention was fixed on Jack's face. He seemed to be listening intently, and I had no doubt he was in fact following the conversation.

"She said that she was thinking about giving up the idea of going back to school. She thought maybe she should go back to cabaret work. It was what she knew and she was good at it." A frown creased his forehead. "She said Miranda was trying to talk her out of it."

"Wouldn't that have been good for you?" I asked. "I mean, didn't you lose your job when Emme decided she was going to study music?"

Jack raked a hand back over his hair. "Hell no," he said. "It was the kick in the pants I needed."

The confusion I felt must have shown on my face. "I've been writing songs for years," he said. "I'm embarrassed to say how many because I haven't done a damn thing with any of them. I don't know if they're any good or if they're crap." He shrugged. "When Emme decided to change her life I realized it was my chance to try to change mine. I showed her some of my stuff. She said some of it was good." He laughed. "Some of it. She also told me I wasn't too old and it wasn't too late. And that's what I told her. Emme inspired me to go after my dream. I didn't want to see her bail on her own."

There was no way this man had had anything to do with Miranda's death, even without the alibi—the bar—that he'd mentioned. "You're a good friend," I said.

"I hope things work out for Emme," he said.

"Me too." Hercules shifted in my arms. He was getting restless. "Thanks for letting me retrieve Hercules," I said. "I'm sorry he stowed away in your car."

Jack grinned. "Best hitchhiker I ever picked up. He didn't

put his bare feet up on the dashboard or sing 'Me and Bobby McGee' around a mouthful of popcorn."

I laughed. "It was good to meet you, Jack," I said.

He nodded. "You too, Kathleen."

I walked over to the truck, fished my keys out of my pocket and got in, setting Hercules down on the seat. He and Owen eyed each other for a long, silent moment. "You're in big trouble, mister," I said as I pulled out my phone to let Maggie know all was well.

Hercules craned his neck in the direction of Jack Spector's car. The man was just pulling out of his parking spot, and he raised a hand in acknowledgment before he drove away. "Big trouble," I repeated.

The cat looked over his shoulder at me and then turned and began to wash his face. It was clear he didn't think he was in trouble—big or small—at all.

chapter 9

Marcus picked me up early the next morning. We were going out to Wisteria Hill to feed the cats. I leaned over to kiss him and then straightened up and fastened my seat belt.

"Good morning," he said. "How did you sleep?"

"I slept well until a certain furball decided it was time to get up a good twenty minutes before my alarm was set to go off and poked me in the eye with a paw."

He laughed.

"No, no, no," I said, shaking my head. "Don't take Owen's side."

"He just wanted to have breakfast with you."

"No, he wanted to have *my* breakfast instead of his own. I was at the table, I got up to get another cup of coffee and he jumped onto my chair."

Marcus was still grinning. "In Owen's defense, I've had your scrambled eggs. They're very good."

"I was having blueberry pancakes."

"Even better!"

Exasperated, I shook my head at him.

"Why are we feeding the cats this morning?" he asked as he backed out of the driveway. "Not that I mind getting a chance to spend time with you."

"Roma and Eddie have gone to get Sydney."

Right before I'd moved to Mayville Heights, Roma had discovered that there was a feral cat colony on the old estate. She'd put together a group of volunteers to help her take care of them and over time had caught and neutered all of the cats and taken them back out to the old carriage house they considered home.

Roma had recruited me to join her helpers and then played matchmaker and paired me with Marcus.

He started up Mountain Road. "I can't believe those two are actually getting married. I was starting to think it wouldn't happen, especially after that whole thing with the band."

That "whole thing with the band" was a very public marriage proposal Eddie had planned at a high school band concert with some help from Marcus and Brady Chapman. Instead of an engagement it had led to Roma ending their relationship because she believed Eddie would come to regret their age difference.

"I'm glad it worked out for them."

"So am I," I said. I smiled, remembering Roma standing up in the middle of my kitchen and proposing to Eddie in front of half our friends. "'I love it when a plan comes together.'"

Marcus sent me a quick sideways glance. "Shakespeare amended for this century?" he asked.

I shook my head. "Hannibal Smith from *The A-Team*." Hercules and I were watching the eighties action-adventure show online. The cat was a big fan of B. A. Baracus, played to perfection by Mr. T. I wasn't sure if it was the hair, the jewelry or the attitude.

I set the big stainless-steel thermos I'd brought with me at my feet.

"Is that coffee?" Marcus asked.

"Yes," I said.

"The way to my heart."

"I thought my blueberry pancakes were the way to your heart."

"Those, too," he said with a smile. He yawned then. "I'm sorry. It's not the company."

"Late night?"

He nodded, flicking on his blinker.

"Miranda Moore's murder?"

"Among other things."

"Do you think it's possible that the person who killed her was really after Emme Finley?" I asked.

"You know I can't answer that," he said, eyes never leaving the road.

I stared out the windshield for a minute. "Will you at least tell me what killed her? You know Bridget is going to find out and it will be in the paper in a day or so anyway." Bridget was the publisher of the *Mayville Heights Chronicle*, and she had a way of ferreting out details the police would just as soon stayed quiet.

I watched the muscles tighten in his jaw for a moment as he clenched his teeth. His mouth moved and then he said simply, "She was shot."

"Shot?" I repeated.

Marcus nodded. "At close range. Two shots. A .38. Please, Kathleen, keep that to yourself."

"I won't say a word," I promised.

Miranda had been shot.

Up close.

It sounded so cold. So personal.

Marcus pulled into the parking area to the left of Roma's house and shut off the SUV. We got out and retrieved the cats' food and dishes from Roma's porch and walked around the old carriage house to the side door.

Because the Wisteria Hill cats were feral, they weren't socialized, although over time they had all learned to associate Roma and her regular volunteers with food. After we put out the food and water at their feeding station, Marcus and I retreated back by the door and waited. I leaned against him and he put one arm around me.

"Do you think Roma will eventually tear this building down?" he asked, his voice low and warm by my ear.

I tipped my head so I could look at him. "I never thought about it," I said. The building was old and ravaged by water and time. Everything at Wisteria Hill had slipped into disrepair in the years the old estate had been abandoned. Roma had done a lot of work on the house and the yard. I'd never asked her what she had planned for the carriage house.

I looked around the space now. There were an old rain barrel in one corner and a large coil of rope nearby. The space was hot in the summer and freezing in the winter, and part of the roof leaked. Still, I had a bit of a soft spot for the old building. When Marcus and I were first getting to know each other we'd had some of our best getting-to-know-you conversations in this very spot.

After several minutes Lucy made her way out to the feeding station. She was the smallest of the cats but she was also the matriarch of the group.

"Hi, Lucy," I said softly.

The little cat turned when she heard my voice. Lucy and I had developed a bond in the time I'd been coming out to help feed the cats. Although I'd never been able to touch her, Lucy would come closer to me than she would to anyone else. Now she made her way across the wooden floor, stopping just a few feet in front of Marcus and me.

I hadn't seen Lucy and the other cats in the colony in several weeks. After Roma had bought Wisteria Hill from Everett she didn't need her volunteers as much.

"Merow," Lucy said, and it seemed to me there was a hint of reproach in the sound.

I leaned toward her just a little. "I know, it's been a while since I came out to see you," I said. "I'm sorry."

She looked at me for a long moment. "Mrrr," she said softly. Then she turned and headed for the feeding station.

"I think you've been forgiven," Marcus whispered.

The other cats began to come out slowly then. We checked each one, looking for any indications they might be hurt or sick, but they all looked well, even Smokey, the oldest of the group.

After the cats had eaten and left, Marcus put out fresh water while I gathered the dishes. We put everything back in the porch and walked over to the SUV. I grabbed the thermos and poured us each a cup of coffee.

"What's your day look like?" he asked.

"I have to see if I can find the rest of our skeleton," I said.

"Excuse me?" One eyebrow went up.

"Abigail and I have been going through the Halloween decorations. Do you remember that plastic skeleton we dressed as a wizard last year?"

Marcus nodded as he took a sip of his coffee.

"Well, it's missing a tibia, a scapula and a couple of phalanges. Other than looking for those pieces, there's nothing special on my agenda."

"How about I bring lunch?" He lifted his face up to the warm morning sunshine.

"I'd like that," I said. I was about to ask if he'd come up with a theory about whether or not Miranda's death had been a case of mistaken identity, when his phone went off. He answered it, walking several steps away from me. Police business.

He talked briefly, then ended the call. "I'm sorry," he said, walking back to me. "We have to head back. I have a meeting with the prosecuting attorney in forty-five minutes."

Marcus dropped me at home, leaving me with a quick kiss and a promise he'd see me at lunchtime. He was gone before I realized I hadn't told him about meeting Jack Spector the night before. Then again, for all I knew, maybe he'd already talked to the man himself.

As promised, Marcus showed up at the library with lunch at about quarter after twelve—pasta salad he had made and s'mores cupcakes from Sweet Thing. And a large coffee from Eric's.

"Lunch, coffee *and* a cupcake," I said, fishing a tiny plump tomato from my salad and popping it in my mouth. "This is really nice."

Marcus leaned sideways and wiped a bit of poppy seed dressing from the corner of my mouth. "I wanted to say thank you," he said, with that smile that still left me weak in the knees.

"You're welcome," I said. "I'm just not sure for what."

He straightened up and reached for his own food. "I talked to Hannah a little while ago. She's on the way to LA to try out for a limited-run part on *The Wild and Wonderful*." Hannah was his younger sister, a very talented actress and writer.

"My mother had something to do with that, I'm guessing."

Marcus nodded. "She shared a video of Hannah with the show's casting director that you had shared with her."

"From that outdoor theater festival," I said, gesturing with my fork. "She played the con artist."

"That's the one," he said. "I already e-mailed your mother to thank her. Now I'm thanking you."

"I love Georgia's cupcakes, so thank you for the thank-you." I stretched up and kissed the side of his jaw.

"Hannah's going to call you tonight."

"I can't wait to talk to her." I speared a chunk of cucumber with my fork. "And I hope she gets the part."

"Me too." Marcus smiled and shook his head. "You know, I can't remember when Hannah didn't want to be an actress. My mother had this big black enamel roast pan. Hannah was maybe two-and-a-half or three. She'd pull that thing out of the cupboard, turn it upside down and stand on it. She'd act out something that most of the time I didn't understand, and then she'd bow and I'd clap for her. Her first love is always going to be theater, but it's fun to see her excited about this."

His words made me think about Emme Finley, which in turn reminded me that while I had told Marcus about seeing Emme arguing with a man in the library parking lot, I hadn't told him about meeting Jack Spector. And more important, I hadn't told him I'd agreed to see if I could uncover anything about Miranda's murder.

I glanced at him. He was studying my face, blue eyes narrowed. "Where did you go?" he asked.

"I was just thinking about Emme," I said. "The man I saw her arguing with in the library parking lot? His name is Jack Spector. He's part of Emme's backup band. I mean, he was part of it. Have you talked to him?"

"I take it *you've* spoken to him," Marcus said.

I nodded. I gave him a brief rundown of Hercules stowing away in Jack's car, leaving out the part about the cat walking through two car windows.

He frowned. "Wait a minute. How did he get out of the truck?"

My stomach did a somersault. "What do you mean?" I asked, spearing another tomato with my fork.

"You said he slipped into this guy's car while he was getting something out of his trunk. But if you were coming out of Eric's, how did Hercules get out of the truck?"

For a moment I didn't know what to say. He walked through the windshield? No. This wasn't the time or the place to tell Marcus about the boys' superpowers. "He, uh, he must have jumped out when I first got out. I was checking my phone and I guess I wasn't paying attention." I shrugged, hoping I didn't look as guilty as I felt.

Marcus looked at me for a long moment. "You know it was a bad idea to follow a complete stranger like that," he finally said.

I held up one hand. "I sent Maggie a text telling her what I was doing along with the license plate of the car." I decided it probably wasn't a good idea to mention the *Save the Bees* bumper sticker. "If he'd gone anywhere out of town or that I thought wasn't safe, I would have called you."

"So I take it you got Hercules back?"

I nodded. "Jack was just going to the marina. After I retrieved Hercules we started talking. He admitted the argument he'd had with Emme. It was because she was thinking about giving up her plans for college. He didn't want to see her do that. And he has an alibi." I explained about Jack mentioning that he'd been sitting in with the band at a bar in St. Paul. "I got the feeling he's staying around for a couple more days."

"Rebecca got to you, didn't she?" Marcus said.

I knew at once what he meant. I nodded. "I should have told you sooner. How did you know?"

"I interviewed Ami. She was very upset. It seemed pretty obvious that she was close to Miranda Moore. And between you and me, we didn't make much headway with a lot of the festival participants. Some of them just don't want to talk to us. I can see they don't trust us."

"Ami came to see me a couple of days ago," I said. "I told her no."

"And Rebecca changed your mind." A hint of a smile pulled at the corners of his mouth. "I know how much faith she has in your abilities."

I set the bowl of half-eaten salad on the desk beside me. "It doesn't mean she doesn't have faith in yours," I said. I studied his face. "Are you upset?"

He shook his head. "No."

I smiled and took a step toward him.

"Just don't do anything stupid. Please."

"Librarian's honor," I said, putting a hand over my heart. I took another step toward him, closing the space between us.

"And remember to share," he added.

"Always," I agreed. I put both hands flat on his chest, stood on my tiptoes because I was wearing flat sandals, and kissed him.

He wrapped both arms around me.

"You're taking this very well," I said.

"This is the new and improved me," he teased. Then his expression grew serious. "This is also who you are, Kathleen. I don't want to change you." He let me go, reached for his lunch and took one of the chairs in front of my desk. I leaned against the desk again and picked up my coffee.

"Did Ami or Ruby say anything about where Emme went?" Marcus asked, stretching his long legs out in front of him. "I'd like to talk to her again. And the ex-boyfriend, for that matter."

"I don't think either one of them know," I said. "I don't think Emme told anyone—including her sister."

"You met Nora Finley?"

I nodded around a mouthful of pasta and tomatoes. "Last night when I was with Ruby. She was out for a walk. It wasn't anything I could put my finger on, but I got the feeling she doesn't have any idea where her sister is, either."

"That's what she told us," he said.

"You don't believe her."

He shrugged. "Nora seems to be very involved in her sister's life. She's her personal manager. It's hard to believe Emme didn't tell her where she was going."

"Does Hannah tell you everything that's happening in her life?" I asked. "Because I know Sara and Ethan don't tell me."

"I'm not managing Hannah's career," Marcus said. "And don't you think it's odd that Nora Finley is still in Mayville Heights and not with her sister?"

"Ruby said that Nora volunteered to help with promotion for the music festival and she wanted to finish what she started."

He didn't look convinced.

"You think Emme is with her ex-boyfriend," I said, jabbing my fork in the air at him. "And I don't mean the history professor. I mean Derrick Clifton."

"I didn't say that."

He didn't have to. The way he turned his attention back to his lunch told me I was right.

"Speaking of the professor, have you talked to him yet?"

"Dr. Hardison? Yes."

I waited for him to say more but he didn't.

"I take it he doesn't know where Emme is."

Marcus shook his head. "He says he doesn't."

I speared a chunk of cucumber and another of dill pickle and ate them. "So does he have an alibi for the time of the murder?"

He looked away for a moment, and I knew he was weighing whether or not to answer my question. Then he shifted his gaze back to me. "I may as well tell you, since you can easily find out. Yes. Dr. Hardison has an alibi. He was teaching a class when Miranda Moore was murdered. Not that he had any motive we know of to have killed her anyway."

He glanced at his watch and made a face. "I'm sorry, Kathleen," he said. "I have to get back to the station."

"If I hear anything about where Emme Finley is, I promise I'll tell you," I said. "But I don't think that Ami or Ruby are likely to share anything with me that they don't want you to know."

"I'm sorry that you get put in the middle of things when I'm trying to do my job," he said.

I shook my head. "I put myself there—at least I did this time. And I'm a big girl. I can handle it."

I spent the rest of the afternoon rearranging the magazine and newspaper section. Harry Taylor had refinished the last of the wooden tables as well as the rack where we kept the current paper copies of a variety of newspapers. I noticed that there were mentions of Miranda's death in the Chicago-area papers, but the focus was more on her connection to Emme Finley than on her life. It made me wonder what it had been like for Miranda to always be standing in her friend's shadow.

After work I headed home. Hercules was sitting in the sunshine on the back step. I reached down to stroke the top of his head. "You're still in trouble for that little stowaway stunt last night," I said.

"Merow," he said. There was nothing repentant about the sound.

"You could at least try to act like you're sorry," I said as I unlocked the porch door.

He blinked his green eyes at me and almost seemed to shrug.

I changed my clothes, had supper and headed down to tai chi. Hercules walked me out and settled on the bench by the window. I leaned down to give him a scratch behind his ears before I left. We both knew he wasn't really in trouble with me at all. If Hercules hadn't climbed into Jack Spector's car, I wouldn't have met the man. Which means I wouldn't have learned that Emme was thinking of changing her plans or that Miranda had been trying to talk her out of it. I didn't know if that had anything to do with Miranda's murder, but I didn't have anywhere else to start.

There were a lot more people on the street than there would usually be on a Thursday night, and they weren't all tourists. The music festival always had a good turnout from people who lived in Mayville Heights, too.

Ruby and Maggie were standing over by the tea table when I walked into the studio before class. Ruby immediately set down the mug she was holding and came across the room to me, folding me into a hug.

"What's that for?" I said. "Were Owen and Hercules especially photogenic last night?"

She grinned. "Actually, they were. I got some great shots. I e-mailed a few to you right before I left the studio. But I wanted to tell you how grateful I am. Rebecca told me that you're going to see what you can find out about Miranda's death. It means a lot. Thank you."

"I'll do my best," I said, "but please don't get your hopes up." I wished Rebecca hadn't said anything to Ruby, but the cat was out of the bag now, so to speak.

"Your best is good enough for me," she said. She was in a much better frame of mind, and I was all too aware that people were counting on me to find answers to questions that might not have any good answers.

We started over to Maggie. "I'm thinking of using Fern's for the next photo shoot," Ruby said.

"So Owen and Hercules would go for Meatloaf Tuesday?" I asked.

Ruby grinned and waggled a finger at me. "Now, see, you're kidding but I think that could work."

I bumped her with my hip. "I can promise they'd happily do it, but I'm not so sure it's something the health department would go for."

She nodded. "I'll check it out. Maybe we could shoot after hours."

Maggie smiled at me. "Would you like some iced tea?" she

asked. "I have that orange-spice blend you like mixed with lemonade."

I wasn't a big fan of tea but Maggie's iced tea/lemonade concoction was delicious.

"Please," I said.

Ruby spotted Taylor King in the doorway. "Later," she said to us. Ruby was giving the teen drawing lessons.

Maggie handed me a glass of the iced tea. I took a drink. "Mmmm, that's good," I said. "Not too sweet, not too tart. Just right."

"I'm glad you like it, Goldilocks," Maggie said with a smile.

I took another drink. "Did you know that a lot of people think *Goldilocks and the Three Bears* is one of Grimms' fairy tales, but it was actually published by a British author, Robert Southey?"

"I did not know that," she said. She smiled. "But I love that you did." She took a sip from her tea and then pointed a finger at me. "I think I found a dress to wear for Roma's shower. I'll send you a picture of it later."

I nodded. "I can't wait to see it."

I was looking forward to the party celebrating Roma's upcoming wedding. Both Roma's mom and Eddie's daughter would be there along with all her friends. The only person missing would be Olivia. When I'd e-mailed Roma's daughter about the shower, she'd sent me a terse e-mail in return saying she wouldn't be arriving in Mayville Heights until after the party. I knew it would mean a lot to Roma to have Olivia there, but I didn't want to pressure her. Not every employer was accommodating about time off.

Maggie moved into the middle of the room and clapped her hands. "Circle, everyone," she called.

My T-shirt was damp with sweat by the end of class, and I was happy to head home for a glass of my own lemonade and a molasses oatmeal cookie from the batch I'd taken out of the freezer before I left. I opened my e-mail and found the photos Ruby had sent before class. I was about to look through them when Owen sprang onto my lap.

"Hello," I said. "I take it you'd like to see the photographs Ruby took yesterday."

He stared pointedly at the screen. That was a yes.

Before I could open the attachments, Hercules meowed loudly from the floor by my feet. "Move over," I said to Owen.

He looked over his shoulder at me, whiskers twitching in annoyance.

"Your brother wants to see them, too," I said. I shifted Owen sideways. He made a couple of huffy noises but he moved. Then I patted my leg. "C'mon up," I said to Hercules.

"Merow?" he said. I couldn't miss the inquiry in the sound.

"No, I'm not picking you up," I said. "You're perfectly capable of jumping up."

He cocked his head to one side, a gesture both cats used when they wanted to seem cute and adorable.

"That's not working." I drummed my fingers on the table.

He made a sound like a sigh and jumped lightly onto my leg.

It took a couple of minutes for both cats to get settled. There was a lot of jockeying for position and several glares back and forth.

"Are you two done?" I asked finally. Sometimes they reminded me of a couple of preschoolers trying to share one cookie.

Hercules murped softly and Owen put a paw on the edge of the laptop.

I opened the images Ruby had sent.

She was right. The photos were wonderful. My favorite one was of both cats looking out over the water with the marina in the distance on the left and the sun low on the horizon ahead of them.

I had to smile at the way both Owen and Hercules studied the computer screen, turning their head from one side to the other and exchanging looks.

I tagged all of our favorites and sent everything back to Ruby. Owen jumped down to the floor and headed toward the living room. Hercules moved over and looked expectantly from the computer to me.

"Want to see what we can find out about Miranda?" I asked him.

Hercules immediately turned all of his attention to the computer screen.

There was very little online about Miranda Moore. She had no social media presence. No Facebook, Twitter or Instagram accounts. I did find her and Emme's high school yearbook. There was a candid shot of the two girls that looked like it was taken at a hockey game. They were wearing knit hats and striped scarves, and they looked even more like sisters.

I rubbed a knot out of my left shoulder. "Well, that was pretty much a dead end," I said. "Do you want to take a look at Emme's website?" If there was a connection between Miranda's murder and Emme, it wouldn't hurt to know more about the cabaret singer.

His response was to tap a paw on the keyboard, which somehow got us to my favorite search engine. Emme's website hadn't been updated recently—neither had her Facebook page—and I didn't learn anything there that I didn't already know. But with a little help from Hercules—who just couldn't seem to keep his paws off the keyboard—we ended up on a fan website with lots of information about her music and dozens and dozens of photos, many of which had clearly been poached from other sources, professional and otherwise. Buried in the photo gallery's archives were several images of Emme with who I guessed was her ex-boyfriend, Derrick Clifton. The time frame was right and he fit the general description Ruby had given me.

"She looks happy," I said to Hercules.

He murped in agreement.

It wasn't hard to find the Facebook page of the club that had posted the photos of Emme and Derrick that Ruby had told me about. In those images Emme looked uncomfortable somehow, her body stiff in her bright green jacket, not like she did in those first photos I'd found of her and Derrick. All I could really make out was the back of her head, her left cheek and the small beauty mark above her lip. There were no clear images of her face. In one of the shots Emme was holding a drink. In another she was kissing Derrick. Derrick definitely looked drunk. I couldn't put my finger on it, but something in those photographs was a little off.

In those first three photographs Emme had truly looked

happy, more so than she did in any of the other shots when she wasn't singing. That made me want to know more about the mysterious Derrick Clifton.

I stretched one arm up over my head and yawned. "We'll start in the morning," I said to Hercules as I set him on the floor. "Right now, I'm having a bath."

I overslept Friday morning, and for a change there were no paws poking my hair or my eye and no cat-food breath in my face. Since I didn't have to go into work until lunchtime I pulled on jeans and a T-shirt and made my way, yawning, down to the kitchen to make coffee and give the boys their breakfast.

Owen and Hercules were sitting by the refrigerator door. I could tell from the way their tails were flicking across the floor that they were annoyed at the delay. "Just give me a second to start the coffee," I said. I reached behind me for the glass carafe, and somehow as I turned around it slipped from my hand and hit the leg of the chrome table before hitting the floor—where it cracked into three pieces.

Both cats took a step backward, eyes glued to my face. They knew what I was like without coffee. I closed my eyes, one hand pressed on the top of my head, and said a word that polite librarians didn't generally utter.

I opened my eyes and pointed at Owen and Hercules, both still watching me with curiosity. "Stay there until I get this cleaned up," I said. I sighed in frustration. *It's only a coffeepot,* I told myself. It didn't help.

I picked up the pieces of the broken carafe and used the

vacuum to get any bits of glass and plastic. Then I cleaned the floor with a damp mop just in case there were any tiny fragments of glass left behind. I didn't want to miss anything the cats might step on.

When I'd pulled out the vacuum, they had both retreated to the living room doorway, where they continued to watch me.

Once I was satisfied that the floor was clean I got breakfast for Owen and Hercules and dropped into a chair to consider my options. I knew I could head across the backyard and mooch a cup of coffee from Rebecca. Or I could make a cup of tea, which I knew wasn't what I wanted.

I watched Owen take each bite of food from his dish by the refrigerator and set it on the floor. He'd eye it suspiciously and then sniff carefully before eating. I wasn't that different from him. I was picky about breakfast. Breakfast in my mind needed coffee. Or maybe that was me who needed it. I caught sight of the note I'd stuck on the fridge door the night before: *Ask Ruby about Fern's*, a reminder to check in in a few days to find out if the health department would let her take photos of the boys inside the diner. I thought about the big breakfasts Fern's served and the huge mugs of hot, strong coffee. It occurred to me that a big cup of coffee and one of the big breakfasts at Fern's might be just what I needed.

I called Marcus but got his voice mail. Then I remembered that he was out running with Eddie and the high school hockey team as part of their summer training. "Next time," I said out loud.

Hercules looked up, gave me a blank look and went back to his breakfast.

I went upstairs, brushed my teeth, put on some makeup and pulled my hair up. By the time I was ready to go, both cats had disappeared. Owen was probably checking on his stash of catnip chickens, and Hercules, I knew, could be anywhere inside or out.

Fern's was a 1950s-style diner that had actually been operating back in the fifties. A number of years ago it had been restored to all its glory, or as Roma liked to put it, "Just like the good old days, only better." She was a big fan of Meatloaf Tuesdays and the diner's yellow layer cake with chocolate frosting.

The building itself was low and long, glowing with neon after dark. There were windows on three sides and black-and-white checkerboard tiles on the floor. The diner had the requisite jukebox complete with 45s, booths with padded red vinyl seats and a long counter with gleaming chrome stools.

I stepped through the door, half hoping to see Burtis Chapman sitting at the counter even as I knew it was a bit too late for him. He had more than one business in town, and most of them were one hundred percent legal.

There was no sign of Burtis, but Harrison Taylor Senior was sitting at a booth on the far wall. He smiled when he spotted me and waved me over.

"What are you doing in my neck of the woods?" he asked as I leaned down to give him a hug.

"I dropped my coffeepot," I said, making a face.

"Before or after your second cup?" My love for coffee rivaled the old man's.

"Before the first cup."

Harrison frowned. "That's serious business," he said. He leaned back to look around me, caught the eye of Peggy Sue at the counter and smiled as he pointed at me. "You got time to join me?" he asked.

"I'd love to," I said, sliding onto the seat across from him.

Peggy, who was the morning-shift waitress and also Harrison's lady friend, headed toward us with a big mug and the coffeepot. "Hi, Kathleen. How are things at the library?" she asked as she set the cup in front of me.

"Busy," I said. "The music festival has brought in a lot of tourists."

"She's down a quart," Harrison said, gesturing at the pot.

"Well we can't have that," Peggy said, filling the mug almost to the top with just enough room for cream and sugar.

"Thank you," I said. Just the smell of the coffee was turning my morning around.

"Just coffee or the big breakfast?" Peggy raised an eyebrow.

I reached for the cream pitcher, a black-and-white china cow. "Big breakfast, please."

Peggy smiled. "How about raisin toast this time?"

I nodded as I added sugar to my cup. "That sounds delicious," I said.

"It'll just be a few minutes." She turned the smile on Harrison. "And I'll bring you another cup of decaf at the same time," she said. "I just put on a new pot."

Harrison eyed me. "Not a word," he said.

I put one hand on my chest. "I wasn't going to say anything other than it's good to see you, Peggy."

Peggy waggled a finger at the old man. "Try to behave yourself," she said before heading for the kitchen.

Harrison's children—especially his daughter, Elizabeth—had been trying to get him to switch to decaf coffee for the last year. They were convinced all the caffeine he drank wasn't good for him, although he seemed well after a brief health scare about a year previous. I had no idea how Peggy had been able to get Harrison to cut back, and I wasn't going to ask.

I took a sip of my own coffee, which was hot and strong, exactly the way I liked it. Harrison smiled at me across the table. "So tell me how Ruby's photo project is going," he said.

"It's going well," I said. "Ruby's photographs are generating a lot of talk online—not just here in Mayville Heights. And there's a lot of interest in the upcoming calendar. I'm just hoping that will translate into more visitors for the town."

He nodded, fingering his snowy Santa Claus beard. "So do I. Talk is cheap."

I pulled out my phone. "Would you like to see some of the photos?"

"I would," he said with a smile.

I scrolled through the dozen images I'd downloaded to my phone. Harrison studied each one, pointing out how Ruby had managed to highlight different aspects of Mayville Heights in each one—the water, the Riverwalk, the architectural detail of the old school that was now home to Riverarts—while still focusing on the cats.

"Ruby is a damn talented photographer and you have a couple of fine-looking cats," Harrison said when we got to the end of the images.

"They seem to like it," I said, putting my phone away and reaching for my coffee. "Sometimes I swear both of them know exactly what's going on and it's like they're posing for Ruby."

"Your boys are Wisteria Hill cats," he said with an offhand shrug, as though that explained everything. And maybe it did.

Peggy came back then with my breakfast and a fresh pot of decaf for Harrison. I couldn't miss the way they smiled at each other, and it made me smile, too.

We talked about the projects I had planned for the fall at the library, and I told Harrison about the great turnout we'd had for Michel's presentation at the library.

"I've been thinking about doing a series of talks about the history of Mayville Heights," I said. "Based on the questions we get at the front desk I think there's enough interest—from tourists and from people who live here." I set down my fork and raised an eyebrow at him. "What do you say?"

"About what?" he asked.

"About coming to the library some afternoon and talking about the town?"

He gave a snort of derision. "I'm damn sure no one wants to listen to me ramble on and on about things that happened long before they were born."

Harrison was a great storyteller, and he knew more about the town and its history than just about anyone, with the exception, maybe, of Burtis Chapman and Mary Lowe—both of whom I also planned to ask to get involved in what I was calling "The History Project," at least for now.

"Care to place a small wager on that?" I asked.

"What do you have in mind?" he asked. The twinkle in his blue eyes told me he was hooked.

"You come and talk for about half an hour about the history of the town—time period to be determined—and then you answer questions. If my meeting room isn't full, I'll treat you to the biggest steak Peggy has out back." I tipped my head in the direction of the diner's kitchen.

"Which room?"

I speared a chunk of potato and ate it. "The big one," I said.

"You're confident," he retorted.

"As someone I know likes to say, it's not bragging if you can do it."

Harrison laughed at his own words being used against him. "You need to start hanging out with a better class of people," he said.

"I like the class I'm hanging out with just fine," I said. "So do we have a deal?"

"And what do you get, Kathleen, if somehow I don't manage to win this wager?"

I raised an eyebrow and favored him with my best Cheshire-cat smile. "You come back and do a second talk."

He laughed. "Well, with terms like that how can I refuse?" He extended his hand across the table.

We shook hands and Harrison picked up his coffee cup again. I mopped the last bit of scrambled egg and fried tomato off my plate with my toast. I realized the old man was studying me over the top of the heavy stoneware mug. "Little bird says you were with Ruby when she found that body down by the Riverwalk," he said.

"Strictly speaking, it was Hercules," I said, gesturing with my fork. "Ruby was taking photographs and he kept looking over toward the bank. Finally, she walked over there to see what had caught his attention." I stopped, swallowing hard as the image of Miranda Moore's body curled up in the tangle of bushes flashed into my mind.

"You figured anything out yet?"

I narrowed my gaze at him.

"Now, don't tell me you aren't at least asking a few questions," Harrison said. He looked over at the counter, smiled at Peggy and held up his cup. "We both know you seem to have a knack for getting pulled into this kind of thing."

A man had just come into the diner. Instead of looking around for a seat he headed for the counter. Take-out order, I decided. Peggy was already on her way over with the coffeepot. She handed the man a menu and I heard her say she'd be right back.

"How about you, Kathleen?" she asked as she topped up Harrison's cup. She indicated the coffeepot. "It doesn't have to be the unleaded."

Something about the man studying the menu was familiar. I'd seen him somewhere before. But where? I concentrated on his profile and suddenly I had it. It was Derrick Clifton. I realized Peggy was waiting for my answer. "Umm, no, thanks. I'm good," I said.

I looked over at the counter again. It was definitely Clifton. He was clean-shaven and he'd cut and dyed his hair since the tabloid photos, but I still recognized him. I could see the scar Ruby had mentioned on his forehead. What were the odds he'd show up here? Maybe better than average. Derrick was in the area probably to stay close to Emme. Fern's was a much better choice for food than anywhere downtown, where he was more likely to run into someone from the festival who might recognize him.

I knew I should call Marcus, but by the time he got to Fern's I knew Derrick would be gone and so would the chance to question him. Peggy was already back taking his order. I was running out of time.

I smiled at Harrison. "I need to get going," I said. "I'll call you about our deal."

"You do that," he said. "It's been a while since I had a good steak." He turned and glanced over at the counter. His smile faded. "You be careful, Kathleen," he said. "Don't do something foolhardy."

He knew, I realized. He didn't know who Derrick Clifton was, but he knew that somehow the man had some connection to Miranda's murder. The old man was sharper than most people half his age.

"I won't," I promised. I slid out of the booth, leaned down and kissed his cheek. Then I made my way over to Peggy. I paid my bill, giving Derrick a quick, offhand glance. I was definitely right on my ID.

I was waiting in the truck when he came out of the diner. It had been pretty easy to figure out which vehicle was his. He also drove a half-ton truck. His was a dark blue, the sides of the bed spattered with mud, as was the back end, which helped obscure the Illinois plates. It seemed clear that he was trying to avoid detection.

When he pulled out of the lot I followed him. I stayed back a reasonable distance just as I would have if we were just going in the same direction. Given the first two turns Derrick took I felt certain that he was headed for the highway just outside of town, albeit via a roundabout path. I took a chance that he was on the way to one of the two motels nearby and chose the more direct route It didn't make sense for him to be going anywhere else.

I was at the air hose at the Kwik Trip station when the dirty blue truck pulled into the driveway of the Red Apple Motel across the road. Pretending to use the air hose let me keep an eye on the Red Apple as well as the Cadillac Motor Inn next door. Derrick parked in front of the last unit. He got out with his bag of takeout, crossed to the motel room door and knocked. He wasn't alone. The door opened and I caught a glimpse of a woman. Was it Emme? Had she lied about leaving the area? I gambled that I was right.

I drove across the street, parked near the front of the motel lot and walked down to that last unit on the end of the squat, stubby building. I thought about pretending to be someone from housekeeping but decided to just be myself. If I was right and Emme was the woman with Derrick, she didn't seem to be there under duress.

I knocked and waited. After half a minute I heard the sound of the security chain being pulled back. The door opened. Emme Finley stood there in a pair of denim shorts and a gauzy yellow peasant shirt. "All we need is—" She stopped, mouth hanging open a little, eyes wide when she saw it was me, and not the housekeeper she had probably been expecting. "Kathleen? What . . . what are you doing here?" she asked. She kept one hand on the door handle and the other on the frame of the door, blocking the opening with her body so I couldn't see around her.

"I need to talk to you," I said.

Her gaze darted sideways for a moment.

"I know Derrick is here with you," I said. I held up both hands. "I just want to talk, that's all."

"About what?"

"About Miranda." I paused, wondering how to explain what I was doing there. "Ruby and Ami are my friends. I care about them and they cared about Miranda."

"I've had some messages from Ruby," Emme said.

I waited for her to elaborate but she didn't.

"I'm just . . . trying to figure out what happened," I said.

She studied me for a long moment and then dropped the hand that had been on the door frame. "Come in," she said.

The space was a typical motel room. A queen-size bed occupied most of the left wall, bookended by two squat nightstands. Each nightstand held a tall lamp topped with an orange shade the color of a traffic cone. The shades had likely been chosen to coordinate with the wild orange-and-fuchsia bedspread.

There was a small drop-leaf table on the other wall, just inside the door, with a chair tucked in at each end. The bag of take-out food was on the table. Derrick Clifton was standing next to it.

"You followed me," he said. He glanced at Emme. "I saw her at the diner."

"Yes, I did," I said.

"Kathleen, this is Derrick," Emme said. Her gaze moved from me to him and she smiled. "My boyfriend."

He offered his hand. "Excuse me for not saying it's a pleasure to meet you, Kathleen," he said. "But you did follow me, so I'm not sure it is."

"I wanted to talk to Emme—to both of you, actually."

"How did you know we were together?" Emme asked.

"I didn't. But when I saw Derrick I realized it was a possibility." I shrugged. "It was mostly a lucky guess."

Derrick moved over to the bed and sat down. I leaned against the wall.

"Everyone seems to think you left town," I said.

The color rose in Emme's cheeks. "That's because I let them think that. I didn't . . . I didn't know what to do. So Derrick suggested we stay here, but not tell anyone until I figured out what my next step is going to be."

I nodded. Her reasoning made sense to me.

"I've had a couple of messages from Ruby, and one from Ami," Emme continued. "They seem to think you might be able to figure out who killed Miranda. Ruby said something about you helping catch the person who killed her teacher." Her voice had an edge of skepticism. I could see the same doubt in Derrick Clifton's eyes and the set of his mouth.

Ruby had been referring to the murder of Agatha Shepherd. I'd discovered who had killed the former school principal, and I'd almost been killed myself when the killer's cabin was destroyed in a gas explosion.

There was no reason for either Emme or Derrick to talk to

me, and now I wondered if tailing him had been a bad idea. Was my showing up going to push them into leaving the area, going back to Chicago or somewhere, anywhere else? The only thing I could think of was to explain why I'd gotten involved in Miranda's death in the first place.

I took a deep breath. "As I said, I care about Ruby and Ami. And they cared about Miranda." Nothing changed in Derrick's expression, but Emme looked down at the floor. "I'm not saying I'm going to be able to figure out who killed her," I continued. "But sometimes people tell me things they don't feel comfortable telling the police. And I remember things that other people forget or don't pay attention to in the first place." I held out both hands and shrugged. "I'm not making any promises." I wasn't sure I was making a lot of sense, either.

Derrick looked up at me, eyes narrowed, head tipped to one side. "I'm pretty much a pariah as far as Emme's family and friends are concerned. Are you here because you think I killed Miranda?"

Emme turned to look at him. "Don't," she said.

I shook my head. "I don't think you killed Miranda."

"What makes you so sure?" he asked, a challenge lighting up his dark eyes.

"You love Emme," I said.

He glanced over at her and a hint of a smile flashed across his face. I was certain about Derrick's feelings for Emme. It wasn't just the way he was looking at her now, the way he couldn't keep that smile at bay. It was also the look in his eyes I'd seen in those photos of the two of them together I'd found in the archives of that fan site online. "You wouldn't have hurt

Miranda, because that would hurt Emme and you would never do that."

"I'm supposed to be the jilted boyfriend."

I took a moment and studied him before I answered. Derrick Clifton was not what I'd expected. He was thoughtful and well-spoken. Nothing about him made me think he was some kind of vindictive ex. Emme didn't seem frightened of him in any way. She seemed stronger with Derrick in the room. She was still profoundly sad and a lot quieter than the previous times we'd met, but she wasn't afraid. "I don't think the two of you were ever really broken up," I said. "At least not for very long."

Emme did smile then. "No, we weren't. I know how hokey it sounds, but we're just meant to be together and what's meant to be will always find a way."

She looked at Derrick, who responded by rolling his eyes. "You're not going to sing, are you?" he teased.

She made a face at him. "No, I'm not."

He reached up and grabbed her hand, giving it a squeeze. Then he turned his attention to me. "So if you're not here because you think I killed Miranda, what do you want?"

I couldn't think of any diplomatic way to phrase things, so I just said the words. "I want to know if you can think of anyone who might want to hurt Miranda . . . or Emme."

Emme blinked a couple of times and turned pale. She dropped onto the corner of the bed. Derrick put an arm around her shoulders. "You think the person who killed Miranda was really trying to kill me?" she said.

I pulled a hand over the back of my neck. "Maybe. I'm not sure."

"Why would someone want to kill Emme?" Derrick asked, frowning. "There's nothing controversial about what she does. She's a singer."

Emme turned to look at him. "But why would someone hurt Miranda? She was my assistant. Everyone liked her." She looked at me then. "I can't think of anyone who would have wanted me dead, but if it wasn't mistaken identity, then the killer was after Miranda and that makes even less sense."

"This whole thing doesn't make any sense," Derrick said. "Yeah, Emme does have some fans who are a bit fanatical, but no one's ever gone so far as to threaten her any more than just saying they're not going to listen to her music anymore. It was more like a kid threatening to hold their breath until they pass out than a real threat."

Emme nodded in agreement. "There were a few people who weren't happy when I said I was going back to school, but Derrick's right, all they did was say they weren't going to listen to my music anymore."

"Do you have e-mails or letters from any of those people?" I asked. I'd been around enough actors to know that some people's adoration could turn from harmless to dangerous overnight.

"Miranda kept a file of them. Just in case."

"I think you should show them to the police," I said. "You're probably right that none of those people are dangerous, but it can't hurt."

"Okay," Emme said. "I guess I can do that."

"What about Miranda's family? Ruby said she has a step-father and a couple of stepbrothers."

Emme nodded. "There's no way they would have hurt her."

Derrick made a snort of derision. "That's the truth. All three of them were always freeloading off of Miranda. They treated her like she was an ATM. With her gone they might have to actually work for a change."

I glanced at Emme.

"Derrick's not wrong," she said softly.

I cleared my throat. "I, uh, need to ask about those photos of the two of you that were taken at that club and ended up online. Obviously *you've* seen them."

Derrick rolled his eyes and Emme ducked her head, rubbing the space between her eyes with the back of a bent finger. "Just one time," she said. "And I didn't look at all of them. The ones I saw made me cringe."

"Once was enough," Derrick added.

"Were you drinking?" I asked.

"I had a beer," Derrick said. He held up a finger. "One beer."

"And I had sparkling water—at least I think I did," Emme said.

"You don't remember that night?"

"Not really."

"What do you remember?" I asked. "Do you remember being at your apartment?"

Emme nodded. "I remember being home. Nora was out and Miranda had a date—someone she used to work with had set her up with a friend and she was nervous. She was supposed to meet him at a restaurant but then he texted that he'd been held up at work. He asked if they could at least meet at this club near his office for a drink."

"So she left and you were home alone."

Emme glanced over at Derrick for a moment. "No," she said. "Clubs weren't Miranda's thing. She was going to cancel and I offered to go with her. I was kind of restless. All I had planned was watching TV and eating a giant bag of chips."

"You were going to be her out if she needed one," I said.

She gave me a faint smile. "If the guy seemed okay, I'd get an Uber. If anything felt off to either one of us, I'd stick around and we'd leave together."

I'd used a similar plan back in college with my friend Lise. We'd even had a code word, "aardvark," which meant, "Don't leave me alone with this guy." "So who got to the club first?"

"We did. Miranda had a glass of wine and I had sparkling water with lime. We'd been sitting there maybe five minutes and Derrick walked in. I couldn't believe it. He looked around, saw us and came right over to the table. He said that I'd sent him a note asking him to meet me there."

I held up a hand. "Wait a minute. An actual note? Not a text? Not an e-mail?" I looked at Derrick. "You didn't think that was odd?"

Derrick shook his head. "No. That was just Emme. She's been doing that for years." I remembered Ruby saying Emme had written her a good-bye note.

She shrugged, almost embarrassed it seemed. "I like writing real notes and letters," she said. "It just seems more personal.

I'll use any kind of paper and just about anything to write with."

"Do you still have the note?" I asked.

"No," Derrick said. "I must have thrown it out."

Emme played with the hem of her yellow shirt. "I didn't send it. I couldn't have. First of all, I didn't know where Derrick was staying, and second, I didn't know I was going to be at that club until Miranda's date asked her to meet him there instead of at the restaurant where they'd planned."

"Which means there's no way anyone else could have known," Derrick added.

"Did you talk to anyone before you left the apartment?"

Emme shook her head. "And neither did Miranda. She couldn't have left a message for Derrick, because she was with me from the time she got the text about meeting at the club until we actually got there. Anyway, she wouldn't have done something like that to get me to talk to Derrick. She was my best friend."

Derrick pulled a hand back over his neck. "I think it was a setup. Some kind of screwed-up fan trying to get back at Emme and make her look bad just because she'd decided to put her singing on hold for a while. It was just bad luck that Emme actually showed up."

I made a face. "You've lost me," I said. "Are you trying to say you think some unbalanced fan of Emme's got you to the club with the plan to somehow get you to do something stupid and, what? Embarrass Emme somehow? That doesn't make a lot of sense."

The two of them exchanged a look. "Not embarrass Emme," Derrick said. "Hurt her. I think the idea was to drug me and take some compromising photos of me with some other woman. When they showed up online it would have hurt Emme. I think the whole thing was just planned out of spite."

I nodded slowly. The whole thing made a weird kind of childish sense.

"And then when Emme showed up out of the blue—"

"The person just changed their plan a little."

It was as good an explanation as any. I turned to Emme. "Do you mind if I ask why the two of you broke up? It's pretty clear you're crazy about each other."

"I listened to other people instead of my own heart," she said. "I know that sounds like a line from a romance novel, but it's the truth."

"And I acted like a jerk," Derrick said with a wry smile.

Emme smiled, then reached up and laid her hand against his cheek for a moment. She shifted her attention back to me. "The last straw, so to speak, happened when I was singing at a club in Grand Rapids. Derrick punched a guy at the bar. Bouncers threw them both out. That was it. I was done."

Derrick didn't say a word. His gaze was locked on Emme.

She glanced down at her feet for a moment. "I didn't find out for close to three weeks that Derrick had actually punched the guy because he was harassing the bartender. Derrick had already told him to leave the woman alone. Guy put his hands on her and Derrick punched him."

"This is where I'm supposed to say I'm sorry," Derrick said.

It was clear he wasn't. And while I thought there were better ways to have handled the situation, I liked how he'd come to the defense of someone being bullied by a creep.

I sighed. "Let's go back to Derrick coming over to your table. What did you do?"

"I told him I didn't want to talk to him," Emme said. "I remember watching Derrick walk over to the bar with Miranda, and that's really the last thing I remember clearly until the next day. Miranda had to fill in the details for me."

"What did she tell you?"

Emme played with the hem of her shirt again. "I told her I didn't want to talk to Derrick. She said she'd text her date and say something came up and we'd go home, but he walked in at that moment. Miranda said I insisted we stay." She shrugged. "That makes sense. She'd been doing so much for me, and I wanted her to give this date a try. Miranda said the guy turned out to be nice. He suggested they get something to eat nearby, and he even invited me to join them. Since Miranda was okay with him, I turned them down. Miranda said we all left together. They walked down the street to a nearby restaurant, and I got my phone out to order an Uber."

I looked up at the ceiling for a moment. There weren't any answers up there. "So you didn't order a ride, or if you did, you didn't use it. You went back inside to talk to Derrick."

Emme shook her head. "I must have, but why don't I remember and why doesn't he? Several people saw me with Derrick. It was definitely me. I was wearing my green jacket and I had my hair up. And apparently I was drinking. I don't drink, Kathleen. I'd just finished doing some public service announcements encouraging people not to drink and drive and saying it was possible to have fun and not drink." She rubbed her forehead with the heel of her hand. "When the photos showed up online, people called me a hypocrite. I was dropped from the campaign. Elliot ended our relationship, and one of the schools I'd applied to rescinded the offer to audition. They'd just started a new Don't Drink and Drive program. The whole thing was a mess."

Derrick put his arm around her shoulders and she leaned against him. "That's kind of why I'm here," Emme said. "I don't know what to do. It really wasn't any kind of a romance with Elliot, but he was my cheering section as far as going back to school and he was getting me ready for all the academic stuff like the French placement test." She blew out a breath. "I didn't even finish my first year when I went to college at eighteen. Maybe I'm not cut out for this."

Derrick kissed the top of her head. "That's crap," he said. "You can do anything."

As I watched the two of them, I didn't see any indicators that they were lying: Both of them held my gaze; neither one of them stumbled over their words. But I couldn't think of a good reason for anyone to go to so much trouble to set them up for a few embarrassing photos, either.

"It seems like a lot of trouble to go to just to hurt Emme," I said.

Derrick shrugged. "Maybe the idea was just to stir up a little controversy and sell some pictures. Emme's a big deal in Chicago. She was doing that public service campaign and then bang! There are photos of the good girl drunk in a club with her tongue down the bad boy's throat." He raised an eyebrow. "Less than twenty-four hours later those pictures were all over the *Good Night Chicago* website, and a day after that they were on three other websites and the so-called entertainment section of the newspaper."

"You suspect the photographer?"

"You're damn right I do." Derrick's face was flushed and anger flashed in his dark eyes.

"We tried to track him down but we got nowhere," Emme said, lifting her head. "Nora even went to see our lawyer, but the copyright on the photographs was owned by some paper company and there was no way to force any of the places that used them to tell us who took them." She gestured with one hand. "Nora said we were just making it worse, drawing more attention to the pictures by trying to find out who took them."

Emme's sister had probably been right.

"It had to be money, at least as far as the photographer was concerned," Derrick said. "It's the only motive that makes any sense."

"But why would some random photographer want to kill me or Miranda?" Emme asked, picking at the pink nail polish on her left thumb. "There's no money in that." She looked at me again. "I'm sorry, Kathleen. I don't know who would want to hurt either one of us."

"I'm sorry you even have to think about it," I said.

I pushed away from the wall. There were a pen and a pad of paper with the motel's name at the top in red letters on the small table next to me along with the takeout, which had to be cold by now. I wrote down my cell number. "If you think of anything, please call me," I said. "Or if there's anything you need."

Emme got to her feet. "I'll send you a text so you have my number." She looked at her chipped nail polish. "There is one thing you can do for me."

I gave her an encouraging smile. "Sure. What is it?"

"I know I can't hide forever, but I need more time to figure things out, to decide what I'm going to do. I don't . . . I don't want anyone—not Ruby, not even my sister—to know where I am."

Or whom she was with, I was guessing.

"I won't say anything to Ruby or anyone else," I said. "But the police do need to talk to you."

"I should have thought about that," she said, still picking at the polish on her thumb. "I'll call them right away."

I picked up the pen again and wrote the number for the Mayville Heights police department on the pad below mine. "Ask for Detective Gordon." I looked over at Derrick. "It was just luck that I happened to see you at the diner. You got rid of the beard and your hair's darker, but I recognized you. Be careful. I found you. So could anyone else."

I left them then, walked across the small motel parking lot and climbed into the truck. I closed my eyes for a moment, leaned back against the seat and let out a long breath. Then I looked over at the door to the motel room. My gut was telling me that Derrick wasn't the bad guy.

So who was?

chapter 10

I headed home with no more answers than when I'd left. Hercules was sitting on the blue Adirondack chair in the backyard again.

"Are you coming in?" I asked, pausing with one foot on the back stairs. He looked around the yard. Scanning for his archenemy, the grackle, I wondered?

"Mrrr," he said. He made no move to jump down from the chair, so I took that as a no.

I found Owen in the kitchen sitting on one of the chairs at the table. I stared at him for a moment. He looked back at me with a slightly guilty expression, it seemed to me.

Did I want to make an issue over this? No, I decided. "I'm going to put my shoes over here," I said, gesturing at the mat under the coat hooks.

I turned and made a production number of taking off my blue Keds and tucking the laces inside each shoe, and when I turned back around Owen was sitting on the floor next to the chrome chair, innocently washing his face.

"Wise choice," I said as I moved past him.

Marcus called about half an hour later as I was collecting the towels to put in the washer. "Emme Finley called me," he said. "She said you gave her my number."

"I know you had more questions for her," I said, sitting down on the edge of the tub.

"I did. And she'd received a few nasty e-mails from unhappy fans. I wanted to see those."

"I don't think Derrick Clifton had anything to do with Miranda's death," I said. At my feet Owen looked at me, head cocked to one side—it seemed to me—in curiosity. "Later," I mouthed, feeling just a little silly, although it wasn't really any sillier than me sharing the photo Maggie had texted of the dress she'd gotten for Roma's shower. Owen had given it an enthusiastic meow of approval.

"I know," Marcus said.

I frowned even though he couldn't see me. "Wait a minute, how do you know?" I asked.

"How do you know?" he countered.

"From watching him with Emme. He's crazy about her and he'd never do anything to hurt her, so he couldn't have killed Miranda." I reached over my head and pulled down a towel I'd left over the shower rod to dry. "I know that's not exactly evidence. It's just an observation."

"It's not nothing, either," he said. "And yes, I know it took me a long time to understand that."

I smiled. "So what do you have?"

"A couple of credible witnesses who put Derrick up at The Brick at the time of the murder." The Brick offered cheap beer and loud music.

Owen poked the pile of towels with a paw. I shook my head at him. As usual he acted like he had no idea what I was objecting to and poked them again.

"Stop doing that," I said sharply.

He turned with a "Who, me?" look on his furry face.

"Stop doing what?" Marcus asked.

"I'm sorry," I said. "I wasn't talking to you. I was talking to Owen."

"What's he doing?"

"Trying to knock over a pile of towels."

"Maybe he's trying to encourage you."

Owen had given up on the towels and had jumped onto the back of the toilet tank. I saw him eye the toilet paper roll. "Try that and it'll be a very long time before there's another funky chicken in your life," I warned.

The cat's whiskers twitched as though he were weighing the merits of ignoring my warning.

"Sorry," I said to Marcus. "I was talking to Owen again. So what do you think he's encouraging me to do exactly? Do more laundry?"

"Maybe he's telling you to keep poking around to see what you can find out."

I laughed. "Or maybe he's thinking he can steal a towel for his kitty lair in the basement." Maggie said Owen must have been a pack rat in a past life.

Marcus laughed as well. "Or that," he said.

"I should get this laundry in the washer," I said. "I still need to get ready for work."

"Have a good day," Marcus said. "I'll talk to you later."

"You too," I said. I ended the call and reached for Owen just as his paw was about to send the roll of toilet paper unrolling onto the floor. "What part of 'don't do that' are you having trouble with?" I asked.

He made grumbling noises low in his throat. I stepped over the towels and set him in the hall. He made a point of not looking at me as he headed for the bedroom.

I collected the towels and headed downstairs. Hercules was in the kitchen. There were some bits of dried grass stuck to his ear. "Ear," I said, pointing at his head.

He immediately swiped a paw over his furry black ear. Problem was, it was the wrong ear.

"Other one," I said.

To my amusement he switched paws and washed his other ear.

Hercules trailed me as I went down the basement steps to the washer. He jumped up onto the dryer as I started the machine and added soap and fabric softener. I found myself relating my visit with Emme and Derrick to him. I talked to the cats about things all the time, rationalizing it by saying that hearing myself talk out loud helped me figure things out. And that was true. It was also true that I was fairly sure both of them understood exactly what I was talking about.

"If neither Emme nor Miranda had enemies, then who killed Miranda?" I said.

Hercules looked up from nosing one of my wool dryer balls across the top of the machine. I think he would have shrugged if he could. He didn't have any ideas, either.

"Maybe it was just a random act of violence."

He wrinkled his whiskers at me and dropped his head to nudge the ball again.

I started stuffing towels in the washer. "It doesn't feel right to me, either," I said.

I closed the lid of the washer, picked up Hercules and went back upstairs to get a cup of coffee and then remembered that I had no coffeepot. I leaned against the counter, and Hercules licked my chin in sympathy.

"You know, I think we're right about Miranda's death. It wasn't random. There haven't been any problems along the Riverwalk other than the occasional drunk trying to climb a tree. So what we have to do is figure out who wanted one of those two women dead."

Hercules made a face and shook his head.

"I guess I'll start with Ruby. Maybe she can tell me who Emme and possibly Miranda spent time with since they got here." I pulled my phone out and sent Ruby a text to see if we could meet. Less than a minute later I got one back. Ruby replied that she had just finished a practice and invited me to stop at the theater in about an hour. She was working on a new version of the final concert program for the rest of the morning.

I finished getting ready for work, put the towels in the dryer, grabbed my messenger bag and set out fresh water and a few sardine crackers for the boys. Hercules came out to the porch and sat on the bench by the window. I scratched the top of his head and told him I'd see him later.

I headed down Mountain Road and decided my first stop was going to be Eric's. I knew Ruby liked their iced tea. Claire was working. "Hi, Kathleen," she said. "What can I get you?"

I smiled back at her. "A large iced tea, please," I said.

Claire's eyes narrowed. She cocked her head to one side. "Okay, who are you and what have you done with the real Kathleen?"

I laughed. "It's not for me. It's for Ruby."

She smiled. "That makes more sense. How about our peach iced tea, then? It has peach syrup and peach puree."

I nodded. "Umm, yes. I think Ruby would like that."

Brady Chapman—Maggie's . . . I didn't really know how to describe their relationship—was at a table by the window with an older man I didn't recognize. He raised a hand in hello to me, then caught Claire's eye and pointed at his cup. She nodded. "Just let me get Brady a refill and then I'll get that iced tea," she said.

"Go ahead," I said, taking a seat at the counter.

Claire grabbed the pot and headed over to Brady's table. She filled both men's mugs. Brady said something to her and she smiled. On the way back to the counter she stopped to top off the cup of another customer, a man eating alone. He was rangy with dirty blond hair combed back from his face and longish sideburns. He was sporting a scruff of facial hair that looked more like he hadn't shaved in a few days than anything intentional. Something about his body language—the tilt of his chin, the way he shifted his body toward Claire, invading her space, and how his eyes lingered on more than her face—sent a cold finger across the back of my neck.

The man said something to her I couldn't hear. She straightened and said something back, and I saw a flash of annoyance on her face. He put his hand on Claire's backside and smirked at her. She smacked it away and took a step back from the table. He grabbed her arm.

From the corner of my eye I saw the door to the kitchen open. Eric came out, glanced at me and smiled. Then he scanned the room. He sized up the situation at once and was at the table before anything else could happen.

Eric Cullen wasn't a big man, but he had presence and he was deceptively strong. I'd once seen him handle an intoxicated and belligerent customer during the Winterfest dinner at the community center, getting the drunk—who had cuffed a kid across the back of the head—out to the parking lot and keeping him restrained until the police arrived. Now he grabbed the customer by the elbow.

The man clenched his teeth. Whatever Eric was doing hurt. "Keep your hands to yourself," Eric said.

"Hey, we're just talking." He had a sullen edge to his voice.

"The conversation is over," Eric said. He didn't raise his voice, but no one who was in the restaurant had any trouble hearing him. Brady had been watching Eric. He got to his feet.

The man let go of Claire's arm.

"You all right?" Eric asked.

She nodded and took a couple of steps back. She put the arm he'd been holding against her abdomen, and I could see the skin was twisted and red.

"You're done," Eric said to the customer, letting go of his elbow.

The man looked at his half-eaten plate of food. "What? Because I was making a little conversation?" He looked at Claire. "Loosen up a little, sweetheart."

"Get out of my restaurant," Eric said. Even someone who didn't understand the English language couldn't have missed the threat behind the words.

I hoped the guy wouldn't be stupid enough to challenge Eric. It would end badly, I knew. But not for Eric.

The man made a sour face, mouth twisted to one side. "Screw you," he said. "Your food sucks anyway." He slid out of his seat and made his way to the door. Once he was outside I let out the breath I hadn't realized I was holding.

Eric said something to Claire and she nodded. He caught Brady's eye and the men exchanged a look. It was a guy thing. Probably the same look two cavemen had exchanged after one had successfully run off a saber-toothed tiger or a mastodon.

Eric looked around the room. "Coffee's on the house," he said with a smile. He picked up the pot Claire had been holding, and they both came back to the counter. He grabbed a fresh pot and shook his head as he passed me. "It's not even Monday," he said.

"Are you all right?' I asked Claire.

She nodded. "Yeah, I'm okay." She rubbed her arm. It was still red. The man hadn't just grabbed her arm; he'd twisted as well. I fished in my bag and pulled out a tiny jar of salve Maggie and Rebecca had made when I'd scraped my leg. "Try a little of this," I said. "It's one of Rebecca's herbal creams."

She took the container, unscrewed the top and smoothed some of the cream on her arm. It smelled faintly of lavender. "Thanks," Claire said. "I'll just go wash my hands and get your iced tea." She headed for the kitchen.

Eric came back then. His pot was almost empty. "You may as well take the last of this," he said. "Like I said, it's on the house." He grabbed a take-out cup, poured the coffee and added cream and two spoonfuls of sugar.

"Do you have any idea who that guy is?" I asked, tilting my head in the direction of the entrance.

He shook his head. "I was going to ask you if you did."

"I don't," I said. "Maybe someone associated with the festival?"

"Let's hope not," he said. "The guy's a dick." He put a lid on my cup.

Claire came out of the kitchen with the iced tea. She held up her arm. The redness was already fading. "Thanks, Kathleen," she said with a smile. "It feels better already."

"Good," I said, reaching for my wallet to pay for Ruby's tea.

"Forget it. We're good," Eric said, making a shooing motion with one hand.

I reached for the cup. "Thanks," I said.

"Be careful out there." Eric's eyes shifted in the direction of the street.

I knew he meant keep my eyes peeled for the man he'd asked to leave.

I nodded. "I will."

I found Ruby in the front office of the theater, head bent over her laptop. I tapped on the open door and she looked up. "Hey, Kathleen," she said with a smile.

I held out the iced tea. "I thought you might be ready for a break," I said.

"I am. As my grandfather used to say, I'm as dry as a covered bridge." She took the cup and had a long drink. A smile lit up her face. "Peach. My favorite. Thank you." Ruby leaned back in the chair and stretched her arms over her head.

"What are you working on?" I asked, dropping into a chair just inside the door.

"A new layout for the final concert program." She gestured at the screen. "With Emme gone, there are some changes to the lineup." She brushed some wisps of hair back from her face. "And everyone wants to acknowledge Miranda's death but not be melodramatic about it, if that makes sense."

I nodded. "It does."

A tiny frown creased her forehead. "So have you come up with anything yet?"

I hated to disappoint her. "No," I said. "I'm still trying to figure out whether the killer was after Miranda or could have mistaken her for Emme."

"Do you think someone could have been after Emme?"

"Maybe. Neither one of them seemed to have any enemies." I folded my hands around my cup. "What about while they were here for the festival? Did either Miranda or Emme strike up a friendship with any of the other participants? Other than Ami and you?"

Ruby took another sip of her iced tea before she answered. "No. It was pretty much just the four of us. And Emme and Miranda still had business connected to Emme's music to take care of, so they were with Nora a lot." She gestured at me with her cup. "You should talk to Nora."

"I'm surprised she's still here, since her sister's gone," I said. "I know that Nora has been helping with promotion and wanted to finish what she started, but she doesn't really have any ties to the festival."

A small smile played across Ruby's face. "Nora Finley is one of those people who likes things done a certain way. That's how she ended up volunteering to work on the promo for the festival in the first place. She kept finding problems with the way the volunteer who was doing it was handling things." The smile turned into a grin. "You know what Mary has to say about her way and the best way? Well, that's Nora in spades."

I grinned back at her. "I understand," I said. I'd heard Mary say—and not completely in jest—that she wasn't a perfection-ist and it wasn't her fault that her way of doing things and the best way happened to be one and the same.

"I think Nora wants to stay in town so she can keep an eye on the investigation into Miranda's death," Ruby went on. "She had a lot of questions for Marcus when we went to get clothes from their apartment, and I got the feeling she would have made some suggestions as to where he should be looking if Marcus hadn't—very diplomatically—shut the conversation down."

"He's good at that," I said. I shifted in my seat. I really wasn't learning anything I didn't already know. "Ruby, did

Emme or Miranda have any problems with anyone that you saw?"

She fingered one of the piercings in her right ear. "I've been thinking about that since we . . . since Miranda's death. Everyone liked both of them. Emme is fun, easy to get along with, the kind of person who shows up for a practice with cupcakes for everyone. And Miranda was just plain nice. She always had Band-Aids and an extra pen in her bag. She never forgot how everyone took their coffee or if they didn't like coffee at all. I don't understand why anyone would have wanted to kill either one of them."

There wasn't much more to say.

"I'll keep at it," I told Ruby. "And I can promise that Marcus is doing the same."

She gave me a hug and I headed out to walk to the library. Nora Finley was standing on the sidewalk, fishing for something in her purse. The older woman gave me a small smile, and I walked over to join her.

"Hello, Kathleen," she said. "I'm glad I saw you. I wanted to say thank you. Ruby told me it was you who spoke to Detective Gordon so we could get into Miranda's room to get . . . her things."

"You're welcome," I said. "I'm glad I could help."

She sighed softly. "We're having a memorial service in a few days back in Chicago. Miranda's stepbrothers are—" She shook her head. "I'm not sure what they're going to do."

I was guessing that Nora was probably about Roma's age, but she seemed so much older. I tried to figure out why. Her clothes weren't particularly old-fashioned—a white cotton shirt with three-quarter-length sleeves and blue capri pants. I couldn't see any gray in her dark brown chin-length hair. It was her manner, I realized. She was reserved in both her responses and her body language, and she had a tendency to frown disapprovingly over her glasses, the way she'd just done when she'd mentioned Miranda's stepbrothers. Burtis Chapman had an expression that seemed to apply to Nora—she was older than her birthday.

We walked to the corner, talking about the weather and how much Nora had enjoyed walking around town, exploring Mayville Heights. "I hope I'll see you again before I leave," Nora said as she indicated she was headed up a side street.

"I do as well," I said. As she walked away I noticed the lace on my shoe was undone and I bent down to tie it, setting my coffee on the sidewalk. When I straightened up I took another drink, looking idly around. Just ahead of me I saw movement in the bushes. A squirrel maybe? Or someone's cat? No, I realized as I kept looking. Not unless a squirrel had a camera with a telephoto lens.

Whoever that was crouching in the bushes, they were spying on Nora Finley. She was too far away to call to, so I eased up behind the bush, unsure of what I was going to do. Swinging my bag at the photographer seemed a bit extreme, but I couldn't just let this person get away with stalking Nora.

A bit of coffee slopped out of my cup. That was it, I realized. I leaned forward and poured the last of the coffee on the person hunkered down in the bushes.

He—it was a young man—jerked upright, swearing and shaking his arms. He swung around to me. "What the hell are you doing?" he yelled. He was in his midtwenties, three or four inches taller than my five foot six, I guessed, wearing jeans and a black T-shirt. He was of Asian ancestry with spiky black hair and coffee spilled on his shirt.

"What the hell is wrong with you, lady?" he shouted, swiping at his left shoulder. With his other hand he snapped the lens cap on the camera slung around his neck.

"I'm sorry," I said.

He pointed a finger at me. "You did that on purpose."

"And you were hiding in the bushes on purpose."

He pressed his lips together and didn't answer.

"Why are you taking pictures of that woman?" I pointed in the direction Nora had gone.

"I don't know what you're talking about." He was a terrible liar. His face flushed and he couldn't quite look me in the eye.

I pulled my phone out of my pocket.

"Hey, what are you doing?" he asked.

"I'm calling the police," I said.

He held up both hands. "Okay, okay, okay. Yeah, I was following her. That's Nora Finley. I was hoping I could get some shots of her sister Emme Finley, the singer. There are a couple of websites back in Chicago that will pay good money for photos of her. Someone tried to kill Emme a few days ago. And she's just dropped off the grid. Her best friend ended up dead instead. I figured her sister would know where she was."

"Why would some website want those photos?" I asked. I really didn't get it.

He looked at me like I was stupid. "You're kidding, right?

Emme Finley is the good girl with the bedroom voice and the bad-boy ex. People eat that stuff up."

His whole demeanor changed when he talked about Emme, I noticed. He smiled when he said her name. This guy was a fan, not a paparazzo. "Her best friend is dead," I said. "Emme needs time to deal with that, not have her grief stuck on a website for entertainment."

"A couple of pictures aren't going to hurt anyone. What's the big deal?" He really did look puzzled, as though he really didn't grasp how wrong what he was trying to do was.

Before I could answer, an SUV pulled to the curb on the other side of the street. I glanced at it and realized it was Marcus's SUV. I wondered what he was doing here as he got out of the car and walked over to us.

"Hi. What's going on?" he asked as he took in the would-be photographer's camera.

The young man suddenly didn't seem to know what to do with his hands. He jammed them in the pockets of his jeans and then pulled one back out to run it over his hair as he shifted from one foot to the other. "Nothing's going on," he said. "Just enjoying the sunshine."

I had the sudden urge to laugh at his discomfort.

Marcus flashed his badge. "Could I see some ID, please?"

"Uh, yeah, sure." He fumbled for his wallet, pulled out what looked to be his driver's license and offered it to Marcus. "Aren't you gonna ask for her ID?" he asked, eyes flicking to me.

"No," Marcus said. He studied the license and then looked at its owner again. "Alec Kane," he said.

"That's me," the young man said with a forced smile. He held out his hand for his license but Marcus ignored it. He looked at me instead. "Everything all right?" he asked in a low voice.

I nodded.

Marcus turned his attention back to Alec Kane. He held up the license. "I'll be right back." He headed across the street to his car.

Alec was fidgeting so badly I thought he was about to bolt up the sidewalk. Suddenly I felt sorry for him.

"He's a good guy," I said, gesturing in the direction of Marcus's SUV.

"Easy for you to say," Alec said, rolling his eyes. "You don't have fourteen outstanding parking tickets."

"What?" I said. Fourteen parking tickets? Had I heard him right?

Turns out I had. Marcus came back and told Alec he needed to go down to the station with him to straighten things out. A black-and-white pulled in beside the SUV a minute later. After he'd put the young man in the backseat of the police car, Marcus grabbed a cardboard box from the front seat of his own vehicle. I walked over to him. "Want to give me the short version of what that's all about?" he asked, turning to look at Alec in the backseat of the cruiser.

"He was following Nora Finley, hoping she'd lead him to Emme."

Marcus shook his head.

"I don't think he's any kind of professional," I said. "More like a fan." I frowned at the box. "What's that?"

He smiled and held it out to me. "It's for you."

I took the carton, eyeing the lettering on the side. "You got me a carburetor?"

"Open it."

Inside the box, in a nest of crumpled newspaper, was a new glass coffee carafe.

I grinned happily at him. "How did you get this?"

"We have half a dozen at the station that don't work with our machine because the guys are always breaking them and then getting the wrong replacement. Don't worry. I put money in the kitty to cover it."

"Thank you," I said. I stood on tiptoe and gave him a peck on the cheek.

"Get a room," I heard a voice mutter through the open window of the police car.

"I'll see you later," I said.

Marcus called late in the afternoon. It turned out that Alec Kane had an alibi for the time of Miranda Moore's murder. He had been in Chicago, taking photos of a well-known actor whose spray tan had turned his entire body Big Bird yellow.

I hadn't really thought that Alec had had anything to do with Miranda's murder, but I was glad to have my feelings confirmed.

"Was he the one who took those photos of Emme and Derrick?" I asked, swinging slowly from side to side in my desk chair.

"I don't know," Marcus said. "I didn't ask, because it doesn't have anything to do with the murder."

I wasn't sure I agreed with him, but I kept that to myself.

Alec Kane was clearly a fan of Emme. A fan who liked to take pictures of her. Did he have anything to do with those photos of Emme and Derrick at that club? I had no proof those images had any connection with Miranda's death. But I had no proof they didn't, either.

"I have to go," he said. "Kane arranged payment for those tickets. We'll be releasing him in about an hour."

I took an early supper break and was waiting for Alec Kane when he came out of the police station, holding a large cup of coffee in my left hand as a peace offering of sorts. When he caught sight of me he made a show of taking a step back and holding up his hands for protection. "Are you going to dump your coffee on me again?" he asked.

"No," I said, offering the take-out cup to him. "I got this for you. Cream and sugar because I didn't know how you took it."

He took the coffee. "Cream and sugar is fine. And it's the least you could do considering you got me arrested."

"Fourteen unpaid tickets got you arrested," I said.

"Yeah, well, there are too many rules about where you can and can't park in Chicago," he muttered.

Alec Kane was more than a bit immature.

"Are you headed back to Chicago?" I asked.

"Might as well," he said. "Coming to Mayville Heights has been a bust. I really was hoping to get a few pictures of Emme but it looks like she left town."

I took a gamble. "You've made money off Emme Finley before, haven't you? You took those photos of her with her ex-boyfriend."

His eyes slid off my face the way they had when I'd asked

about Nora at our earlier encounter. "I don't know what you're talking about."

I shook my head. "I hope you don't play poker, Alec."

He made a face. "Fine. I took the photographs. I got a tip to go to the club, and when I got there Emme was all over a guy who sure as hell wasn't her boyfriend." He made a face. "And I don't get what she saw in the guy. She's beautiful and smart and, man, can she sing. She could do a lot better." He gave a snort of derision. "Not that Dr. Tightass Professor was much of an improvement."

I stifled a smile at the name he'd given to Emme's ex-boyfriend. Alec definitely had a crush on her, I realized. He got a goofy smile on his face when he talked about her. And he didn't like her former boyfriend.

"Why do you sneak around taking pictures of people you don't know?" I asked.

"Photographers take shots of people they don't know all the time."

"Those people are professionals and even they cross the line sometimes, too. Doesn't that bother you?"

He shrugged and took another sip of the coffee. "I'm a good photographer. I've been taking photos since I was a kid. I even know how to use film. I wanna be a celebrity photographer—in Los Angeles—but I need a portfolio if anyone's going to hire me. So I've been taking pictures of celebrities in Chicago. Sometimes the clubs will buy my pictures for Facebook or their websites because it's good publicity for them. And I've sold stuff to a couple of entertainment websites. All I need is one photo for my big break."

"So you took the photos of Emme and her ex at that club. Then what?" I asked. We had started walking in the general direction of Eric's Place.

Alec looked away again. It was such an obvious tell. "Nothing happened," he said.

"You're lying again."

He scratched the back of his head. "Yeah, well, you make my head itch," he retorted. "Fine. I got an e-mail from someone who knew I had them and wanted to buy them. I figured it was probably someone at the club, you know, trying to draw some attention to the place. The money was good, so I took it."

"So someone else sold the incriminating photos that turned up on the *Good Night Chicago* website and on the club's Facebook page? Not you."

Alec nodded. "Yeah. Whoever it was bought everything from me."

I knew the answer to my next question before I even asked it, but I asked anyway. "Did you meet this person face-to-face?"

He shook his head. "Uh-uh. The whole thing was done by e-mail."

I stopped walking and stared at him. "Did it ever occur to you that you were being used? That someone wanted those photos to hurt Emme in some way?"

He ducked his head for a moment before giving me a sideways glance. "Not at the time, but later, yeah, it did."

"Do you have any idea who you were dealing with?" I asked.

"Nah," he said. "I thought maybe someone wanted to break up Emme and that professor guy she was seeing, Elliot Hardison, and if they did, it worked, because he dropped her like a hot tamale."

We started walking again. "But what would anyone get out of that relationship ending?"

"Well, the professor was helping Emme with her application to that college she wanted to go to—not with the singing part but with the academic stuff. You know she wanted to learn French, right?"

I nodded. Ruby had told me that Emme had applied to the ultra-selective musical theater program at Penn State School of Theatre, and Emme herself had told me she wanted to study French.

"But who would benefit if Emme gave up the idea of college?" I said.

He gave me a "well, duh" look. "Her agent, Lucie Pope. Who else? You want to find the person who wanted those photos, talk to her."

We were in front of Eric's then.

"Thank you for answering my questions," I said.

"Well, thanks for the coffee," he said. He held up the cup. "At least this cup."

I walked back to the library, thinking about what Alec had told me. Could Emme's agent have gone to such extreme lengths to get her to change her mind? Could she have come to Mayville Heights to talk to her client and somehow been involved in Miranda's death? It seemed like a stretch, but I knew people had been killed for less.

Mary was at the circulation desk when I got back. She'd

been away at a kickboxing tournament—she'd won her division—and I hadn't really had the chance to talk to her.

"Congratulations," I said.

"Thank you." She smiled. "I wasn't so sure I was going to win anything this time. There were some tough boxers, but I finally managed to get a leg up on the competition." Her blue eyes twinkled.

I groaned at the pun and shook my head and she laughed.

"I missed you," I said. "It was way too quiet around here."

The grin faded from her face. "I heard about that nice little Miranda Moore," she said. "That's so sad."

"It was."

"And she was here in the library just before it closed the day she was killed."

Miranda had been at the library the day she died? Confused, I stared at Mary. "I don't remember her coming in. Are you sure it was last Saturday?"

Mary frowned, brows knit together. Then her face cleared. "You had to go over to Henderson Holdings, remember?"

I nodded. Next spring I wanted to expand the gardening project Abigail and I had been doing with some of the kids in Reading Buddies. Harry Junior and I had put together a proposal, and Harry had done drawings to scale. I had taken it all over to Lita so Everett, who had offered to fund the project, could take it with him on a business trip to read.

"She asked about the Riverwalk," Mary said. "She wanted to know if it went all the way to Wild Rose Bluff, because she wanted to walk out there and take some pictures." She pressed a hand to her chest for a moment and I could see the sadness in her eyes. "I explained that the boardwalk went part of the way and the trail the rest of the way. It's just so sad that those were the last hours of her life and she didn't know it."

It was true, I thought, but someone likely had known it. The question was who?

chapter 11

Marcus was sitting at my kitchen table when I got home, eating a pulled-turkey sandwich with the boys at his feet. I set my new coffee carafe on the counter, put my arms around his neck and kissed him. "Thank you again for the coffeepot," I said. "I didn't get a chance to properly show my full appreciation before."

He trapped my arms with one of his and kissed me a second time. "I appreciate your appreciation," he said with a grin.

I straightened up and went to the fridge for some lemonade.

There was no lemonade in the refrigerator, and then I remembered that I'd finished the last of the pitcher while I was doing the laundry.

Hercules rubbed against my leg and I bent down to scratch the top of his head. Owen gave an annoyed meow. I knew it had nothing to do with me paying attention to his brother. "Forget it," I said over my shoulder. "Marcus isn't going to feed you two any more turkey now that I'm home."

Marcus looked down at his plate. Hercules looked over at his brother. Owen studied a spot on the floor. They all looked a little sheepish. Finally, Owen stretched and headed for the living room.

I gave Hercules one last scratch behind his ear and turned my attention back to Marcus.

"Do you want part of my sandwich?" he asked.

I nodded and he pulled the remaining half sandwich into two pieces and gave me the larger one.

"Thank you," I said, dropping into the chair across from him.

"What do you want to drink?" he asked, getting to his feet.

"Hot chocolate, I guess," I said. Hercules hopped up onto my lap and looked expectantly at me. "Hey, I already told you that you weren't getting any more turkey."

He put a paw on my chest and gave a low murp.

Marcus laughed. "He's right, Kathleen."

I frowned up at him. "What do you mean?"

"You said that *I* wasn't going to give them more turkey, not you."

Hercules looked from Marcus to me. "So the two of you are using semantics against me?"

The cat licked his whiskers, and I would have sworn there was just a hint of smugness on his furry black-and-white face. There definitely was more than a hint of smugness on Marcus's face. They knew they had won.

"Oh, for heaven's sake," I said. I pulled a tiny bit of turkey from my sandwich. "Do not tell your brother," I warned, shaking a finger at him. The cat took the bit of meat with a soft mrr of satisfaction.

Marcus brought me my hot chocolate and sat down opposite me again. "So how was the rest of your day?" he asked.

"I talked to Alec Kane," I said.

He nodded. " I know."

"I mean after you released him."

He picked up the remains of his sandwich, which Hercules had been eyeing across the table. "I know," he said again.

I frowned at him. "What do you mean you know? Were you lurking by the police station door?"

He pulled a slice of dill pickle out of his sandwich and popped it in his mouth. Hercules watched his every move.

"Forget that," I told the little black-and-white cat. "It will give you pickle breath."

He made a disgruntled mutter.

"No, I wasn't lurking anywhere," Marcus said. "But I *was* the one who told you when Alec Kane was going to be released. So what did he tell you?"

He'd told me on purpose. Just when I thought I knew everything about the man, he'd do something to surprise me.

I put a hand on Hercules to steady him and tucked one leg up underneath me. "Alec Kane took the photographs of Emme and her former boyfriend, Derrick. The ones that might have derailed her chances to get into the music program she was applying to."

"He has an alibi for the time Miranda Moore was killed.

And frankly that would give Emme Finley a motive to want to hurt him, not the other way around."

"Someone paid him for those incriminating photos," I said, reaching for my cup.

"I don't see how that connects to whoever killed Miranda. Someone from the club probably bought the pictures." Marcus ate the last bite of his sandwich. "I did a little digging, and it got some decent publicity from the scandal—*free* publicity—or maybe not quite free."

I found myself shaking my head.

"There was no other reason for someone to want those photos," he said. "No one benefitted."

I remembered that Alec had pointed out that Emme's agent could have benefitted.

I glanced at my watch. It wasn't that late in Boston. "I need to call my mother," I said to Marcus.

"This has something to do with the murder, doesn't it?"

"Yes."

He got up and took his dishes over to the counter.

"I promise I'll tell you everything I find out," I said.

He leaned over and kissed me. "I'm going to have a shower." He dropped another marshmallow in my cup. "You know you wanted three," he said. He smiled and headed for the stairs.

I watched him go, thinking how well he'd gotten to know me. Hercules shifted on my lap. I looked down at him and felt a twinge of guilt because Marcus didn't know *all* of my secrets.

I gathered the cat and my hot chocolate and headed for the living room. I curled up in the big chair with Hercules settled on my lap and my drink close by. It was my favorite spot for calling Mom and Dad, and I'd usually end up with a cat on my lap, making it even more cozy.

My mother answered on the fifth ring. "Hi, Mom," I said.

"Katydid! I was just talking about you," she said, and I could hear the pleasure in her voice. "Your ears must have been burning."

I felt a small twinge of homesickness the way I almost always did when I called. "So what were you saying about me?" I asked.

"Your brother and I are going through photos to make a photo book for your father's birthday, and we found one of you dressed as Dr. Dolittle for Halloween with Ethan and Sara dressed as monkeys. You're all so adorable."

I laughed. "I remember that. While I may have been able to talk to the animals, it didn't mean those two monkeys listened!" I felt a pang that I couldn't be in Boston to help them with this gift for Dad.

"Sweetie, will you look through your own photos and see if there are any you want to add?" Mom asked.

"I will," I said, thinking that there was a photograph of the five of us on the Boston Common that my friend Lise had taken that would be a perfect addition to the photo book.

"I wish you were here, but when we get the book put together I'll send you and Sara the link so you can look at it before it's printed."

"Thanks," I said. I felt better knowing I could be a small part of the project.

"So what's up?" Mom asked.

Hercules laid his head on my chest and as I stroked his fur

he began to purr. "I'm guessing you read about Miranda Moore's death in the *Chronicle*?" Mom had been reading the Mayville Heights paper online every day since I'd moved here.

"I did."

"Do you know a woman named Lucie Pope? She's Emme Finley's agent."

"I'm sorry, I don't." I imagined Mom shaking her head. "Maybe your brother does."

Ethan knew a lot of people in the music business.

"I'll let you talk to him," Mom said. "I love you. Give Marcus a hug from me."

"Love you, too, Mom," I said.

After a moment Ethan came on the phone. "Hey, what's up?" he asked.

"I hear Mom found a photo of you in your monkey suit," I teased.

He laughed. "Yeah, well, it's not as much fun as the one she found of you in your birthday suit."

"You better not be serious," I said. Hercules lifted his head and gave me a curious look.

Ethan was still laughing. "I am dead serious, big sister," he said. "You're running down the hall holding a pair of socks in one hand, and that's the only clothing you have."

"That picture is not going in any photo book," I said hotly.

"Yeah, keep telling yourself that," he said. Then his voice grew serious. "So Mom says you wanted to ask me something about some music agent."

"Lucie Pope. I don't suppose you've heard of her."

"Sure I have," he said. "Remember that festival we played at last year up in Maine?"

My foot was going to sleep so I shifted my leg, which annoyed Hercules. He glared at me before settling himself again. "The all-acoustic one. Sara filmed you, didn't she?"

"Yeah, that's the one. Pope had a singer and I think a band performing. She's your age, I'd guess."

I waited for Ethan to make an old joke. He loved to tease me because I'd been a teenager when he and Sara were born, but for once he didn't.

"Does this have anything to do with another murder you've gotten mixed up in?"

"Kind of," I said. "Lucie Pope is the agent for a cabaret singer from Chicago named Emme Finley, but Emme may be going back to school and making a career change."

"Yeah, well, Lucie might be making some changes herself. There's a rumor going around that she has a deal pending for a reality show for one of her clients and as part of it she's getting a producer credit. If it's true, losing a singer wouldn't be a big deal."

"Do you think she'd talk to me?"

I knew I was getting fixated on those photos of Emme and Derrick, but like Miranda's murder, the amount of effort someone had put into getting those images didn't make sense to me. I knew at best it was a tenuous connection between the two events. I was hoping maybe Emme's agent would know if the singer had made any enemies.

"I don't see why not." I imagined him shrugging as he

perched on a stool at the kitchen counter, assuming he wasn't actually sitting on the counter. "I think I still have her card. Want me to call her and see if she'll talk to you?"

"Yes, please." I recited the phone number at the library. "And you can give her this number and my cell as well."

"Hey, no problem," he said.

"I owe you."

Ethan laughed again. "Oh man, I like that."

And he'd make me pay up, I knew. Not that there was anything I wouldn't do for him or Sara anyway. "I love you, brat," I said.

"Love you, too," he retorted.

We ended the conversation, and I got up with Hercules and my mug to warm up my hot chocolate, which was now more like lukewarm chocolate.

Marcus was just coming down the stairs wearing nothing but a pair of gray sweatpants. His hair was damp.

"Did you talk to your mother?" he asked.

"I did."

"Did you find out anything useful?"

He had to ask twice because I was staring at his bare chest and didn't hear him the first time. "Uh, maybe," I said. "I'm not sure."

He grinned and kept advancing on me as I tried to tell him that Ethan was going to try to put me together with Emme's agent. I backed into the kitchen, managing to bump into the door frame and the table because I kept getting distracted because he was gorgeous without his shirt. Not that he wasn't gorgeous with it.

Hercules wriggled in my arms and I set him down, putting my mug on the table as I straightened up. Marcus was directly in front of me now.

"Is there anything else you need to tell me?" he asked.

I nodded. "Yes."

"So are you going to tell me now?" he said.

I shook my head. "No."

He pulled me into his arms, and just like that scene in *Wuthering Heights* when Heathcliff kissed Cathy, the birds flew over the heather.

chapter 12

It was quiet on Saturday morning at the library, so I decided it would be a good time to start choosing which books we were going to use for our Banned Books display in September.

Mia was helping me work our way down the list we'd made the previous year.

"*The Adventures of Huckleberry Finn* and *The Catcher in the Rye* for language, right?" Mia asked me. As usual, the teen was dressed in a conservative black skirt and a white shirt with the sleeves rolled back.

"Absolutely," I said, adding both titles to the pad in front of me. "And I think we should add *Fahrenheit 451.*" In more than one library Ray Bradbury's classic had had words blacked out. "Did you know that the postal service refused to mail *For Whom the Bell Tolls?*" I asked.

She nodded. Her hair was shaded with purple streaks like a grape Popsicle. "We learned that in English class."

"I bet you didn't learn that the *Captain Underpants* books are among the most banned books in the country," I said.

Mia looked surprised. "But why? I loved Captain Underpants when I was a kid."

"I know," I said, setting down my pen. "The series is one of the most popular with the Reading Buddies kids. The books have been challenged for, among other reasons, encouraging kids to disobey parents and teachers."

"That's why the books are so much fun," she said. "Because the boys are always doing things they're not supposed to do."

Abigail poked her head around the workroom door. "There's a call for you," she said. "Someone named Lucie Pope?"

That was fast. I did owe Ethan.

I got to my feet. "Thanks," I said. "I'll take it in my office."

I sat on the corner of my desk and reached for the phone. "Ms. Pope, thanks for calling," I said.

"Please, call me Lucie," she said. She had a warm, husky voice. "Your brother said you have a couple of questions about Emme Finley."

"I do. You probably already know what happened to her friend Miranda Moore."

"Emme called me. I'm not sure how I can help you. I can't share anything private with you."

Behind me the sun was streaming through the window. It felt off to be talking about murder on such a beautiful day.

"I understand that," I said. "I'm wondering if you can think of anyone who might have wanted to . . . hurt Emme. Does she have any enemies?"

"Wait a minute. Are you saying whoever killed Miranda was really after Emme?"

"Maybe," I hedged. "I don't know."

"You've met Emme?" Lucie asked.

"Yes, I have."

She made an approving murmur on the other end of the phone. "Then you know the kind of person she is. She doesn't have any enemies, because she doesn't make enemies. Yes, there were a few club owners and some fans who were disappointed by her choice to go back to school, but no one was so put out that they'd try to kill her. For the record, that includes me."

I decided to go for broke. "Ethan says you have a deal in the works that could—" I hesitated.

"Bring me a boatload of money? Yes, I do."

I couldn't help smiling. "I was going to say, that could lead to your own career change."

"You obviously have much better manners than I do," she said with a laugh. Then her tone changed. "I would never have hurt Emme or Miranda. Miranda was a quiet little thing. I didn't really know her, but what I knew I liked. And for the record, I was in a little hole-in-the-wall club in Portage Park listening to a band when Miranda died."

I made a note on the pad on my desk. Marcus would be able to check that alibi pretty easily.

"Kathleen, I find it hard to believe—no, impossible to

believe—that anyone would want to kill Emme Finley," Lucie said. "I don't know if this will help, but Emme's sister, Nora, once mentioned Miranda's family was messy. Maybe you'd be better off trying to see what you can find out about them."

Maybe I would.

chapter 13

Roma hadn't wanted a traditional wedding shower, so Maggie and I, as maids of honor, were hosting an afternoon tea for her at Briar House, a new bed-and-breakfast I'd discovered just outside of town that offered a traditional English tea—or close to it—in their dining room.

The owner of the bed-and-breakfast, Vera Webb, who was originally from the British midlands, was waiting for Maggie and me when we arrived. She was in her late fifties, in a simple navy skirt and white blouse with three-quarter-length sleeves, her thick gray hair pulled back into a smooth twist. Her half-frame reading glasses hung on a chain around her neck.

"Kathleen, it's good to see you again," she said in her crisp British accent.

"It's good to see you, too," I said. Vera had been indispensable in planning the party, and the moment I'd seen the dining room, I'd known it was the perfect place to celebrate Roma's upcoming wedding. "You remember my friend Maggie."

Vera offered her hand. "It's nice to meet you in person," she said.

"You as well," Maggie replied with a smile. "Your house is beautiful."

"Why don't you both come and see the tea room?" Vera said.

We followed her down the short hall to the left. She opened the sliding wood-panel door and Maggie gave a gasp of happiness. "Oh, this is wonderful," she exclaimed, clasping her hands together.

It wasn't the first time I'd seen the room, but like Maggie, I was captivated by how perfect it was.

"Thank you." Vera beamed.

The high-ceilinged room was filled with light from the vintage wrought-iron chandelier with its white glass shades, as well as from the high, wide windows with their lacy curtains. The dark walnut trim around the windows stood out against the pale blush-colored walls decorated with a collection of vintage mirrors and delicate watercolors. The wide-planked floors gleamed.

Small square tables that could seat four people each were covered with soft green-and-coral-flowered tablecloths, with small bouquets of garden flowers in a variety of cut glass vases in the center of each one. In the middle of the room was a small table just big enough for two, covered with a white lace tablecloth. A tea set of delicate white china with deep pink roses and edged with gold was waiting for Maggie and me to pour for the guests as hostesses.

With Vera's help we'd decided on a menu that included two of the sixteen choices of tea the B and B offered: Earl Grey, a black tea flavored with oil from bergamot oranges, I'd learned; and rooibos—or red bush—tea, which was naturally caffeine free. Maggie had made those choices since she was the tea drinker. The rest of the menu consisted of traditional English scones with homemade jam and clotted cream; cucumber, smoked salmon and cream cheese sandwiches; and a sour cream lemon pound cake with lemon glaze and bits of candied lemon peel sprinkled on top. I felt certain all our guests would be pleased.

Roma had wanted to forgo gifts altogether, but as Maggie had pointed out, no one was going to be happy with that. "People want to celebrate with you," she'd said. She was also the one who came up with the idea we finally settled on—a recipe shower. Maggie had given each guest a four-by-six piece of cardstock and asked them to share a favorite recipe. She'd also asked each person to bring a favorite photo of Roma. Maggie had already created a beautiful handmade book to hold the recipes and photos.

She turned to me now and gave me a quick hug. "Thank you for finding this place. It's perfect," she said. "Roma's going to love it."

"I wish Olivia could have been here," I said.

A cloud seemed to pass over Maggie's face. "Are you sure she's okay with Roma marrying Eddie?"

I looked at her in surprise. "What makes you say that?"

She shrugged. "It's not a big deal, but I e-mailed Olivia to see if she'd send me a recipe since she couldn't make it for the shower. She said she was too busy."

"Maybe she was," I said. "She probably has a lot to do before she gets here."

Maggie nodded. "You're probably right." She smiled. "Has Marcus seen you in that dress?"

I felt my cheeks get warm. "Yes," I said. When I'd come down the stairs earlier I'd gotten a long wolf whistle.

We'd decided that we'd all dress up a little. Maggie was wearing the deep blue sundress she'd texted me the photo of. It had short flowy sleeves and a gathered waist, and she'd chosen low-heeled rainbow sandals. I had decided on a sleeveless raspberry shift with a band of lavender-and-white flowers around the hem and my favorite white sandals with their oh-so-comfortable rubber soles.

Rebecca and the Kings—Ella and her daughter, Taylor— were the first to arrive, all wearing pretty summer dresses.

"This is perfect," Rebecca exclaimed as she hugged first me and then Maggie.

Ella, who was a talented fiber artist as well as an accomplished seamstress, had noticed a needlepoint sampler on the wall and was asking Vera about it.

I held up the small clutch purse Taylor had loaned me from her collection of bags. "Thank you for this," I said. "It's perfect with my dress and shoes."

She smiled at me. "I thought it would be, and it holds more than you'd think by looking at it."

I smiled back at her. I tended to carry a lot in my bag, whether it was my messenger bag or a tote bag. Taylor had offered to lend me a small purse when we'd decided to dress up for the party and had very diplomatically suggested that I didn't need one of my big bags this one time.

Mary and her daughter, Bridget, showed up next. "What recipe are you sharing with Roma?" I asked, pointing at the envelope Mary was carrying. I'd been trying for ages to get Mary to tell me what the secret ingredient in her cinnamon rolls was. She refused and kept telling me to go experiment in my kitchen. I'd been doing that but I could never quite get it right—not that Marcus seemed to mind eating my "experiments."

"None of your beeswax," Mary told me now, with a smile.

Out of the corner of my eye I saw Susan appear in the doorway. Mia was with her. Instead of her usual updo, Susan had pulled back the front of her hair, holding it in place with a small paintbrush and leaving the rest of it long. She wore a wild black-and-white geometric-print ballerina-length dress and heels that added a good four inches to her normally tiny height. Mia had chosen one of her ubiquitous black skirts—a short circle cut— and a lavender top that matched the streaks in her hair.

As planned, Roma arrived last with her mother, Pearl, and Eddie's daughter, Sydney. Roma swallowed a couple of times and then wrapped Maggie and me together in a hug.

"I don't know how to thank you," she whispered.

"Just be happy with Eddie," I said, blinking a couple of times so I wouldn't cry. Maggie nodded in agreement, and I noticed her eyes were bright with unshed tears, too.

Pearl took one of my hands in both of hers. Pearl Davidson Carver was a tiny woman. She had short, naturally curly white hair and the same warm smile as her daughter. "Everything looks absolutely wonderful," she said. "I'm so happy Roma has both of you"—she looked around the room—"all of you as friends."

"We're lucky to have her," I said. I meant every word. Roma had been more than just a good friend. She'd bandaged me up more than once, teasing me that I wasn't the type of animal she usually treated. Like Maggie, she'd nudged Marcus and me together, and she always took excellent care of Owen and Hercules, neither one of whom was a very good patient.

"I'm so happy my girl and Eddie are getting married," Pearl said. "I'm getting a great son-in-law and another beautiful granddaughter."

We both looked at Sydney, talking to Rebecca and gesturing with both hands the same way her father did when he was talking.

"She looks so much like Eddie," Pearl commented.

She was right. Not only did Sydney have a lot of her dad's mannerisms, she also had his eyes and his smile. I guessed that the child's mass of golden curls had come from her mother.

"I'm in awe over how hard Eddie and Roma *and* Sydney's mom have worked to make a loving family for her," I said.

"It's a parent's job to put their child's happiness and well-being first," Pearl said. "You do whatever is necessary." She turned back to me, and as our eyes met I got the feeling she was remembering the sacrifices she'd made to keep Roma safe when she was barely more than a baby.

I thought about the period of time when my mom and dad were divorced, before Ethan and Sara were born. They had always put me first, even when I'd treated them—especially my mom—badly.

Vera caught my eye then, raising an eyebrow. I nodded and touched Maggie on the shoulder, our cue that it was time to get people seated. Vera came back with the tea, while a young man about Taylor and Mia's age followed with the scones and sandwiches.

Maggie and I took our seats. Vera set a teapot in front of each of us, both of them in quilted green tea cozies. "Yours is Earl Grey," she said to Maggie. "And yours is the rooibos," she told me.

We ate and talked and laughed, and the scones and the tiny finger sandwiches just seemed to disappear like magic because it seemed like we were all so busy talking there couldn't have been any time left to eat.

After everyone had had a slice of the cake, we gave Roma our gifts. I had shared my salmon roll recipe, which was one of Roma's favorites. The photo I'd chosen was one of the three of us—Roma, Maggie and me—that Marcus had taken at Winterfest last year.

Roma looked at the recipe and the photo and then jumped up and hugged me. "Thank you for the gift, all of this, for today, for always being my friend."

I nodded wordlessly and hugged her back, knowing if I tried to say anything, I'd lose it.

Maggie had chosen her pizza recipe for Roma. I thought about all the times the three of us had spent eating pizza and talking in Maggie's apartment. Her photo was also from Winterfest, the first one I'd attended. It was Roma, posing with Faux Eddie, the full-size replica of the real Eddie that Maggie had created for a display during the festival, the same replica that had indirectly been responsible for Roma and Eddie getting together.

Roma pressed a hand to her mouth, and then she got up again and wrapped Maggie in a hug.

All of the recipes and photos were special. Rebecca had copied out her mother's instructions for beef stew. Her photo was of Roma as a little girl. Abigail shared a recipe for apple turnovers. Pearl's recipe was for blueberry pancakes. And Mary gave Roma the instructions for her cinnamon rolls.

I looked over Roma's shoulder and read the ingredient list. I didn't see anything that I hadn't tried in all my attempts to replicate the recipe. "I don't see the secret ingredient," I said.

Mary raised an eyebrow, gave me a devilish smile and leaned over to whisper in Roma's ear. A smile spread across Roma's face. She put her right hand over her heart. "I swear," she said solemnly. She looked at me, lips pressed together so she wouldn't laugh.

I shook my finger at Mary and glared at her. "One of these days I'm going to figure out that recipe," I said.

"Make an honest man out of that poor boy and maybe I'll give it to you," she countered.

Everyone laughed and I felt my cheeks get red.

After the gifts were all opened and everyone had had a chance to look at the photographs, we continued to mill around talking.

Mia and I were trying to decipher the name of the artist of one of the watercolors when Roma joined us. She smiled at Mia. "I'm honored that you shared the coffee cake recipe you used to make with your grandfather."

"Grandpa liked happy endings," Mia said. "I think he'd be happy I shared the recipe with you."

Roma looked at me. "I've already said this to Maggie. Thank you for talking me into this. It was perfect; this place, the food, all the wonderful recipes, and don't get me started on the photos or I'll cry."

Syd joined us then. She leaned against Roma, who put her arms around the child's shoulders. "I like your hair," she said to Mia.

"It's not that hard to do," Mia said. "I do it myself."

"Could you teach me?" Syd asked.

"Sure," Mia said. Then she made a face and looked at Roma. "I mean, if that's okay."

"You have to check with your mom," Roma said.

Ruby joined us then. "Little hint," she said. "Start with just one colored streak because it won't freak out the grown-ups. Then before they know it your whole head is green."

Syd grinned, and she and Ruby exchanged high fives.

"Ruby," Roma said, an edge of warning in her voice.

Ruby raised her eyebrows and grinned. "What? You think I started out like this?" She patted her copper-colored hair.

"When I turn eighteen I'm going to have this stupid mole lasered off," Sydney said, touching the beauty mark on the right side of her face near her lip.

"Why?" Ruby asked. "That's a beauty mark and lots of beautiful women have them."

The child rolled her eyes. "Yeah, my dad says the same thing, but all the women he named are about a hundred years old or dead. And the boys at school always say I have pen on my face."

"The guys at school are a bunch of dweebs," Mia said.

Syd nodded. "My dad said that, too."

Ruby held up a finger. "Kate Upton," she said. She continued with fingers and names. "Blake Lively. Scarlett Johansson. My friend Emme Finley. Ansel Elgort."

"Ansel Elgort is a boy," Syd said, an edge of disdain in her voice.

"That's not his fault," Ruby retorted. "You want me to keep going?"

Syd shook her head. "No, I get the point."

"Don't do stuff because of dumb boys," Ruby said. The rest of us nodded. "When you get to be my age you'll wonder why you ever cared what they think. I promise."

That evening I filled the bathtub with hot water and bubbles and stretched out for a long, relaxing soak. A black-and-white paw poked around the bathroom door, which I'd forgotten to close all the way—not that closing the door would have stopped Hercules. The little cat jumped up onto the back of the toilet tank and began to wash his face.

"How was your afternoon?" I asked.

"Mrrr," he said without missing a pass of his face. Translation: "Okay."

I thought about Ruby mentioning Emme's birthmark as I told Hercules about the party. Then I remembered that feeling I'd had that something was different about Emme in the Facebook photos. I'd put it down to thinking it was just that there were no clear shots of her face, but now it occurred to me that it might be something else, something my eye had seen but my brain hadn't quite registered.

I got out of the tub, dried off and put on my pajamas. I retrieved my laptop and, with Hercules looking on, brought up the photo of Emme and Derrick kissing. I centered the image and increased the magnification. Then I went to Emme's website, found a headshot of her and did the same thing. I studied the two images side by side on the screen. "That's it," I said to Hercules.

I pointed at the photograph of Emme and Derrick. The cat leaned in for a closer look and then looked at me. It seemed to me that he got it.

"I'm right, aren't I?" I said.

"Merow!" Hercules said with enthusiasm.

Emme's mole was not in the right place. It was slightly higher than where it should have been, just above her lip. It wasn't something anyone would probably notice with just a cursory look at the photo, because the misplacement was slight. But it was there. Maybe I'd noticed it because I'd spent so much time watching my mother and father change the way they looked with makeup. If Emme had taken more than a quick look at the pictures, she probably would have realized it wasn't her in them.

"That was Miranda," I said. She was the only person who could have been masquerading as Emme.

As crazy as it seemed, that was Miranda. But why?

chapter 14

Miranda had pretended to be Emme. It made no sense whatsoever. "Why would she do that?" I said to Hercules.

He didn't seem to know, either.

"Okay, so what do we know so far?" I held up one hand, counting on my fingers the way Ruby had done earlier. "Alec took photos of Miranda, pretending to be Emme, making out with Derrick at that club. Those photos ended up on the club's Facebook page and website and on *Good Night Chicago*'s site and some other places. A small scandal ensued."

Hercules bobbed his head. He was with me so far.

"Emme and her professor boyfriend broke up. Emme started having second thoughts about going back to school." I groaned. "Why is that such a big deal? Why did it matter whether or not Emme Finley went to school?"

I knew very little about Miranda other than what Ruby had told me. Her mother and father were both dead. She had a stepfather and two stepbrothers whom she wasn't close to. She and Emme had been friends since elementary school, and the two of them were as close as sisters.

"Was that it?" I asked Hercules. "Was Miranda afraid of losing her best friend? Was that why she tried to derail Emme's plans?"

I pulled a hand back through my hair. That just didn't fit with the woman I'd talked to. Miranda had pretended to be Emme. That I was certain about. Had that masquerade gotten her killed? I wasn't sure that made sense, either.

"If Miranda was trying to derail Emme's plans, the only person who had a motive to kill her was Emme herself," I said out loud.

Hercules cocked his head to one side and seemed to consider my words.

"Emme had an alibi." I remembered Nora saying they'd gone home at four thirty and stayed in all evening.

I sighed and set the computer on the floor beside me. Hercules immediately climbed onto my lap and nuzzled my chin. "This isn't working," I said as I stroked his fur. "I don't know what to do next. I wish the answer would just fall from the sky somehow."

He yawned and so did I. "It's getting late and we're both tired," I said. "And as Scarlett O'Hara said, 'Tomorrow is another day.'"

An answer didn't fall from the sky, but some help did come in the form of Emme herself, who walked into the library just before lunch on Monday.

"Hi, Kathleen," she said. "Do you have a minute?"

I glanced behind me at the checkout desk. "I'm fine," Susan said. "Abigail is in the stacks if I need her."

I led Emme over to the far end of our computer room. "I wanted to tell you that Derrick and I are back in Mayville Heights and I'm staying here until the person who killed Miranda is found. I'm not running away and hiding anymore. Miranda deserves better." There was a determined look in her hazel eyes and a new confidence in her stance.

"You were allowed to take some time to grieve," I said carefully. "You and Miranda were close." Should I tell her I believed it had been Miranda posing as her in those photos with Derrick? No, I decided. Not until I could tell her why Miranda had done it.

She smiled. "Thank you for saying that. You're right. Miranda and I were as close as sisters. Closer in a lot of ways than I am to Nora, because there are so many years between us."

I thought about Ethan and Sara. There were a lot of years between us as well, but we'd always been close. I was lucky, I realized.

"I just wanted to ask if you've been able to come up with anything," Emme continued.

I shook my head and felt my stomach do a flip-flop. "I'm

sorry. I don't have anything to tell you yet." It was as close to the truth as I could get.

She put a hand on my arm. "Please don't give up, Kathleen," she said. "Both Ruby and Ami say you're good at this kind of thing. And I think people are more likely to talk to you than they are to the police. If someone is talking to you, it's just a conversation. With the police even the most innocent questions feel like an interrogation. Trust me."

I didn't have to take her word for it. I remembered my first encounter with Marcus, which oddly enough had happened because of a death connected to the music festival. His questions had felt like an interrogation because they were. When he was working on a case every conversation was an interrogation.

I sighed softly. If I was going to destroy Emme's beliefs about her best friend, I needed to at least be able to explain Miranda's actions. "I won't give up," I said, "but I'm not making any promises."

"That's enough for me." She played with the elephant charm she was wearing on a silver chain around her neck.

I tried to recall what Ruby had told me about Miranda's family. "Miranda's mother is dead," I said.

"That's right," Emme said. "Our moms were close, but I think we would have been friends anyway. Miranda never knew her father. He was killed in a car accident just before she was born. Her mother remarried, and then she died when we were freshmen in high school. I guess maybe I kind of understood what she was going through. Our mother—mine and Nora's—died of cancer when I was eight. The difference was I had Nora, and I still had my dad then. He was wonderful. Miranda was left with her stepfather and two stepbrothers. It wasn't Cinderella, but it was close for a while—except there was no prince or fairy godmother to save her." She continued to finger the tiny silver elephant.

"Nora and I had always planned to move to Chicago when I graduated whether or not I went to college. There was no way I was going to leave Miranda behind. So two days after graduation we packed everything we could into the car and we left and we never looked back."

"How did Miranda end up working as your assistant?" I asked.

"It was just a temporary thing. She lost her job about six months ago. But she had a job in the registrar's office at the University of Chicago starting in September, and she was planning on taking courses, too. She wanted to eventually become an accountant." She stopped, swallowed and cleared her throat. "I'm sorry," she said, her voice husky with emotion. "Sometimes it just hits me that I'm never going to see her again."

Miranda didn't sound like someone who would have been trying to derail her best friend's plans. Was I wrong? Was it someone else impersonating Emme? No. Miranda was the only person who made sense. "What was her relationship like with her stepfather and stepbrothers?"

She shrugged. "Her stepfather pretty much just ignored Miranda. Her stepbrothers were always mooching off her. She'd save a few hundred dollars, and then one of them would show up and it would be gone. Neither one of them ever seemed to be able to hold a job for very long. Brent—he's the older one—always had some get-rich-quick plan. Not that any of them ever worked out."

"Emme, do you have a photo of Miranda I could have?" I said. "I've been thinking that maybe I'd try to reconstruct her last few hours." Actually, it had just occurred to me, but it was still a good idea.

She nodded. "I have lots of them." She pulled out her phone and began scrolling through her photos. She stopped on one image and smiled. "That's us at graduation," she said, turning the phone so I could see. I leaned in for a closer look.

She and Miranda in their blue-and-gold caps and gowns looked so young and so happy, arms around each other's shoulders. A younger Nora, without glasses and with hair that was lighter and longer, stood next to them.

"You both look happy," I said.

She nodded. "We were." She looked at the photo again. "Nora looks so young." She glanced up at me. "She's always been so responsible. Me going back to school meant that Nora would get a chance to have her own life."

"You don't look a lot alike," I said.

"Nora looks like our dad. She has his hair and his long fingers—piano-player fingers, she always said. I take after Mom. We both get our hazel eyes from her." She smiled. "I wish I had a photo of him to show you. He was the best dad."

She started scrolling through the pictures again. "Here's one of Miranda from a couple of months ago." She shook her head. "No, that's no good."

I glanced over her shoulder. The photo looked fine to me. It had been taken outside. Miranda was sitting on a set of steps that looked to be part of a gazebo.

"That's from before she dyed her hair."

I took a better look at the image. Miranda's hair was a deep, coppery red. "Her hair was really pretty," I said.

Emme nodded. "I thought so, too, but one day she just showed up with it dark brown. She said she was tired of being called 'Red' and she just wanted a change." A smile spread across her face. "We really looked alike after that."

Was that the reason Miranda changed her hair? So she'd look even more like Emme?

Emme continued to go through the pictures. She suddenly stopped and went back several images. "I forgot I even had this," she said, more to herself than me. She shook her head; getting rid of an old memory, maybe? Again she turned the phone so I could see the screen. "Miranda's brothers. Brent and Nick. There was a barbecue after graduation at the school. They came. Probably for the free food, not for Miranda. I'd forgotten I'd taken the picture or that I'd transferred it to this phone."

She said something else but the words didn't register. All my focus was on the screen in front of me. "I saw him," I said slowly.

Emme frowned. "What do you mean you saw him? Saw who?"

"Him." I tapped the phone screen with one finger, indicating the taller of the two young men in the photo. He was the obnoxious customer Eric had kicked out of the diner.

"That's Brent," she said. "Brent Pearson."

"He's still here," I said. "At least, he was a few days ago."

She looked at me wide-eyed. "Why on earth would Miranda's stepbrother be here in Mayville Heights?" she asked.

That's what I wanted to know.

chapter 15

Emme found a more recent photo of Miranda and sent it to my phone. She was going to check in with Marcus, and I asked her to tell him about Miranda's stepbrother. She promised she would.

Roma's daughter, Olivia, arrived late Monday afternoon. Maggie had invited Roma, her mom, Olivia and Sydney to join us for breakfast at Eric's Tuesday morning. I was the last to arrive. Nora Finley was alone at a table by the far wall. She smiled a hello at me from across the room.

"I'm sorry I'm late," I said as I got to the table where Maggie and the others were sitting. "Owen managed to upend his water twice, the second time on Hercules's foot."

Maggie, who was stirring her tea, made a face. "There's no way that was good."

I nodded. "Let's just say 'mad as a wet cat' is a very accurate saying." I smiled across the table. "Hi, Olivia," I said. "It's good to see you."

"Hello, Kathleen," she said. I noticed two things at once. First of all, her wavy hair, the same dark chocolate-brown shade as her mother's, had been cut into a collarbone-grazing bob. Second, and more important, she wasn't happy. The smile she gave me was forced, and when she wasn't faking a smile there were tight lines pulling at the corners of her mouth and eyes.

I glanced at Roma, noting the tension in her shoulders. She was turning the large silver ring she wore on the index finger of her right hand around and around in circles. Something was wrong.

"Kathleen, can I come see Owen and Hercules?" Sydney asked.

"Absolutely," I said. "They'd love to see you." The boys had first met Sydney on shot day at Roma's clinic. She'd rewarded their so-called "good" behavior with their favorite fish crackers, and they'd adored her on sight.

"Can I bring them a treat? Roma said I have to ask first."

I smiled at her. "Yes, you can bring them a treat as long as it's not pizza. Roma gets annoyed if I let them have pizza."

"One tiny bite of pepperoni isn't going to hurt them," Maggie said, peering into the little stainless-steel teapot in front of her.

"First of all, it's never just one bite," Roma said, gesturing at Mags with her spoon. "And second, Owen and Hercules are cats. Cats, Maggie. Not people. Cats eat cat food. And pizza is not cat food." She and Maggie had had this conversation before. Although I suspected that given their other "abilities,"

Owen's and Hercules's digestive systems weren't like most cats', I wasn't about to share that supposition with Roma—or anyone else, for that matter.

"See why it's a good idea to ask?" I stage-whispered across the table to Syd.

She grinned at me.

Nic arrived then with coffee for me. "Do you need a menu, Kathleen?" he asked.

I shook my head. "No thanks. I know what I'd like."

We ordered, and when Nic went back to the kitchen Maggie clinked the side of her cup with her fork. "Okay, there are a few details that need to be taken care of."

I stifled a smile. Maggie could be almost obsessive when it came to taking care of all the details involved in displaying her artwork. She was turning out to be just as obsessed when it came to her role as maid of honor. She turned to me. "Kath, do you have your shoes?"

I nodded. "Yes. I picked them up yesterday." The store had been out of my size and they'd had to be specially ordered and then were back-ordered. "And yes, they fit just fine."

"Perfect," she said.

"Sydney, you need to try your dress on." The child had gone through a growth spurt, and her dress had had to be lengthened. Luckily, Ella King was a whiz with a needle and thread.

"We're going out to Ella's right after breakfast," Pearl said, exchanging smiles across the table with Sydney.

Maggie turned her attention to Olivia. "Olivia, you need to look at your dress right away and try it on for Ella so she can make any adjustments it might need."

"I don't think I can do that today," Olivia said.

Maggie sent me a look across the table. I remembered her asking me at the shower if Olivia was okay with Roma getting married.

"Sweetie, the wedding is less than a week away," Pearl said. "We don't have a lot of time."

Olivia shrugged. "I can't help that. It's what happens when people get married in a big rush." The look she gave her mother across the table was almost defiant. This was not the Olivia I'd met before.

"You can wear whatever you want," Roma said. "That's not a problem."

"But we won't match," Sydney said, giving Roma a stricken look. "We have to match. It won't look right."

"You'll match Kathleen and Maggie," she said.

Sydney's dress was the same pale green color as the dresses Maggie and I were wearing. Like ours, her dress was sleeveless and fastened at the waist with a wide satiny ribbon. But where our dresses were floor length, hers had a fuller ballerina-length skirt. Olivia was supposed to be wearing a similar dress to mine and Maggie's only with a slightly lower neck and thin spaghetti straps.

"We're all bridesmaids. We're all supposed to match," Sydney said stubbornly.

"I don't have to be a bridesmaid," Olivia said. She sounded more like a petulant child than Sydney did.

Sydney bit her lower lip. She turned to Olivia. "I won't have anyone to walk with if you're not a bridesmaid."

"You can walk with Kathleen and me," Maggie offered.

"Or you could go first instead of me," I said.

The child turned to me. "Really?"

I nodded. "I'm a little nervous about walking in first. Have you seen my shoes?" I held up my right thumb and index finger about three inches apart. "I'm a little wobbly on those heels."

Maggie grinned. She began to walk two fingers across the table with very shaky steps. Sydney laughed.

I made a face at Maggie and then I looked at Syd. "See? If you go first and I fall off my shoes, everyone will be looking at you and no one will notice."

Maggie leaned sideways. "Yes," she said. "So please, will you go first?"

Syd nodded. "Okay, I'll do it," she said with a happy smile.

"Thank you," Roma mouthed at me.

"Sweetie, could you show me where the ladies' room is?" Pearl asked. "It's been a while since I was here, and I'm not sure I remember."

"Sure," Sydney said, sliding out of her chair. "They have the best hand dryer. When it blows it wrinkles up your skin and sends it moving right across your hand."

Pearl took her hand and they started for the washroom. "I'm not sure I like that," I heard Pearl say. "I already have quite a lot of wrinkles."

As soon as they were out of earshot Roma turned her attention to her daughter. "You're acting like a child."

"I think Sydney's doing a pretty good job of that," Olivia said.

"No," Roma said. "She's acting like a ten-year-old who's excited to be in a wedding. You're acting like your underwear is stuck somewhere uncomfortable. It's pretty clear you don't want me to marry Eddie. Why?"

"I don't see what the rush is." Instead of looking at her mother she looked out the window.

"We've been engaged for a year. We're not rushing." Roma studied her daughter, eyes narrowed. "What's the real problem, Ollie?" she asked.

Olivia's mouth moved but for a moment no words came out. Then she finally turned to her mother. "I don't see why you have to get married at all. You're not exactly a kid. And anyway, Eddie is way younger than you. You know it won't work out."

"We're getting married because we love each other." Roma smiled then. "I know I'm not a kid and I know how much younger Eddie is." She looked over at Maggie and me, and I put my hand on her arm and gave it a squeeze. "For a long time I wouldn't say yes, because I *was* afraid things wouldn't work out. I was wrong." She took a deep breath and let it out. "I'm marrying Eddie and I really want you to be there and to be happy for me."

Olivia pushed her chair back from the table. "I have to go," she said. She was on her way out the door as Pearl and Sydney came back from the washroom.

"Where did Olivia go?" Syd asked.

"There was somewhere else she had to be," Roma said.

"She's mad." Sydney looked over at the door.

"No," Pearl said.

"Yes," Roma countered. She looked at her mother and gave her head a little shake.

"She doesn't like me."

"That's not it," Roma said. She got out of her seat, came around behind me and took both of Sydney's hands. "Sometimes people get mad when things are going to change."

"That doesn't make sense," Sydney said. "Change isn't bad. My mom says 'change' is just another way of saying 'new adventures.'"

Roma nodded. "Your mother is right. But just because something is an adventure doesn't mean it's not a little scary. I was scared about marrying your dad."

"Dad said you were stubborn as a cow."

Roma laughed. "That, too. The thing is, all these changes scare Olivia. So she acts mad. She'll get over it."

"Okay," Sydney said, although I thought she didn't look completely convinced.

Our food arrived then. We ate and Maggie entertained us with a funny story about a customer at the co-op store who had bought one of Ruby's big acrylic abstracts because he "liked the kangaroo."

After we'd all finished eating I went over to the counter to get a cup of coffee to take to work with me. Nic was just making a fresh pot.

Nora Finley, bill in hand, joined me. "Good morning, Kathleen," she said.

I smiled. "Good morning."

She gestured at the table by the window. "Is that your family?" she asked.

"In a way," I said, following her gaze. "They're not my biological family. They're my family of the heart."

"Not everyone understands what makes a family," she said. "Or what's important."

For some reason her words felt like a criticism. She had to have seen Olivia stalk out. "Sometimes family is complicated," I said.

"In a family, the needs of the many outweigh the needs of the one," Nora said. I immediately thought of Mr. Spock in the *Star Trek* movie *The Wrath of Khan* saying almost the same thing, although I didn't really see Nora as a *Star Trek* fan. It was possible she was thinking of the English philosopher Jeremy Bentham, who'd expressed a similar sentiment, although not as eloquently as the late Leonard Nimoy, I was sure.

Nora paid her bill, wished me a good day and left.

My gaze drifted back to the table, where Maggie was having an animated conversation about something, waving her fork wildly in the air while Pearl and Sydney laughed. Roma looked pensive. I thought about what Captain Kirk had pointed out in *The Search for Spock*: Sometimes "the needs of the one outweigh the needs of the many."

Roma and Sydney showed up for tai chi that night without Olivia.

"I thought Olivia was coming," Ruby said.

Roma shook her head. "She had something else to do."

"Tell her I missed her," Ruby said over her shoulder as she headed toward the middle of the floor.

"It's because Olivia doesn't like me," Sydney said.

Roma sighed. "That isn't true."

"It's hard for some kids when their parents remarry," I said.

"Olivia is a grown-up, not a little kid, and she isn't even here most of the time. So why does it matter to her?"

Maggie set her tea down. "Syd, do you know anything about tai chi?" she asked.

"You're trying to change the subject."

"Yes, I am," Maggie retorted. "This is a place where we leave our outside problems where we leave our outside shoes." She pointed at the door. "It all stays out there." She looked at Sydney again. "You ready?"

Sydney nodded. Maggie clapped her hands and called circle.

I put an arm around Roma's shoulders. "What can I do?" I asked.

"I don't know," she said. "Olivia has been acting like a temperamental five-year-old since she arrived. I don't understand what her problem is. Syd's right. Most of the time she won't even be here."

"When my parents remarried I went from only child to big sister to two siblings," I said. "Not to mention right in front of me every morning was the irrefutable proof that my mother and father had been sneaking around having sex. I know nothing about being a parent, but I do remember how it felt when mine told me they were getting married again. Maybe Olivia just needs to work it out in her head."

"I hope so," Roma said as we took our places.

As we started warm-ups I remembered what I'd said to Nora Finley: Sometimes family was complicated.

chapter 16

Late morning I took an early lunch break and walked over to the Stratton. Uncle Mickey had invited me for coffee. He'd be leaving soon and I wanted to spend a bit more time with him. I found him onstage bent over the piano, making notes on some sheet music with a pencil. I watched him work for a minute, humming snatches of melody and muttering to himself. It reminded me of the way my mother worked when she was taking a script apart, although in her case she would do all the characters in different voices.

Michel looked up, saw me and smiled. "Kathleen, you're here," he exclaimed, coming down from the stage to give me a hug. "Come back to my office slash dressing room," he said, making a dramatic swoosh through the air with one hand when he said "slash."

The space, painted all white with a tiled floor, had a mirrored vanity on the back wall and a long table to the right that Michel seemed to be using as a desk, coffee station and general dumping ground.

"Is coffee all right?" he asked. He smiled. "I don't have any hot cocoa."

"Coffee would be wonderful," I said. I gestured at the coffeemaker. "What is that thing?"

"That, my dear, is a Technivorm coffee machine," he said. "It's Dutch."

"And that's a good thing?"

"If you're discriminating about your coffee, it's a very good thing."

I couldn't honestly say *I* was discriminating about my coffee. Oh, I'd savor a cup of the good stuff, expertly brewed, but I'd also happily drink a cup of gas station brew if that were all there was.

I looked at the photos Michel had stuck to the vanity mirror. There was one of Ruby and Ami frowning as they studied a piece of music and another of Emme grinning as she sang. I recognized quite a few other people as well.

When the coffee was ready he poured me a cup. He'd gotten cream from the mini refrigerator, and there was honey and sugar. "I should warn you," he said. "I'm turning into one of those pretentious coffee snobs. I expect you to be suitably impressed."

I took a sip from my mug and groaned with pleasure. Then I smiled at him. "You? Pretentious? Never! But I am impressed."

We sat and talked a little more about the music festival and what Michel's plans were for the rest of the year. Michel rubbed a hand over his chin. "I'm so sorry about what happened to Miss Moore and that Emme Finley felt she couldn't stay after everything."

"Did you know Miranda?" I asked.

"Not very well. She helped get the schedules passed out, and I needed copies one day and she offered to make them for me. She seemed kind."

I nodded. "From what I know about her, she was."

His expression turned thoughtful. "I saw her the night she died, you know," he said. He held up a hand. "And yes, I told your detective."

"When?" I asked. My detective hadn't told me that.

"It was around six thirty," Michel said. "I said good night to Nora and the others who were in the office. I was just heading back to the hotel. I offered Miranda a ride, but she said she wanted to walk because it was such a nice night." He smiled then. "She was in a good mood. She told me she had a new job to start in a couple of weeks and she was going to be a whole new person. I wished her good luck." He shook his head.

I swallowed down a lump in my throat. "I didn't know Miranda well, either," I said. "But I liked her. I'm happy to know she had so much to look forward to, but sad, too."

"I am as well," Michel said.

I glanced at my watch. It was time to head back to the library.

Michel walked me out to the auditorium. Backstage was a rabbit's warren of set pieces, risers and chairs. I could see staging toward the right side of the stage. Michel rolled his eyes. "If the fire marshal ever comes back here, we're going to be shut down," he said. "I keep saying we need to move all of this out of the way and I keep being promised that it will happen, but I've come to the conclusion they're just humoring me."

I gave him a hug and promised I'd come backstage after the closing concert. "Give my love to your mother," he said. I promised I would, although I'd do it when my dad wasn't in earshot. As far as he was concerned Michel had always had designs on my mother. And he was probably right.

I stopped at the main doors to check my phone, and as I looked outside I saw Brent Pearson ending a conversation with Nora. *What was Miranda's stepbrother doing here?* He was gesturing with his hands while she shook her head. I watched as he turned away and strode down the sidewalk while Nora went in the direction of the parking lot.

I wondered what they were talking about—maybe the service for Miranda? They both looked angry. Maybe Pearson was after money. I remembered Emme saying he used to ask his stepsister for money. Somehow, given what I knew about Nora, I doubted he'd get it from her.

When I got back to the library I discovered that Brent Pearson had gotten there ahead of me. He was using one of our public access computers. I tidied up the magazine area while surreptitiously watching him. Finally, I decided to go speak to the man. Up close he was younger than I'd thought—late twenties probably.

"Mr. Pearson," I said, "I'm Kathleen Paulson. I knew your stepsister, Miranda. I wanted to express my sympathies."

"Uh, yeah, thanks," he said.

I wanted to keep the conversation going. "I was wondering when the service will be."

"I'm not sure about that." His eyes darted back to the computer screen. I was at the wrong angle to see what he'd been accessing.

"Will you be letting Emme or Nora Finley know what you decide?" I asked.

He abruptly turned back to the computer, clicked a few keys and stood up. "I have to go," he said. Before I could say anything else, he'd left the building.

I sat down and checked Pearson's browser history. He had been looking at new, fully loaded half-ton trucks. Interesting for a man who was always trying to get money from his sister.

I was getting nowhere, running around in circles chasing dead ends the way Owen chased leaves in the yard. I still believed those photos Alec Kane took were the key to figuring out who killed Miranda. So what I needed to do was figure out who had used Alec to take the photos.

Midafternoon I joined Abigail at the front desk. "I'm going to take an hour of personal time."

"Go ahead," she said. She gestured around the space. "It's not exactly a beehive of activity in here today." Midweek, especially this time of year, could be quiet and today was no exception.

Alec Kane met me for coffee at Eric's. When I'd called him he'd told me he'd decided to stay around for a while. He'd been taking photos of what he called "real people" and found he liked that a lot better than hiding in the bushes.

"I'll have mine in a cup," he said to Claire when she came to our table with the coffeepot. She looked confused.

"Inside joke," I said with a grin.

"So you want something," Alec said once Claire had moved on.

I nodded. "I want all the e-mails you got from the mystery person who bought the photos. And the original e-mail that tipped you off to where Emme was going to be. If you have them." I crossed my fingers that he did.

"Do I have them? My e-mail box is the electronic equivalent of The Container Store. What are you going to do with them?"

"Try to figure out who sent them."

"You some kind of computer whiz?" he asked.

I shook my head. "No. But I know someone who is." At least I hoped he was.

I called Gavin Solomon when I got back to the library. I'd met the security expert when the library had hosted an art exhibit with some very rare and valuable pieces. Gavin was engaging and handsome, and he shamelessly used his charm with every female over the age of eighteen. He had thick red-gold hair, a close-cropped beard and a ready smile. I had never been sure if he actually needed the dark-framed glasses he wore, or if they were just for effect.

I had a feeling that Gavin had the skills I needed and if he didn't, he would know someone who did. He was surprised to hear from me but didn't seem unhappy about it. "Kathleen, this is a wonderful surprise. How are you?"

"I'm well, Gavin," I said.

"Security is all right at the library?"

"It is," I said. "We've been testing the system you suggested, and it's working well so far."

"Good to hear," he said. "So is this a personal call or professional?"

How could I explain what I was looking for? "Some of both," I settled for saying.

"Now, that sounds interesting." Gavin could be a bit of a flirt—or a lot of a flirt if he felt it could get him what he wanted. From what I'd seen while working with the man, his charm took him a long way.

"I'm looking for someone who can trace some e-mails for me," I said.

"When you say 'trace,' what exactly do you mean?"

"I mean I'd like to find out where they came from." I swiveled in my chair so I could look out over the water.

"Were those e-mails sent to you?" Gavin asked.

"They were sent to a friend of mine." Alec and I were friends now, weren't we? "He sent them to me. Do you know anyone who can help me?"

"I can," he said.

"Really?"

"Really."

I'd been hoping Gavin would say he could help me. I'd suspected when we worked together that the man had skills he didn't advertise. "I don't expect you to do it for nothing," I said.

"I'm pretty sure we can work something out," he replied, a teasing edge to his voice.

"You haven't changed," I retorted. I couldn't help smiling.

Marcus didn't really like Gavin. "He's too slick," he'd said. And then there was the flirting with me.

Gavin reminded me of a big friendly dog. He was fun to spend time with as long as you kept it in the back of your mind that he might try to jump up on you at any moment.

He laughed now. "Some things never change. I'm eternal, like the tides."

I laughed.

"Seriously, Kathleen, I'd be happy to help you. And you don't owe me anything." The teasing edge came back to his voice. "Someday, maybe I'll call upon you to do a service for me," he said, paraphrasing Don Corleone's usually misquoted line from *The Godfather*.

"As long as I don't have to put a horse's head in someone's bed, I think we're good," I said.

"We'll see." He gave me an address to forward the e-mails to and said it would probably take a day or so. "I'll call you when I have anything."

I thanked him and said good-bye. Maybe, at last, I was getting somewhere.

I was restless after supper, checking my phone several times even though Gavin had said it would take him a day or so to get back to me. Finally, I decided to take back the purse I'd borrowed from Taylor. She was working out at her dad's storage business on the highway.

I started for the truck and Owen trailed behind me. I stopped at the porch door. "Did I invite you to come along?" I asked.

"Merow," he said.

"Funny, I don't remember that," I said, opening the door so he could go out ahead of me.

Owen sat on the passenger seat watching traffic through the windshield as we drove up to the highway. When we arrived, Taylor was working on a laptop behind the reception counter. Keith was in his office, phone to his ear. He waved hello and I waved back.

"Thank you for the purse," I said. "Everything I own is big enough to hold a laptop or a cat. Or both." I pointed over my shoulder at Owen looking out through the passenger-side window of the truck.

Taylor waved at the cat and laughed. "You can borrow something anytime you need a bag."

"I might want to buy a bag for my friend Lise for Christmas," I said.

Taylor nodded. "Think about what you want, or you can tell me a bit about your friend and I can pull a few bags that might work."

"Thanks," I said.

"That was a great party," she said. "And that cake was awesome!"

"I know. I had two pieces."

Keith hung up his phone then and came out to the counter.

"Hi, Kathleen," he said. "How are the new shades working?"

Keith was on the library board. At the start of the summer they had paid for new shades for the meeting rooms to keep out the afternoon sun and hopefully reduce the air-conditioning bill.

"The rooms are definitely not as warm as they were," I said.

"It's a start." He looked at Taylor and his head seemed to tip just slightly in my direction.

Taylor pressed her lips together and glared at her father.

"What's going on?" I asked.

"Nothing," Taylor said.

Keith opened his mouth, glanced at his daughter—who looked like she might whack him with the purse I'd just given her—and seemed to think better of whatever he'd been going to say.

I leaned forward and peered over the waist-high counter.

"Did you drop something?" Keith asked.

"No," I said. "I was checking to make sure there wasn't some intruder back there, because the two of you are acting a little off."

"Ask her," Keith said to his daughter.

"I sort of have to now, don't I, Dad?" she replied in the aggrieved teenager tone that I heard all the time in the library when some teacher decided the students had to use an actual physical book for a project.

"I'm applying to the University of North Carolina," Taylor blurted out. "I want to study pre-med there."

"That's wonderful," I said, grinning at her. "The program has an excellent reputation."

"It's kind of competitive and . . . well . . . I was wondering if you would write me a letter of recommendation?" She held up her hands. "You can say no if you want to."

Taylor had volunteered for several years with the Reading Buddies program at the library, she'd helped with our fundraisers and she had worked with Ruby on our summer art and reading club. She was friendly, well-mannered and a hard worker. It would be easy to write a reference for her.

"I'd be happy to," I said.

"I told you she'd say yes," Keith said, a huge smile spreading across his face.

Taylor rolled her eyes. "Dad, you're getting annoying."

He looked at me. "I've been told I'm turning into one of those parents." He made air quotes around the word "parents." "You know, the ones who look for any chance to brag about their kid." I could see how proud he was of Taylor.

I thought about my own dad, who was always quick to talk up the three of us, even when the accomplishment was, say, not blowing up the school science fair for once—Ethan, by the way, not me.

"Hey, give your dad a break," I said. "It's not his fault there's so much to brag about."

"Exactly," Keith said. "Not only is she a great student and a hard worker, she's also a genuinely kind person."

Taylor blushed and ducked her head, but I could see how happy her father's words made her. She and Keith had butted heads in the past and likely would again—Mom and I had. But we were both lucky to have loving families. I felt a twinge of sadness thinking of Emme and Miranda, who had both lost so much of theirs.

As I waited for the traffic to pass so I could turn left out onto the highway from the driveway to Keith's storage business, I saw Miranda's stepbrother Brent Pearson go by in an old truck. Why was he still here?

An idea had been niggling in the back of my mind since Emme had told me Miranda's bracelet hadn't been with her body. Had he killed her? Did the bracelet have some significance we didn't know about? I'd assumed Pearson was better off with Miranda alive. What if I was wrong?

I hesitated and Owen meowed loudly. Translation: "Go!" So I turned right instead of left. There were a couple of vehicles between Pearson and me, but it was easy to keep the faded red half-ton with the broken left taillight in sight.

We followed him to a shabby, rundown motel I hadn't realized existed. The attached bar seemed to be doing a lot more business than the motel. I drove by, turned and came back in time to see Pearson go into a room on the top level of the two-story building. Even though it was late there was still a cleaner, a stocky middle-aged woman, up there doing the rooms. I pulled into a parking spot close to the road.

"Now what?" I asked Owen. I was very aware that I'd followed Brent Pearson at the urging of a cat.

"Mrrr," he said. His golden eyes were glued to the door to Pearson's room. At least that's how it seemed. After three or four minutes Pearson came back out. He stopped to talk to the cleaner, effectively blocking her way and standing way closer than he needed to. I could tell from her body language that she didn't like the man. She was leaning sideways, shoulders hunched in on herself.

Pearson finally headed down the covered walkway to where another man was leaning against the railing drinking what looked to be a can of beer. After a brief conversation the two men headed down to the bar. The cleaner moved on to Pearson's room, leaving the door open. She went inside and returned with the garbage cans, which she emptied into the trash bag on her cart. She looked at her supplies. I could see she was almost out of towels. Her shoulders sagged. She made her way down the stairs and started across the parking lot in the direction of the main building, without closing the door.

I looked at Owen. "This is so wrong," I said.

He climbed across my lap, put a paw on the door handle and gave me a pointed look. Wrong or not, it seemed we were doing this.

I put him back on the passenger side. "Stay here," I said. I climbed out of the truck and dashed across the poorly lit parking lot and up the side stairs to Pearson's room. If I found anything, I was going to have a hard time explaining that to Marcus, but now that I was so close, I had to know if Miranda's stepbrother had her bracelet. I looked around and slipped into the room, just in time to hear a cat sneeze. Owen suddenly appeared in front of me.

"Why is it you understand the word 'pizza' but you don't understand the words 'stay here'?" I asked.

He gave me a blank, unblinking look. It's hard to win an argument with a cat.

I looked around the room and saw no sign of any jewelry. I saw no signs of anything much personal at all. Interestingly there were a couple of brochures for new half-ton trucks tossed on the bed. It seemed Brent Pearson was in the market for a new vehicle. I wondered how a man without a steady job was going to pay for it. Was there any chance that Miranda's death was going to mean some kind of payout for her stepbrother, or was I just grasping at straws?

I checked the drawers, which were empty, and rummaged through a backpack, which seemed to be the only thing belonging to Pearson in the room. There wasn't so much as a toothbrush in the bathroom. I even checked the mini-fridge, but all it held was four cans of beer and a half-eaten package of beef jerky.

Owen stuck his head inside and sniffed the beef jerky. "Focus," I told him.

I heard voices then. It was the cleaner thanking someone else for guessing that she was low on towels and folding them for her. *Crap on toast!* Now what?

I looked around for somewhere to hide. Owen was just slipping under the bed. There was no way I was joining him. I didn't want to think what might be lurking under there—dead or alive.

Outside on the balcony I could hear the maid telling her companion that she could slap Carla for calling in sick again and sticking her with all the rooms. The other woman offered to help her finish.

I didn't have a choice. I dove under the bed with Owen.

The two women quickly finished the room with what Mary would have called a lick and a promise. Since they weren't doing a very thorough job they didn't bother to vacuum under the bed. It had been a long time since the space had seen a vacuum. Owen and I were stretched out in what looked like a dust bunny convention. About three inches in front of my nose was what looked like a crumpled receipt. Owen reached out and swatted it with a paw. I glared at him and closed my hand over the wrinkled bit of paper.

Once the women were gone I rolled out from under the bed and stood up. There was dust on my jeans and dust in my hair. Owen poked his head out and looked around. There was a dust bunny clinging to his left ear.

I smoothed out the receipt and looked at it. No surprise, it was for beer and pizza from a place in Minneapolis. Dated the night Miranda had been killed. So assuming this was Brent's receipt—and given the motel's cleanliness standards, that wasn't certain—Brent Pearson hadn't killed his stepsister. That didn't mean he didn't know something about her death, though. Marcus would say my gut feeling wasn't enough, but it was for me.

Suddenly I heard someone at the door. I motioned for Owen to move and we rolled under the bed again. Brent Pearson came into the room. I recognized him from his shoes. Okay, this might be bad.

He went to the bathroom—thankfully closing the door—without stopping to wash his hands afterward. Then he grabbed all four cans of beer from the fridge and left again.

I'd been holding a sneeze the entire time and I couldn't hold it any longer. Owen glared at me. We waited a full sixty seconds but Pearson didn't come back.

"We have to get out of here right now," I told Owen. "It was stupid to sneak around in here in the first place."

I went over to the window next to the door and eased the curtain back a crack. Pearson and the other man I'd seen before were leaning on the railing by the top of the stairs, each with a beer, the other two cans waiting at their feet. "This is not good," I said.

I looked around, wondering why there wasn't a second door leading to an interior hallway. Then I realized that there likely was no inner hallway. The parking lot for the bar was on the other side of the wall. The only way out was via the door I was standing next to.

I pushed away a rush of panic. This wasn't the stupidest thing I'd ever done, but it was going to make my top-ten list. If I stepped out the door now, Pearson and his friend would see me. But if I didn't get out soon, he'd find me when he came back. I looked down at Owen, wishing I had the ability to vanish. Then it occurred to me that maybe *I* didn't need it.

I crouched down next to the cat and pointed at the door. "You have to distract them," I said.

His response was to swipe at the dust bunny on his ear.

"I know you understand what I'm saying." I picked Owen up, nudged the curtain aside again and showed him the two men. I felt a little foolish, but it wasn't any crazier than the one-sided conversation I was already having.

"All you have to do is go down there and knock one of those cans of beer through the railing."

Since they only had four cans in total, I was banking on them chasing after it.

"They won't be able to see you," I said.

He swiped at his ear again.

So this was how it was going to be. "One can of sardines," I said. "And you don't have to share with your brother." I set him on the floor.

He gave me the same blank, unblinking look he'd given me before. I thought about Owen walking across the hood of the truck, invisible except for the dead vole in his mouth that seemed to be levitating a few inches above the dinged metal surface.

"This is extortion."

His expression didn't change. I was running out of time and ideas, and the little furball knew it. "A can of sardines and a funky chicken."

As quickly as a finger snap he winked out of sight. I eased the door open and after a moment pulled it almost closed again. Then I tugged the edge of the curtain back, crossed my fingers and hoped for the best.

The two men were drinking and talking, folded arms propped on the railing. As I watched, Pearson started and brushed at his leg with his free hand. Just as he was about to take another drink he jumped again, slopping beer onto the front of his shirt.

"Hey! Knock it off," I heard him say in a loud voice to his buddy.

What the heck was Owen doing? I wondered. The men were arguing now. Pearson was up in the second man's face, jabbing his finger at him. All at once I saw one of the two cans of beer sitting by their feet begin to move. Since they were still arguing neither Pearson nor his buddy noticed.

The can stopped at the edge of the concrete walkway. The other can began to move. Pearson was still punctuating whatever he was saying with jabs from his finger, moving his friend backward.

"Stay there, stay there," I whispered.

Suddenly the second man gave Pearson a shove. At the same time the two cans of beer toppled over the edge.

Pearson swore and took a swing at his buddy. He didn't connect. He pushed past the other man and scrambled down the stairs. For a moment his friend just stood there. Then he took the last swallow from the can, yelled something at Pearson in the parking lot below and went down the steps.

I bolted from the room and ran down the walkway. "Let's go," I said as I passed the spot where I thought the cat might be.

I kept my head down as I hurried down the stairs, but I risked a quick glance to my left as I reached the bottom step.

Both of the cans of beer had exploded when they'd hit the parking lot pavement, and now Brent and his drinking buddy were yelling at each other, red-faced and angry. A crowd had already started to gather.

I turned right at the bottom of the stairs and went all the way around the back of the building, through the bar's parking lot, to get to the truck. As I got closer I could see Owen sitting on the hood. I was so glad he was safe.

I scooped him up with one hand and pulled out my keys with the other. Then I unlocked the door, dumped Owen on the seat and started the truck while pulling on my seat belt with the other hand. It wasn't until I was driving down the highway, the motel no longer visible in my rearview mirror, that I let out the breath I was holding.

I glanced over at Owen sitting next to me. I couldn't help smiling at him. "As Ruby would say, that was awesome," I said. He looked at me and I was pretty sure he was smiling, too.

※

I was sitting at the kitchen table with a cup of coffee and an apple spice muffin watching Owen dig into his stinky dish of sardines when Marcus called.

"How was your day?" I asked.

"It's not over yet," he said. "I'm still at the station doing paperwork. And if we're going paperless, why is there actually more of the stuff?"

I knew he wasn't really expecting an answer. "Any chance you'll be getting away soon?" I asked. "I have apple spice muffins and I'll rub your shoulders."

"Ummm, I like the sound of that," he said.

He was probably sitting at his desk, a bit of stubble on his cheeks and his hair mussed from all the times he'd run his hands through it. "So?" I said.

"Give me half an hour, maybe a bit more."

I stretched my legs out onto one of the other chairs. "Before I forget, Miranda's stepbrother Brent Pearson came into the library. He was using one of the computers."

"You're looking in the wrong place, Kathleen," he said.

"He knows something," I said. "He was evasive and uncomfortable, and all I did was ask about the service for Miranda."

"Well, whatever the reason was he was acting that way, it wasn't because he killed his sister. He has an alibi."

I rubbed the space between my eyebrows with my thumb. This didn't seem like a good time to tell him what Owen and I had done. I settled for "Are you sure?"

"Very," he said. "He was in jail."

"Jail?"

"Yes," he said. "Brent Pearson was arrested for being drunk and disorderly at a pizza place in Minneapolis."

So that was his receipt I'd found under the motel room bed.

"Pearson got into an argument with another customer about the White Sox of all things. Bartender called the police. Pearson was in jail at the time of the murder, sleeping it off. It's an unimpeachable alibi."

"Why is it that every good suspect in this case has an alibi?" I groused.

"Because they're all innocent," Marcus said gently.

I shook my head even though he couldn't see me. Somewhere out there was someone who wasn't innocent. How was I going to find them?

chapter 17

Thursday made up for the previous day at the library being so quiet. The books I'd ordered for Reading Buddies arrived, we had an unexpected visit from two daycares—probably because it was raining—several tourists came in to use our Wi-Fi and to get out of the rain and half of Mayville Heights seemed to have run out of reading material.

At lunchtime Maggie dropped off some photos she'd had printed that had been taken at the tea. She was on her way to the Stratton Theatre to meet Brady for the lunchtime concert. "Bach and Roll," she said with a smile. "Modern songs that are really variations on classical pieces."

"Sounds like fun," I said.

We spread the photos on the circulation desk and looked at

them with Mary. There was a wonderful one of Mary and Sydney. "Could I get a copy of that, Maggie?" Mary asked.

"Absolutely," Maggie said.

Mary smiled. "She's a great kid."

"She is," I agreed. When Roma and Eddie had broken up, Roma had stayed in Sydney's life. Sydney in turn had done everything she could to try to get them back together, including telling Roma that she and Eddie being apart was just too traumatizing.

Maggie glanced at the clock. "I need to get going," she said. "I'll see you tonight."

"I'll be ready," I said. Maggie had canceled tai chi because she, Rebecca and I were going out to Wisteria Hill to decorate for the wedding, which was only three days away now. Actually, Maggie and Rebecca were the decorators. I was just the unpaid labor, although Rebecca had promised me a lemon meringue pie.

It was good to have something happy to focus on.

Maggie picked up Rebecca and me in her Bug after supper. There were three large boxes in the backseat and barely enough room for me to squeeze in and fasten my seat belt. "What's all this?" I asked.

Rebecca turned and looked over her shoulder. "Did you get everything?" she asked, blue eyes sparkling.

Maggie nodded.

"Even the lights?"

"Four sets," Mags said, holding up four fingers as she started to back out of my driveway.

"Splendid," Rebecca said with a grin that made her look like a mischievous little girl.

Maggie and Rebecca talked about their plans for decorating the living room of the old farmhouse as we drove out to Wisteria Hill. At one point Mags gestured over her shoulder with one hand. "There's a drawing in the top box next to you," she said. "You can have a look and see what we're talking about."

I lifted the flap on the carton and felt around inside. My hand touched what felt like a glass vase before I grabbed the sheet of paper with Maggie's plans. And they looked to be fairly detailed plans, I discovered as I studied the equally detailed drawings she'd done. That was the way Maggie was. I knew the living room of the old farmhouse would be beautiful by the time she and Rebecca had worked their magic.

Rebecca shifted in her seat and looked back at me. "I'm glad Roma and Eddie decided to get married at the house," she said. "I think it's a wonderful place to begin their marriage."

"And you're not at all biased," I said, smiling at her. Rebecca's mother had worked at the old estate, and Rebecca had pretty much grown up out there, along with Everett, who had been in love with her his whole life. She and Everett had been married in that same room.

"Not in the slightest," she said solemnly, and then she laughed.

Rebecca and Maggie talked about the decorations all the way out to Wisteria Hill. They were still talking about lights when Maggie parked the car and we got out. She grabbed two of the boxes and I got the other one. Rebecca led the way to the side door of the old farmhouse. Roma answered our knock.

The first thing I noticed was that she seemed distracted. She was wearing a sleeveless tank and loose sweatpants rolled at the ankles. Her feet were bare and her hair was pulled back in a stubby ponytail.

"Hi, guys, she said. "You can just stick those in the living room."

I followed Maggie and Rebecca into the room and set my box on the floor. Maggie had already set down her two cartons and was standing in front of the fireplace, hands on her hips. Rebecca was turning in a slow circle, lips moving, counting silently to herself, maybe?

"Where's your mom?" I said to Roma.

"Mary swooped in to take her shoe shopping," she said.

I put an arm around her shoulders. "Everything all right?" I asked.

She shook her head in frustration. "Not really. I'd say Olivia is acting like a child, but she didn't behave like this when she was one. Syd, on the other hand, is trying way too hard to be the perfect child." She tucked a loose strand of hair behind one ear. "Last night Eddie joked that he had a full tank of gas in the truck and there was still time to elope, and I almost took him up on it." She pulled a hand over her neck. "At least I think he was joking."

"I'm sorry," I said.

She leaned her head against mine for a moment. "I never thought Olivia would react this way. She always seemed to like Eddie. I thought she'd be happy for me. When I called her to say we were getting married she really seemed good with it."

She looked over at Maggie and Rebecca, who seemed to be

having a very serious discussion about the fireplace mantel. "And now decorating fairies have taken over my living room." She gave me a wry smile.

I laughed and put both arms around her. "What can I do?" I asked.

"Keep your truck gassed up," she said. "That eloping idea is getting better by the minute."

I gave her another hug.

"I'm going to tell Sydney you're here and get some shoes," she said. "I'll be right back."

I walked over to Maggie. "What can I do?" I asked her.

"There are four strings of fairy lights in one of those boxes," she said, making a vague gesture over her shoulder. "Could you find them, please?"

I was sitting on the floor straightening out a string of lights, when I heard raised voices coming from the kitchen. I glanced up at Maggie, who was standing on a stepladder attaching removable hooks to the wall. She made a face.

Olivia was standing in the doorway now. I could see Roma just beyond her. She'd pulled on a denim shirt and was holding one sock.

"Why?" Olivia said. "Because you're rushing things. You're not some love-struck teenager. You're a grown woman." Her voice got louder and angrier with each word. She took a couple of steps into the room. "This is silly," she said, making a sweeping dramatic gesture. "Decorations and lights and stupid frou-frou."

"You don't even live here anymore," Roma said, and I could see how hard it was for her to keep her voice reasonable. She was clutching the lone sock so tightly in her hand the skin was stretched white over her knuckles. "I have a great new life ahead of me. I'm happy. Why are you so angry?" I saw movement behind her and realized Sydney was standing there, listening to it all.

"It's not just your life," Olivia shouted. "It's my life, too. Why do you have to change everything? Things were fine the way they were. *We* were fine."

Something changed in Roma's expression. "Wonder Woman and Supergirl." She smiled at her daughter. "You're right. Life was wonderful when it was just you and me, and I wouldn't trade that time for anything. It was the best time of my life, and nothing will ever change that."

"So why are you changing everything?" Olivia said, brushing angrily at the tears slipping down her face.

"Because life with Eddie and Sydney and you is also the best time of my life, and nothing will ever change that, either." I could hear the love in her voice.

Eddie came up behind her and put his arms around her. "Best time of my life, as well," he said, kissing the top of Roma's head.

"That doesn't make any sense." Olivia sounded more like a child than a grown woman.

"Do you remember when we went to the state fair and rode the Ferris wheel for the first time?" Roma asked. It seemed like a strange question to ask now.

Olivia nodded, wiping tears off her chin.

"Do you remember what you said about that day?"

"Best day ever," Olivia said in a low voice.

"Do you remember the day you won the part of Anita in *West Side Story* and all your friends cheered and clapped? What did you tell me about that day?"

"I said that was the best day ever." Realization began to show on her face.

"And they were," Roma said.

"You don't just get one best day in your life," Eddie said.

Roma looked up at him and smiled before turning her attention back to Olivia. "The best day ever was the day I married your father. We were so young and we thought we owned the world. The best day ever was the day you were born, because I thought I could never love someone as much as I already loved that tiny person they put in my arms."

I felt a tear slip down my cheek.

Roma put a hand on Eddie's arm. "The best day ever was when I asked Eddie to marry me in the middle of Kathleen's kitchen and he said yes. And the best day ever will be when we actually get married and make our two families into one. And then when you get married and when Sydney does and when I get to be a grandmother. Do you see what I'm saying?"

Olivia nodded her head. "I'm a brat," she said, and then she burst into tears.

Roma folded Olivia into her arms and Eddie wrapped his around both of them. After a minute Olivia lifted her face and Roma wiped the tears away with her hand. She gave her mother a shaky smile. "Can you forgive me?" she said.

"Always," Roma said, kissing her forehead.

Olivia sniffed a couple of times and looked at Eddie. "Can *you* forgive me?" she asked.

"We're family," he said. "It's what we do." Then he laughed. "This is my circus." He gestured with one hand. "And you're one of my monkeys."

Olivia went to wash her face. Eddie announced to the room in general that he was going to put the kettle on, and Maggie, Rebecca and I wrapped Roma in a group hug.

Rebecca patted her cheek. "I'm going to help Eddie make tea." She smiled at me. "And a pot of coffee."

"And I'm going to start putting up froufrou," Maggie said with a grin.

"I think we're okay," Roma said to me.

I nodded. "I think you are."

She looked around the room. "I'm getting married in three days."

I laughed. "You just figure that out?"

Roma laughed. "It just suddenly felt real." She looked over her shoulder. "Wait. Where's Sydney?"

I pointed toward the doorway. "She was right there just a couple of minutes ago."

"Hang on a minute," she said. She left the room, and I heard her calling Sydney's name with increasing anxiousness in her voice.

I stepped out onto the side veranda. There was no sign of Syd anywhere in the yard. I went back into the house.

Roma was standing in the middle of the kitchen, a stricken expression on her face. "Sydney's gone," she said.

chapter 18

"First things first," Eddie said. "We'll check the house again." He looked at me. "Kathleen, please check upstairs." Maggie was in the living room doorway. "Maggie, down here, please." He turned to Roma, who had been joined by Olivia. "You two check the yard. I'll check the basement."

It very quickly became clear that Sydney wasn't anywhere in the house or the yard, either.

"I don't understand," Roma said. "Why would she run off?"

"We were fighting," Olivia said, shamefaced.

Maggie nodded. "She was standing behind you. I could see her from the ladder. She heard some of what you said, but I don't think all of it."

Roma closed her eyes for a second, and the color drained from her face. "So she could have heard me say that when it was just Olivia and me it was the best time of my life and not heard anything that came after that."

Eddie pulled out his phone. "I'm calling Marcus," he said.

We split up to search the woods. Eddie stuck his head in the carriage house and called Syd's name several times. There was no response. "She's not here," he said.

Rebecca stayed at the house in case Sydney came back and to wait for Marcus. Eddie and Roma went up the embankment behind the carriage house and headed for the old well in the woods. Maggie started down the driveway, toward the road. Olivia and I cut across the field and started searching both sides of the brook.

We checked the bushes and the long grass and called out Sydney's name. There was no answer and no sign of her.

"This is my fault," Olivia said. We'd walked farther along the edge of the brook, farther than Sydney could have gotten, and had started back, spreading out beyond its banks. Olivia was just ahead and she turned back to look at me. "I was acting like a child."

I grabbed her by the shoulder and swung her around to face me, probably not as gently as I should have. "This is not helping," I said. "You're the person closest in age to Sydney. Think like a child. Where would she go?"

Olivia didn't move. She didn't say anything. I let go of her shirt. Her eyes were focused on something beyond my right shoulder.

Suddenly she looked at me. "I know where she is," she exclaimed. She started running, up the slope from the brook and back across the field. I ran after her.

Olivia pushed open the door to the carriage house and bent over, hands on her thighs, to catch her breath. Then she straightened up. "Sydney, I know you're in here," she called.

There was no response.

Olivia beckoned to me. We moved to the area where the feral cats had their feeding station. She pointed across the space to the hayloft on the far wall across from the cats' shelters. We walked across the wooden floor.

"Syd, I know you're up there," Olivia said.

"Go away," a small voice replied.

"You know I'm not going to go away," Olivia said. "Everyone's looking for you. Your dad is worried and my mom is scared to death."

"I don't care," Syd said.

"Yeah, that's a lie."

I saw movement up above us. How had she gotten up there? I looked around. A rickety ladder was lying on the ground. Syd was stuck up there. "I hate you," she said.

"First true thing you've said," Olivia replied. I touched her arm and pointed to the ladder. She nodded.

Sydney sniffed a couple of times. "I heard what Roma said, that the best time of her life was when it was just you and her." It was impossible not to hear the accusation in her voice—or the hurt.

"Yeah, she did say that," Olivia agreed. "But if you're going to be any good at listening in on people's conversations, the first thing you need to do is learn to listen to the whole thing. Because she also said the best day of her life was the day she asked your dad to marry her and he said yes. And she said that Sunday will be the best day of her life because we're all going to be a family, and we need to be a family because you really need a big sister."

"Do not," a petulant voice said.

Lucy had come out from her shelter and was watching us, head cocked to one side.

"Do too!" Olivia retorted. "I already told you, you suck at spying on people. And I bet you don't know how to get ice cream out of them when Mom already said no."

"Roma says too much ice cream isn't good for your teeth."

Olivia looked at me and smiled. "Oh, squirt, do I ever have a lot to teach you," she said. She let out a breath. "Look, I was a brat and I'm really sorry. Please, give me another chance. I really did always want a sister."

We waited, and after a long moment Sydney sat up. "I always wanted a cat," she said, looking down at Olivia.

"Cats are good," Olivia agreed.

Syd shrugged. "Better than sisters."

Olivia laughed. "Okay. I deserved that. Now can you please come down because everyone is freaking out?"

Sydney stood up and took a step toward us, and the board beneath her feet cracked.

"Syd, sit down, please," I said immediately.

She did as I asked.

"One of us needs to go up and get her," I said.

"No offense, Kathleen, but it should be me," Olivia said. "I'm the smaller of the two of us."

I nodded.

We got the ladder and set it up to the edge of the hayloft.

Olivia climbed, but as soon as she put a foot on the platform there was another loud crack and her left leg went through a board.

"Olivia!" Syd cried, reaching for her. The whole platform made a groaning sound.

"Nobody move," I said. The hayloft was listing to the right. The whole structure was in danger of coming down. No one had been up there in years. Syd's weight had been enough to loosen the old boards, and Olivia's could make everything collapse.

"Olivia, lie down, very slowly," I said. "It'll spread your weight out."

She stretched out as directed.

"Okay, Sydney, you too," I called.

"I don't want to fall," she cried.

"That's not going to happen."

"Lie down, Syd," Olivia said. She reached a hand across the platform. Sydney grabbed it and stretched out on her stomach.

"Good job," I said, trying to sound reassuring even though I didn't feel that way. "Olivia, can you pull your leg free?"

"I think so," she said. She shifted her weight onto her side and pulled her knee toward her chest. Her foot came free but the platform canted to the side a bit more.

"We're going to fall," Sydney said.

"No, you're not," I said. I remembered seeing a coil of rope over near the cat shelters. I spotted it and went to get it.

"I don't think I can climb down a rope, Kathleen," Olivia said.

"You won't have to." Lucy had disappeared. All the commotion had probably unsettled the little cat. I looked around. I needed a counterweight.

"Syd," I called. "I need your help."

"I'm scared," she said in a small voice.

"Me too," I said, "but I still need your help. Lift your head just a little bit, then look around and tell me if you can see anything that looks big and heavy."

She lifted her head and slowly scanned the room. "I don't see anything," she said after a moment. My heart sank. "The only thing I see is some chain in the corner back there."

Chain. That might be enough. "No, that's good," I said. I hurried across the floor.

The chain was rusted, covered in dust, cobwebs and animal droppings. It was forged with oversized heavy links. It just might work.

It took all my strength to drag the length of chain so it was positioned under the beam closest to the hayloft.

"What are you doing?" Olivia said.

I was knotting the rope through one end of the chain. "I'm going to use the chain as a counterweight. All you have to do is fasten the rope under your arms, and I can lower you down. I can use the beam as a fulcrum."

"Okay," she said. Her voice said she felt anything but.

I tied two large knots in the other end of the rope to give it some heft. It took three tries, but I managed to throw it over the ceiling beam and catch the other end.

"Olivia, can you tie a bowline?" I asked.

"Yes," she said. She was a scuba diver. I'd figured she could.

The platform gave another groan. I was running out of

time. I couldn't go for help. I had to do this by myself. I pushed my sweaty hair back off my forehead. "I'm throwing the end of the rope to you," I said. "Tie a bowline. Get the rope around Sydney. I'll do the rest."

I stepped a little closer and threw the rope up to her. Olivia came up on one arm and caught it on the first throw.

"Good catch," I called.

She quickly untied my two knots, fastened the bowline and gave the rope to Syd. The child slipped it over her head and Olivia explained how to tighten the loop.

"Okay, kiddo," I said. "I need you to crawl to the edge of the platform and roll off."

"No! I'll fall," she cried.

"No, you won't," Olivia told her. "Kathleen has the other end of the rope and she would never let you fall. You're going to swing and she's going to let you down. To the ground."

Sydney lifted her head. "You promise?"

I put a hand on my chest. "I swear."

She nodded. "Okay."

"Hold on to the rope with both hands," I said. The rope was over the middle of the beam. The other end was tied to the chain. I was holding on with two hands. I could minimize the swing. It would work.

Sydney crept over to the edge. She grabbed the rope with both hands. And rolled off. The rope jerked in my hands, and the sudden movement almost pulled me off my feet.

Almost.

She swung out farther than I'd intended, but I got control of the swing and was able to ease her down to the ground. I knelt beside her and she threw her arms around me. "It worked!" she exclaimed. "You're really smart."

"And you're really brave." I gave her a hug. "Now we need to get Olivia down."

She was already pulling the loop of rope over her head. I took it from her. "Okay, Olivia, here it comes."

It took me two tries before she caught the rope. As she pulled it over her head I showed Sydney where to stand. I'd need her help to control the swing with Olivia's weight at the other end of the rope. "Hold tight with both hands," I said, "and when I say 'pull' you pull as hard as you possibly can."

She nodded, a determined set to her face.

"We're ready," I called.

Olivia crab-crawled to the edge of the platform. She eased up into a sitting position.

"Go," I yelled to Olivia. "Pull," I told Syd.

We both yanked on the rope as hard as we could. Even with my two feet on top of it, for a moment I thought it would slip through my hands, but I managed to keep my grip. Even so, Olivia swung out in a long arc. "Okay, start to let the rope out," I said to Sydney.

Sydney nodded and we eased Olivia down to the floor. Her injured leg touched the ground first and the leg buckled, so she fell the last foot. Sydney ran to her and my hands let go of the rope. My arms had stopped working. I couldn't even push my hair back off my face.

The side door to the carriage house swung open. Marcus was standing there.

At the same time, as if in slow motion, the hayloft began to fall forward. The sound of splintering wood filled my ears. Marcus covered the space between us in seconds. Olivia thrust Sydney at me, and somehow I found enough strength to catch her and scramble forward. Marcus grabbed Olivia by the shoulders and pulled her toward him. The hayloft made one last, desperate groan and fell in a heap of twisted, splintered wood. Jagged pieces of wood and dust rained down on us, sticking to our hair, our clothes, our skin. But we were all clear.

Sydney's face was against my shoulder. I'd folded one arm over her head. She lifted it now, pushing her hair back out of her eyes.

"You okay?" I asked.

She nodded, coughed a couple of times and looked around. "Olivia?" she said.

Marcus had literally folded his own body over Olivia. He straightened up and Olivia leaned around him, stretching out a hand. Sydney caught it, gave me a smile and then crawled to Olivia, who wrapped both arms around her, resting her chin on the top of the child's head.

"Are you all right?" Marcus said to her.

She nodded. "Are you?"

"I'm fine." He made his way over to me on hands and knees and pulled me against him. "Tell me you're okay," he said.

I leaned back against his chest. We were safe. Scraped and bruised and very dirty, but we were all safe. "I've never been better," I said. And I meant every word.

chapter 19

We stumbled out of the carriage house and Marcus called for the others. Roma and Eddie came running, and when I saw their faces I had to keep swallowing so I wouldn't cry.

We made our way back to the house, where Maggie and Rebecca were waiting. Maggie brushed slivers of wood out of my hair. "Oh, Kath, your hands," she said. The rope had scraped the left one in particular, raw.

"You need to go to the hospital," Marcus said.

I shook my head. "I don't need a hospital."

"Yes, you do," Roma said. She looked at Olivia, who was sitting on a kitchen chair, her leg propped up on another. "And that leg needs stitches."

"I'm all right," Olivia said.

"Neither one of you is in a position to argue," Roma said. She was right.

In the end it was decided that Roma and Eddie would drive Olivia to the hospital and Marcus and I would follow them. Rebecca offered to stay with Sydney. "Bath first," she said to the child. "After that, brownies."

"What could I do to help?" Mags asked.

"We're having a wedding in three days," Olivia said. "You better get going on that living room."

When we got in the car, my arms were so wobbly Marcus had to fasten my seat belt. After he'd finished, Eddie stuck his head in the open door. "I don't know how to properly thank you," he said. His eyes were suspiciously bright.

My throat was suddenly tight and for a moment I couldn't speak. "I know it's corny, but just be happy," I finally said.

He nodded. "I can do that." He leaned over and kissed my cheek. Then he walked back to Roma's car.

Marcus reached across me and pulled the door shut.

"How did you know we were in the carriage house?" I asked.

"Lucy," he said.

I looked at him. "The cat?"

He nodded as he put the SUV in reverse. "She came across the yard and she wouldn't stop meowing. I knew it had to mean something. I just didn't know what."

Lucy. I'd always felt I had a connection with the little cat. I was going to make her a batch of sardine crackers as soon as I got home.

"There's something special about the Wisteria Hill cats," Marcus said as we followed Roma down the driveway.

"Yes, there is," I agreed. And it was long past time that I shared exactly what that meant.

An ER nurse cleaned both of my hands and bandaged the left one. Part of my palm had been rubbed raw, but overall my injuries weren't as bad as they'd seemed at first glance. In fact, I was able to head into work at lunchtime the next day, over Marcus's very strenuous objections.

"I'm fine," I assured him for what seemed like the tenth time as he stood in the middle of my kitchen, arms folded over his chest, flanked on each side by his furry sidekicks.

"I'm driving you," he said.

"I'd like that," I told him, standing on tiptoe to kiss his cheek before heading upstairs to get dressed.

"You're stubborn," he called after me.

"I never said I wasn't," I countered.

It felt like half of Mayville Heights came into the library to check on me. It was midafternoon before I had a chance to look at my e-mail.

There was one from Ruby with photos attached.

I forgot to send you these. They're some possible sites for more photo shoots. Let me know what you think.

I scanned quickly through the photos. They had been taken earlier on the night we'd been at the marina taking photos. The night Ruby had found Miranda's body. No wonder she had forgotten to send them.

The outside terrace at the hotel was promising. So was the exterior of the bank. Tourists were always taken by the stonework on the old building, especially the gargoyles on the corners of the roof.

In one of the bank images I saw a figure I recognized: Nora Finley. She was standing at one of the ATMs. Based on the lighting it looked to be early evening. No, that had to be wrong. Nora was Emme's alibi. What had she said? *We went home at about four thirty. We didn't even go out for supper. We ordered in.*

I rested my head against the back of my chair and closed my eyes. Nora was her sister's alibi.

I opened my eyes again, and the first thing I saw on my desk was a flyer that had promoted Michel's talk here at the library. I remembered our last conversation. He'd told me he'd left the theater at about six thirty, stopping to offer Miranda a ride. But before that he'd said good night to *Nora* and the others in the office.

No.

I didn't want to believe that Emme had killed her best friend. But for at least part of the time that night Nora Finley had been at the bank, which meant Emme had no alibi. Unless . . .

I didn't stop to think about it. I just grabbed the phone and punched in the number. It rang half a dozen times before Emme answered. "Emme, it's Kathleen," I said.

"Oh, hi," she said.

I cleared my throat. "I need to ask you a question about the night Miranda was killed."

"Okay," she said.

"I know you weren't with your sister. Where were you?"

For a moment there was silence, then I heard her sigh. "With Derrick at the same hotel where you found us. We were"—her voice broke—"together, and my best friend was dying."

It was what I'd suspected. "Did Nora know where you were?" I asked.

"I told her. She said it would look bad if anyone knew I was with Derrick after all the uproar over the photos and the Don't Drink and Drive campaign that went wrong. She offered to say I was with her all evening and . . . and she did. Please don't blame Nora. She only lied to protect me. I'm sorry." Her voice dropped to a whisper.

"I understand," I said, and really I did. "You need to call Detective Gordon and tell him the truth."

"I will," she said. "I promise."

I hung up the phone and stared at the ceiling. All Emme had really done was trade one alibi for another. I thought about what Nora had done. Would I lie like that to protect Ethan or Sara? I didn't think so.

Nora Finley was extremely invested in her sister's life, I realized.

I got up, rubbing a hand over the back of my neck, and my cell phone rang. It was Gavin.

"I found the person who sent the e-mails to your friend," he said. "The same person sent all the e-mails."

I'd pretty much guessed that. "It didn't take you very long," I said.

He laughed. "I'm that good. And she didn't do a very good job of covering her tracks."

"Her?"

"Uh-huh. I tracked everything back to an account belonging to a Nora Henry Finley. Does the name ring a bell?"

I sank onto a corner of the desk. "It rings all sorts of bells," I said. "Thanks for your help, Gavin."

"Hey, anytime, Kathleen," he said.

We ended the call and I set my phone on the top of my desk.

It was Nora. It was the only explanation that made sense.

I tried to sort out what I knew. I could see why Nora might want to keep Emme close. She was more of a mother than a sister, and Emme's life was her life. It was Nora who had the most to gain if Emme broke up with her professor boyfriend and gave up the idea of going back to school. I remembered Emme saying that this would give her sister a chance to have her own life. But what if Nora liked the life she already had?

But why had Miranda helped her? That didn't make sense.

I paced around my office. Marcus's former partner, Hope Lind, used to say that in the end someone's motive for committing a crime came down to one of three things: love, hate or money. I didn't see how love or hate applied in Miranda's case. That only left money.

I spent the rest of the afternoon trying to convince myself I was wrong. I didn't call Marcus to tell him what I'd learned from Gavin, because I wasn't sure he'd take it seriously given how he felt about the man.

Maggie showed up after work to drive me home.

"I have to go out to Roma's to change a string of lights," she said, "but if you need anything, text me."

I promised I would.

I made pasta salad with sun-dried tomatoes I'd gotten from Harry Taylor for supper. I had just finished the dishes when I got a text from Ruby asking me to bring Hercules down to the Stratton Theatre. She wanted to take some shots of him on the piano, and Michel had given her the okay to do it while everyone else was out of the building.

My right hand felt fine and the left just stung a little. There was no reason I couldn't drive downtown. I knew Marcus would easily be able to come up with five or six reasons, which was why I decided not to tell him.

I found Hercules upstairs in my closet nosing around my shoes. "Ruby needs to take a few more pictures," I said.

He immediately dropped his head and began washing the large white patch of fur on his chest. I knew a yes when I saw it.

I pulled my hair back in a ponytail, added lip gloss and tucked my wallet in the pocket of my shorts. I grabbed the carrier bag from its hook and lifted Hercules inside. He poked his head out and looked around the kitchen before turning to me with a questioning meow.

"I'm perfectly safe to drive," I said.

He studied me for a moment, seemed to decide I was telling the truth and settled in the bag.

Ruby had told me to use the main entrance. There was no sign of her in the lobby but I could see lights inside the auditorium. We stepped into the main space of the building, and I walked past the six rows of seats in the back section of the theater. I lifted Hercules out of the bag and set it down on the floor at my feet.

"Hey, Ruby, where are you?" I called. She wasn't onstage. "Maybe she's backstage," I said to Hercules.

"Ruby isn't here," a voice behind me said.

I felt as though I'd been punched in the chest. I turned around slowly. Nora Finley was standing there, pointing a gun at me. Miranda's bracelet was around her wrist.

"Hello, Kathleen," she said.

"Emme told you I called her." My hands were shaking. I tightened my grip on Hercules, hoping Nora wouldn't notice the trembling. "She told you that I asked about her alibi and that she told me the truth."

"Emme is a very trusting person."

"You didn't offer to say she was with you to give her an alibi. You did it to give you one." It was hard to keep my focus on Nora's face and not the gun.

"We're family. We take care of each other," she said.

"That's how you figured out I was onto you."

Nora gave me a cold smile. "I pay attention to details. Like where people set down their phones, for example." She pulled Ruby's cell phone out of her pocket, held it up and then dropped it onto a nearby seat.

"This won't work," I said. I glanced over her shoulder, hoping Michel might have decided to come back and do some work.

"You're wasting your time," she said. "The door is locked and no one is coming." She took a step toward me and I took one backward. The gun gave her a big advantage, but I wasn't going to let her get close enough to grab me.

"How did you get Miranda to impersonate Emme and drug her and Derrick so those incriminating photos could be taken?" I asked. If I kept her talking long enough, maybe someone would show up or maybe Marcus would miss me and come looking for me.

"You figured that out." She spoke as though she were almost impressed by my efforts.

"She drew on the beauty mark. It wasn't quite right." I touched my cheek. "It wasn't obvious at first glance."

Nora gave an elaborate shrug. "It's hard to get good help."

"What did you give them?"

"Did you know if you tell your doctor you're suffering from anxiety, there are a number of drugs he or she can prescribe?"

I looked at her without speaking.

"You have to be careful, though," Nora went on. "Some of those drugs make you forget things."

"How did you force Miranda to help you? It had to do with money, didn't it?" The wheels were turning in my mind. Both Emme and Ruby had mentioned Miranda's affinity for numbers and how she was always a soft touch for her freeloading stepbrothers. I took a leap. "She took money from her last job."

She nodded approvingly. "Very good."

"Because of her brothers."

"The older one got arrested for driving under the influence almost a year ago. Miranda bailed him out and found him a lawyer. Those two weren't even her real family." It was impossible to miss the disdain in Nora's voice.

"She didn't get caught?"

"Miranda was always good with numbers. She managed to put it all back with no one the wiser."

Hercules was watching Nora just as intently as I was. "No one but you," I said.

"I pay attention," Nora said, just a hint of a smile on her face. "One month, Miranda was a little short."

I gestured at the hand holding the gun. "That's Miranda's bracelet."

"My bracelet now," she said. "A reminder that silly sentimentality will get you nowhere in life." She glanced at her wrist. "This is actually worth quite a bit of money. But Miranda would never sell it. It was all she had from her father."

She waved the gun at me. "All I got from *my* father was this." She favored me with a cold smile. "Which has actually turned out to be quite useful."

Part of me ached for her; she was so hurt, so bitter. I was trying to slip all the puzzle pieces into place and keep her talking. "I don't understand. Why didn't Miranda just tell Emme the truth about the money?"

"Considering that sorry excuse for a man she's involved with, you might be surprised to know that my little sister can be quite the goody-two-shoes, especially when it comes to drinking and driving. The truth is our father was killed in a drunk-driving accident. He was the drunk."

"I can't believe Emme would be that judgmental," I said. Where was everyone? Why hadn't someone come to the theater by now?

"She can be a very black-and-white person," Nora said. "As

I told Miranda." She laughed. It was an angry sound with no humor in it.

Nora had played with Miranda's emotions. I wasn't surprised.

I swallowed. My mouth was dry and there was a lump in my throat. "All the same, it must have been difficult to keep secrets from your sister."

"Don't go all Oprah on me," Nora said. "It won't work."

She took another step toward me and I stepped back again. I was getting closer to the main section of seating and farther from the door.

"Miranda was going to tell Emme the truth and take the consequences," I said.

Nora let out a breath. "Yes, she was."

"But I don't understand why you had to kill her." That was true. I really didn't.

"I didn't want to. But Miranda wouldn't listen to reason. She had an attack of conscience."

"She wanted to tell Emme about the photos."

"And other things." Just for a moment Nora's eyes flicked away from my face.

I could feel the warmth of Hercules's small furry body underneath my hands. Somehow I was going to get us out of here. "What other things?" I asked.

Nora shook her head. "It doesn't matter."

"It mattered to you."

I thought she wasn't going to answer. Then she spoke. "Miranda had figured out some of my . . . business dealings with some of the clubs in Chicago."

Another puzzle piece snapped into place. "You were taking kickbacks from some of the clubs Emme was singing at. What did you do? Tell her agent Emme preferred one venue over another for some reason?"

"I was protecting her career. I was making connections."

You were using your own sister, I added silently.

The whole time we'd been talking she'd managed to slowly back me up to the last row of seats in the front section of the theater. I could feel a seat back cold against my legs. I glanced sideways. The only thing I saw was a backpack on the aisle seat two away from me.

"Emme told me Miranda's stepbrother came to see her in Chicago just before you all came here," I said. *Keep her talking. Just keep her talking.* "Somehow he figured it out—I mean about the photographs."

That would explain why Brent Pearson was still in town— he was trying to weasel money out of Nora. Enough, it seemed, to be able to buy a new truck. If she managed to kill me, he'd be next.

"It was just stupid bad luck. Robert Burns was right: *The best laid schemes of mice and men . . .*"

"*Go often askew,*" I finished.

"He was at the club that night and he saw Miranda wearing Emme's jacket. He put it all together. He was blackmailing her, taking pretty much every cent she could get her hands on. She was going to tell Emme the truth. Everything." She straightened up. "She didn't leave me any choice." She made a move-along gesture with the gun. "Now walk," she said.

I squared my shoulders and held on tightly to Hercules. "No."

"You do see that I have a gun and all you have is a cat, don't you?"

"You won't kill me. Not here." I was faking a confidence I didn't feel, hoping she couldn't see how badly my legs were shaking. "If you shoot me here, you'll be caught—too much blood and too hard to explain."

"Shooting a cat wouldn't make that much mess," Nora said. She reached for Hercules, ignoring or forgetting the warning she'd gotten the first time we'd met. He turned into a whirling dervish of claws, hissing and fur. I grabbed the surprisingly heavy backpack and swung it at Nora as hard as I could. It hit her shoulder, knocking her off balance as books spilled onto the floor. Hercules gave a loud yowl and bolted for the stage. I knew where the stage door was, and we'd be able to get out that way.

I raced after him.

chapter 20

Once we were backstage I could see that I was wrong. The set pieces that had been piled up there the previous day when I'd had coffee with Michel were still blocking the way.

Hercules was already making his way to the stairs at the far right of the backstage area. I paused for a second, trying to catch my breath. The stairs. We could go up, across the top where the dressing rooms were, and take the far-end stairs to the stage door. That would work.

But the stairs were blocked off with staging. It looked like some of the stairwell ceiling had come down. Nora was on the stage now. In a moment she'd see us and have a clear line to shoot. The only place to go was the basement. I seemed to remember Ruby mentioning an old coal-cellar door down there, and I decided it was a better option than facing Nora and that gun. I bent down, snatched up Hercules and bolted down the stairs.

The basement was dark and dank, and the smell of age and dust and mold and old paint hung in the air. The ceiling was very low, no more than six feet, maybe even less, and it felt to me like it was pressing on the space above my head, pressing all the air out of the room. I didn't do well in small spaces. Hercules nuzzled my cheek and I gave a muffled squeak. For a moment I'd forgotten I was holding on to him.

I picked my way across the basement, almost tripping over a wooden rocking chair. As my eyes adjusted to the darkness, I saw that the space was piled with old props and costumes, some of them on dressmakers' dummies, which made it look like an army of headless bodies was guarding the space.

What had Ruby said about the old coal chute? It was on the end of the back wall, but which end? I couldn't see anything here where we were, which meant it had to be on the other end. That meant heading deeper into the space to look for it.

The old stone walls were thick, but it was still cold and I shivered in my shorts and long-sleeved T-shirt. I could hear the squeaks and rustling of some kind of rodents. If they'd gotten in, then there must be a way to get out, I told myself.

I heard Nora on the stairs. I crouched behind an old travel wardrobe and a group of several mannequins all dressed in Victorian holiday garb and made myself as small as possible. If she came anywhere near me, I was going to push the wardrobe or one of the mannequins over on her and hope I could get the gun. I realized it wasn't much of a plan.

Nora had found a large flashlight somewhere. She was

sweeping it in wide arcs in front of her. The light glinted off the blue steel finish of the gun in her other hand. I held my breath, ignoring the throbbing in my bandaged left hand. Whatever she did next, I was going down swinging.

She didn't see us. She walked right by us, and as her light swept over the far-end wall, I saw a small room off to my left. And I thought I caught a glimpse of some kind of opening in the wall. The coal chute maybe?

Nora kept going deeper into the basement. I listened to the sound of her footsteps and decided to make a break for the steps. I eased around the mannequins and at the same time her footsteps stopped. I could see the light swinging back in the direction of the stairs. I dropped to the floor and scuttled, crablike, toward the relative safety of a stack of boxes. I was too far away now to make it to the stairs. The only option was to see if I'd been right about that opening I thought I'd seen in that small room.

Herc and I worked our way sideways, hiding behind boxes and furniture and discarded set pieces. Nora called my name a couple of times. She was working her way back to the front of the basement. There was an open space of about twenty feet between where we were crouched behind a large paper screen and the room. It was now or never. I wrapped both arms tightly around Hercules and ran.

The small room had damp stone walls like the rest of the basement. Two sets of shelves lined its outer walls. Those walls looked scorched even in the dim light, as though there had been a fire at some point in the past. Midway along the longer wall of the room, just above the second shelf, was a small opening. There was no way to tell where it went. Maybe into the coal chute. Maybe I'd fall onto the floor. Maybe I could reach up or climb up and get out. Or maybe I'd get stuck and the walls would close in and crush me.

Nora was getting closer, making her way back across the basement, the flashlight sweeping in ever-closer semicircles. I felt my stomach roll over. It was the gun or climbing through that hole. It was an easy choice.

One hand clutching Hercules, I climbed through the square opening in the stone wall. I put a hand above me. There was nothing but ceiling. I reached in front of me and found nothing but air. We had climbed into another small room that seemed to be located behind a partly demolished wall. Most of the space was taken up by a furnace so old its giant leads made it look like an octopus in the faint light.

I noticed two things right away. First of all, the opening on this side had what I thought might be a metal coal chute lid, fastened up and out of the way. I pulled it down over the hole. It might buy us some protection or at least some time. And there was definitely a bit more light, which told me there was a window or windows nearby, which meant a way out.

I looked around for something I could use to break the glass, feeling around in the darkness. The air was stuffier. I was breathing heavily and I felt light-headed. "There's lots of air," I told Hercules. "It's just a little stale, that's all."

"Mrrr," he said softly.

We made our way past the partly demolished wall, and on the floor near the furnace I found a loop of copper wire and a roll of what seemed to be wallpaper, maybe four inches or so in diameter. I slung the coil of wire over my shoulder, thinking it might come in useful for something, and grabbed the wallpaper. It was heavy and satisfyingly solid in my hand.

There were two small windows on the back wall but they were both covered with rusted grates. I yanked on them in frustration but they weren't going to move. I could feel panic wrapping around my chest like a vise, choking the air out of my lungs. I took several raspy breaths. There wasn't enough air in the small space. The only thought I had was *I can't breathe!*

Hercules stirred in my arms and I felt his fur against my face. I imagined my mother smiling and telling me, "You can do anything you set your mind to, Katydid." I put one hand against my chest and forced myself to take slow breaths. In and out. In and out. I swallowed down the sour taste of bile at the back of my throat. The only way out of this was to stop Nora.

"Let's go get her," I said to the cat.

We made our way back to the small room. I could hear Nora on the other side. She was going to come through the opening any minute. Maybe we could use that. I set Hercules on the floor in front of the open hatch and crouched beside him. I hoped he was as smart as I'd always believed. My life was depending on it. "I need you to make noise," I whispered. "Lots of noise." He looked down at the floor with distaste. I had a feeling him making noise wouldn't be a problem.

I straightened up and stepped back. I slipped the coil of wire off my shoulder and raised the wallpaper roll. "Now!" I whispered to the cat. He gave a pitiful meow followed by another and another.

I gave him a thumbs-up.

"Here, kitty. Here, kitty," I heard Nora call. I imagined the disdain that was probably on the cat's face at the moment. As though he'd fall for that. He meowed again.

Although I happily cheered for the Wild during hockey season and the Vikings starting every September, growing up mostly in New England meant my baseball heart had always belonged to the Boston Red Sox and Big Papi, David Ortiz. Hands shaking, stomach churning, I pictured him making his way to the plate from the on-deck circle. *It's the bottom of the eighth inning, game two of the American League Championship series against the Detroit Tigers,* I told myself. I could hear Nora climbing through the chute, pushing at the cover. But in my mind I was seeing the Tigers' reliever, Joaquin Benoit, do his windup. The chute lid opened and Nora's head and shoulders came through, followed by the rest of her. I was seeing Big Papi go into his swing.

The roll of wallpaper connected with the back of Nora Finley's head as I remembered Ortiz hitting the game-tying grand slam. Nora dropped like a rock, the gun skittering across the floor.

And the crowd went wild. At least I and one small cat did.

I dropped the wallpaper roll and used the wire to restrain Nora. She was out cold, but she had a pulse and she was breathing. It was a lot better than she had been planning for me.

Hercules was sitting next to the gun. He meowed loudly at me. "Yes, I see it," I said. I picked it up carefully. It was a Colt Detective Special, a .38. I was fairly sure I knew how to take the bullets out. I'd spent some time with the prop-master when my dad had been in a production of *Some Like It Hot*, and he'd taught me about gun safety.

I kept the revolver pointed at the ground and managed to remove the bullets. I stuffed them in one pocket and the gun in the other. I picked up the roll of wallpaper again and dropped it through the hole in the wall. I started to cough, and I had to stop then for a moment and catch my breath.

I reached for Hercules but he had decided it was faster to just walk through the wall. I took a breath and climbed through to the other side.

We were safe.

Hercules was sitting next to the wallpaper roll. I picked up both of them and started across the basement. I was wheezing from the exertion. The air wasn't any better on this side of the basement.

"We're going to Eric's," I rasped at the cat. "We're going to buy coffee in the biggest cup they have and not decaf; I don't care what time it is. And I'm going to get you the biggest piece of fish they have, and I don't care whether or not cats are allowed in there."

He meowed his enthusiasm for the idea.

As we got to the bottom of the stairs I heard voices above me. I raised the roll of wallpaper—it was some kind of blue flocked design, I noticed for the first time—ready to go all Big Papi on whoever it was. But it was Marcus with a giant flashlight.

"Oh, good Lord, Kathleen!" he exclaimed. He bolted down the stairs and grabbed my shoulders. "Are you all right?"

I nodded. "I'm fine." I pointed in the general direction of the hole in the wall, swaying because I was suddenly light-headed. "Nora Finley not so much."

"She killed Miranda Moore," he said.

I nodded, which made the room swirl around me like I was on a carousel ride. "I know," I said.

He frowned. "How do you know?"

"Gavin figured out she sent the e-mails to Alec."

"Gavin?" he said. He frowned. "Wait. Gavin Solomon?"

I nodded again. The room spun faster. "Uh-huh," I said. "I may have to put a horse's head in someone's bed someday."

I tried to focus on his face, which like everything else kept going out of focus. "How did you know?"

"We finally got the security footage from the marina. At the edge of one frame you can just make out Nora Finley with Miranda."

I started to cough and Marcus put an arm around my shoulders. "We need to get you up into some fresh air," he said.

"Here," I said. I pulled the gun and the bullets out of my pocket and gave them to him.

He helped me up the steps and sent two patrol officers down to find Nora. As we headed through the auditorium I saw the backpack I'd hit Nora with on the floor, books spilling out of it. *Captain Underpants.* That seemed strangely appropriate.

There was an ambulance outside, lights flashing. Paramedic Ric Holm and his partner were waiting.

"I think she needs some oxygen," Marcus said. "She's been in the basement breathing some pretty bad air." He gestured at my hand. "And I think that needs to be re-bandaged."

Ric smiled, easing me down onto the wide bumper of the ambulance. "Hey, Kathleen," he said. "It's been pretty quiet lately. Good to see you."

I reached behind me and set Hercules on the floor. He jumped up onto the stretcher, shook himself and looked around with curiosity.

"Get a piece of jerky out of my backpack for him," Ric said to his partner, indicating the cat. "But whatever you do, don't touch him."

He winked at me and I started to laugh, which just made me cough again. "It's Hercules, right?"

I nodded.

"Hey, Hercules," Ric said to the cat.

He meowed hello and took the jerky Ric's partner was offering.

Ric got oxygen on me as his partner moved to take my blood pressure.

It's over, I thought. *We're safe and it's over.*

A crowd was gathering and I could see Emme and Derrick among them. I started to cough again and my chest ached with the effort. I knew it would pass. For Emme, the pain was just beginning.

chapter 21

Nora had a concussion—I'd hit her harder than I'd realized—so she spent the night in the hospital, handcuffed to the bed with a police officer at the door. Emme came to the house to see me early Saturday morning. She was pale and there were dark circles under her eyes, and she held Derrick's hand the entire time.

"I'm sorry, Kathleen," she said, her voice cracking. "I'm not trying to make excuses for Nora, but this isn't the sister I grew up with."

"You don't have anything to apologize for," I said.

She wiped away a tear. "It turns out I didn't know my sister at all and maybe not my best friend, either."

"Miranda made a mistake," I said, choosing my words with care. "And she was trying to fix it when she died."

Emme nodded.

"Hey, you see the best in people," Derrick said. "That's not bad. You saw the best in me." He smiled.

"And that worked out pretty well," I said, smiling at him. I liked Derrick. He was a good man and it was clear he loved Emme very much. In time I hoped everything would work out for them.

I went to work over Marcus's very strenuous objections.

Rebecca and Ami showed up at the library just before we closed at lunchtime. Ami hugged me. "Thank you for finding Miranda's killer," she said. "I'm glad you're okay." She handed me a bag of organic cat treats. "For Hercules," she said with a smile. "I'm glad he's all right, too."

Rebecca wrapped me in a hug. "I'm so glad that woman didn't hurt either one of you," she said. She handed me an envelope.

I shook my head. "No."

She made an exasperated sound. "Don't give me that look, Kathleen. You don't even know what it is."

I gave her a mock glare. "I know you've done something you shouldn't have done."

"I'm always doing something I shouldn't have done," she said, raising an eyebrow. "It's one of the perks of getting older."

I opened the envelope. It contained a check for a very large amount of money made out to the Reading Buddies account.

"I can't take this," I said.

Rebecca gave me her most innocent look. "But it's for the children."

Ami leaned her cheek against Rebecca's. "How can you deprive little children of books?" she asked.

They were in cahoots and they'd bested me.

"You did this on purpose," I said, shaking my finger at them in mock annoyance.

Rebecca smiled. "Yes, I did," she said.

I'd never won an argument yet with her. I wasn't sure why I even tried.

"Are you all right?" Marcus asked as he headed up the walkway to the theater entrance that evening.

My stomach had done a couple of flip-flops when we'd pulled into the parking lot, but now, as I thought about the wonderful music we were about to hear, mostly all I felt was happy anticipation.

I gave his hand a squeeze. "I'm fine," I said.

An usher showed us to our seats. I remembered the first time I'd come to one of these concerts. Maggie had been supposed to meet me, but she'd conspired to make sure that Marcus had ended up with her ticket instead. It hadn't exactly been the start of a beautiful friendship.

I smiled and gave Marcus's hand another squeeze. "Remind me I need to put my name on the list for CDs. I promised my mother I'd send her one."

He nodded just as the overhead lights flashed to signal five minutes before the concert began.

I looked around the auditorium, pushing away the image of Nora Finley holding a gun and backing me against the seats, and replacing it with one of Burtis and Lita waving from four rows back.

I waved back and turned just as Maggie and Brady appeared, taking the two seats in front of us.

"How's your hand?" she asked.

"A lot better," I said, holding it up so she could see. Roma had stopped in before we left and changed the bulky dressing Ric had put on for a smaller one.

She smiled. "I'm glad."

"Is everything ready for tomorrow?" I asked. Twenty-four hours from now we'd all be at Roma and Eddie's wedding.

Mags nodded. "I think so. And Roma would be happy to get married out on the lawn in jeans and her rubber boots anyway."

"I think jeans and rubber boots were what she was planning on wearing until we took her dress shopping," I said with a grin.

Almost everyone was seated now. There was one empty seat on the aisle, across from me and one row down. Just as the lights began to dim a man slipped into it. He glanced in my direction and then raised a hand in hello.

It was Derrick. And he was alone.

Did that mean what I hoped it meant? I felt a bubble of warmth in my chest.

The curtain rose and Michel bowed to the audience as the sound of applause filled the space.

I scanned the massed choir. I spotted Ami, and a row ahead of her I caught sight of Ruby. And there, on Ruby's right side, was Emme, standing tall and smiling. Michel lifted his baton, and I put my head on Marcus's shoulder and let the music wash over me.

One day later, on a warm Sunday evening, Roma Davidson and Eddie Sweeney were married.

"You look wonderful," I said as Pearl adjusted the neck of her daughter's dress.

"She's right," Olivia said. She looked beautiful in her pale green bridesmaid dress, which Ella King had hemmed with time to spare.

There was a knock at the door and Pearl opened it to Maggie and Sydney. Syd took a step into the room. She stopped and stared at her future stepmother. "You're the most beautiful bride I've ever seen," she exclaimed.

"And you're the most beautiful flower girl," Roma told her. Then she noticed the small box tied with silver ribbons that Sydney was holding.

"I thought we agreed we weren't going to do this," she said, frowning. "No superstitions."

"We didn't agree to anything, dear," Pearl said. "You talked, we nodded. That's it."

"And it's not a superstition," Maggie added. "It's a tradition." She looked at Pearl. "Go ahead."

Pearl smiled. "Something old," she said, offering a small box.

Roma opened it. "Oh, Mom," she whispered.

The box held a short strand of pearls. "They belonged to your grandmother," Pearl said. "After the wedding, if you want to, you could have them restrung into two bracelets for your girls."

Roma hugged her mother. "You're going to make me cry," she said.

"I'm next," Maggie said. She reached under the bed, pulled out a long flat box and handed it to Roma.

"I'm kind of afraid to open this," Roma said as she undid the ribbon bow that was keeping the box shut. She lifted the lid and immediately pushed it down again. Color flooded her face as she looked at Maggie.

"For the honeymoon," Maggie said, green eyes gleaming.

"Kissing stuff?" Sydney asked.

"Yes," Olivia said.

"Something borrowed," I said, quickly offering my gift. Roma's cheeks were still pink.

She took the blue velvet bag I held out. Inside was the braided silver bracelet Mom and Dad had given me when Ethan and Sara were born, to represent the new family we were making. She pressed a hand to her mouth, understanding the symbolism of the gift. "Thank you, Kathleen," she said, fastening it around her arm.

"Our turn," Sydney said, bouncing up and down with excitement. She handed over the ribbon-trimmed box. "This is from Olivia and me. Something blue."

Olivia held up a hand. "It was all her idea," she said. Then she grinned. "And a very good one, too."

Roma untied the ribbon and opened the small rectangular box. And smiled as she lifted out a lacy blue garter.

"We made it," Sydney said with shy pride.

"It's perfect," Roma said, struggling not to cry. She held out her arms and hugged them both. Then she stretched out her right leg, lifted her skirt and slid the blue lace-and-ribbon garter to a spot just above her knee.

"Beautiful," Pearl said. Then she clapped her hands together. "Stand up, ladies. I need to check your dresses. We have a wedding waiting for us downstairs."

Roma caught my eye as I got to my feet, smoothing the skirt of my dress. She smiled and I smiled back at her. I thought about one of my mother's favorite sayings: *"Everything will work out in the end. And if it doesn't, it's not the end."*

Everything had worked out and it wasn't the end. It was just the beginning.

Maggie had done a beautiful job of decorating the living room. It was filled with all of Roma and Eddie's favorite people. Sydney led the way down the stairs and down the makeshift aisle to the fireplace, where her father waited with Marcus and one of Eddie's former teammates. Olivia was next, followed by Maggie and then me.

Roma walked down alone, eyes locked on Eddie's face the entire way. Pearl and Neil, Roma's stepfather, were waiting just before she reached the fireplace. She stopped to kiss them both. And then she was standing with Eddie and they looked so happy it made my chest hurt. I caught Marcus watching me and he smiled.

And then they were married. Roma pulled two flowers from her bouquet. She gave one to me and the other to Maggie. "Don't wait too long for your own happy endings," she said.

She turned and looked teasingly at Lita, standing with Rebecca. "Don't even think about it," Lita warned.

A smile spread across Roma's face. She swung around in the

other direction. "Burtis, catch," she called, tossing him the bouquet.

He was so surprised he automatically reached up to snatch it out of the air. Everyone laughed and clapped.

Marcus came up behind me and slipped an arm around my waist. I looked over at Roma leaning against her new husband with one hand on Olivia's arm and the other on Sydney's shoulder. "And everyone she loved the most was close enough to touch," I said softly.

"Shakespeare?" Marcus asked.

"No," I said as I laid my head against his chest. "Just me."